I0661192

LIES AT ANY PRICE
THE COMPLETE CASES OF
GILLIAN HAZELTINE, VOLUME 1

OTHER BOOKS IN THE ARGOSY LIBRARY:

THE PHANTOM IN THE RAINBOW
SLATER LAMASTER

THREADS OF EVIDENCE: THE COMPLETE
CASES OF RIORDAN, VOLUME 1
VICTOR MAXWELL

MASTERS OF DARKNESS
MURRAY LEINSTER

HE RULES WHO CAN
ARTHUR GILCHRIST BRODEUR

THE HOUSE OF THE EGO: THE COMPLETE
CABALISTIC CASES OF SEMI DUAL, VOLUME 3
J.U. GIESY AND JUNIUS B. SMITH

DEATH TO A TENOR
FRED MACISAAC

MURDER'S MASQUERADE: THE COMPLETE
CASES OF MIKE & TRIXIE, VOLUME 1
T.T. FLYNN

THE LAND OF LIMPING LAW: THE COMPLETE
CASES OF CALHOUN, VOLUME 1
EDWARD PARRISH WARE

COCKED DICE: THE COMPLETE CASES
OF DAFFY DILL, VOLUME 1
RICHARD B. SALE

LIES AT ANY PRICE
THE COMPLETE CASES OF
GILLIAN HAZELTINE, VOLUME 1

GEORGE F. WORTS

COVER BY
STOCKTON MULFORD

ILLUSTRATED BY
ROGER B. MORRISON

POPULAR PUBLICATIONS · 2021

© 2021 Popular Publications, an imprint of Steeger Properties, LLC

First Edition—2021

PUBLISHING HISTORY

"Lies at Any Price" originally appeared in the December 11, 1926 issue of *Argosy All-Story Weekly* magazine (Vol. 182, No. 6). Copyright © 1926 by The Frank A. Munsey Company. Copyright renewed © 1954 and assigned to Steeger Properties, LLC. All rights reserved.

"The Love Bandit" originally appeared in the June 18–July 2, 1927 issues of *Argosy* magazine (Vol. 187, Nos. 1–3). Copyright © 1927 by The Frank A. Munsey Company. Copyright renewed © 1954 and assigned to Steeger Properties, LLC. All rights reserved.

"About the Author" originally appeared in the December 10, 1932 issue of *Argosy* magazine (Vol. 234, No. 5). Copyright © 1932 by The Frank A. Munsey Company. Copyright renewed © 1960 and assigned to Steeger Properties, LLC. All rights reserved.

"Who Did Kill Ezra Klagg?" originally appeared in the January 7, 1928 issue of *Argosy All-Story Weekly* magazine (Vol. 191, No. 6). Copyright © 1928 by The Frank A. Munsey Company. Copyright renewed © 1955 and assigned to Steeger Properties, LLC. All rights reserved.

ALL RIGHTS RESERVED

No part of this book may be reproduced or utilized in any form or by any means without permission in writing from the publisher.

Visit argosymagazine.com for more books like this.

TABLE OF CONTENTS

LIES AT ANY PRICE

1

TWINKLING IS A function of the stars, but Mr. Yistle, the new district attorney, had the trick, somehow, of making his gray eyes twinkle, or seem to twinkle, especially at his sternest moments. His twinkling trick made what he said seem vitally important.

His eyes were twinkling now, but there was no mirth visible or audible elsewhere about his person. He was pounding softly on his desk with a mighty fist.

One of the prerogatives of a district attorney is to hand down ultimatums, and Mr. Yistle was handing down an ultimatum. A square-built man, with a strong, judicial forehead surmounted by a mop of iron-gray hair, and a massive pair of jaws surmounted by an iron-gray mustache, Mr. Yistle was a commanding figure. He was extremely ambitious, and hoped some day to become Governor of the State.

"Be sure of your evidence—then step on the gas," said Mr. Yistle to his new assistant, Mr. Bullock. "Hit the line and hit it hard. Don't let any grass grow under your feet, or any dust accumulate on your coattails. That is going to be the motto of this office, now that I am in charge, Mr. Bullock. I am not knocking my predecessor, but I am saying that this office is going to show some results. Know your evidence is right—then *biffo!*"

Mr. Bullock, who was a pale, thin young man with kind

blue eyes, a disappearing chin, and a prominent Adam's apple, said "Yes, sir!" effusively, and clinched his statement with "You're absolutely right, Mr. Yistle."

The new district attorney, looking at him, knew that Mr. Bullock would employ the word "yes" in his dealings with his fellow men more frequently than any word in his lexicon. Mr. Bullock looked like a yes-man, and, as chance would have it, he was a yes-man—to the tips of his fingers.

His kind blue eyes were radiant with yeses. He would sometimes hesitate before uttering yes, to give it added emphasis. His Adam's apple would dive down, as if it were plunging into a storage bin of inexhaustible yeses, and return with a firm, flavory, well-ripened yes.

"The public elected me to this office," Mr. Yistle confided, "not because they love me, but because they expect results. And results I am going to give them, Mr. Bullock. The people want criminals convicted, and I am going to convict them!

"Politics, Mr. Bullock, had nothing to do with the retirement of my predecessor. In the words of the poet, he was simply one of the men who did not fit in. Have you read

any of Robert Service's poems, Mr. Bullock? You should. They are full of fine ideas and inspiration.

"Now, my predecessor hesitated to use all of the instruments of justice which were at his hand. I am not going to hesitate. When I am convinced that a man is guilty of the crime of which he is charged, I am going to move heaven and earth to have that man convicted. I believe in interpreting justice broadly, Mr. Bullock."

"So do I," Mr. Bullock put in quickly. "I don't want to knock the old district attorney, either, Mr. Yistle, but what you say is certainly—"

"Exactly," Mr. Yistle interrupted him. "Now, take the first case that the grand jury has handed over to us—the People *versus* McArthur. That is what I call a tough case. There is absolutely no question in our minds but that Compton McArthur killed Jake Plovak. Everybody knows it. To send that man up for twenty years, as he deserves, ought to be a mere matter of routine, but it won't be, Mr. Bullock.

"The McArthur family is rich. They are going to have an array of legal talent in that court room, Mr. Bullock, that will be positively dazzling. We are going to have the fight of our lives to win that case, and we have got to win it, because we, ourselves, will be on trial. The public will watch our every move, to see what kind of a district attorney they have voted into office. We cannot afford to start off with a black eye. Are we going to win that case, Mr. Bullock?"

"Yes, sir!" said Mr. Bullock in ringing tones. "I understand the McArthurs have retained Gillian Hazeltine."

Mr. Yistle nodded. He had the greatest respect for Gillian Hazeltine, the respect, say, that Mr. Georges Carpentier had for Mr. Jack Dempsey. Mr. Yistle had been ousted in more than one court room bout with Gillian Hazeltine. Sometimes referred to in legal circles as "the Silver Fox," largely because of his native cunning, Gillian Hazeltine was perhaps the smartest criminal lawyer in the State. He was a silver-tongued orator, a clever actor, a wit, and a master of surprise.

He was a hard drinker, and his methods were commonly known to be unscrupulous, but he was popular with the public. It was said, darkly, of Gillian Hazeltine, that he had bribed judges and bought juries; that he had employed, at one time or another, enough illicit tricks to disbar a dozen lawyers; but he generally took the part of the underdog, and that made him liked. He had never been caught at any of his tricks; he was too smooth.

"Nothing would please me more than to grease the skids for that scoundrel," said Mr. Yistle. "There's nothing he won't stoop to to bring in a verdict for McArthur. Mr. Bullock, we have got to win that case!"

"Yes, sir!" said Mr. Bullock warmly.

"We will win it!" cried Mr. Yistle.

Mr. Bullock's emotions were easily aroused. Tears stood

in his kind blue eyes, and his rather inconspicuous chin trembled.

"Yes, *sir!*" he echoed, tremulously.

The two men shook hands rather dramatically. Mr. Yistle had handed down his ultimatum.

He had brought enthusiasm to this office. Mr. Bullock would, in turn, convey this enthusiasm to the clerks, to the stenographers, to the office boys. There is nothing like setting the right kind of example, and Mr. Yistle had started off his first day as district attorney in the right way.

"Do you want to see that young fellow who was around when you came in, Mr. Yistle? His name, he says, is Willie Applegate, and he wants to see you privately about the McArthur case."

"Send him in," said the district attorney crisply.

2

WILLIE APPLEGATE WAS a clean-cut young man with tanned cheeks, fine brown eyes and smoothly brushed black hair. He was dressed in dark gray tweeds. He had slender, dark-red lips and when he smiled, he showed even rows of good white teeth.

He was handsome in a collar ad sort of way, but wholesome looking. There was an air of universities about him. He was the kind of man who would smoke a pipe.

"I was just wondering, Mr. Yistle," said Willie Applegate as Mr. Bullock withdrew and left the two men alone, "how you are fixed for witnesses for the McArthur trial?"

"Did you see the accident?" Mr. Yistle wanted to know.

Willie Applegate gave him a curious, knowing smile.

"I may have," he said.

"I see," said Mr. Yistle. "Go ahead and tell me what you may have seen."

"I was standing on the corner of Maple and Market Streets when the car driven by Compton McArthur came along and struck down Jake Plovak," the young man obliged. "McArthur was driving recklessly. Obviously, he was under the influence of liquor."

"We should like to prove that," said Mr. Yistle. "Are you quite sure he was drunk?"

"I should say positively that he was drunk. He was steering all over the street. Jake Plovak stepped out from the curb to cross the street, and Compton McArthur, with a wild turn, drove right into him and ran over him. Then he drove away."

"What did you do then?"

"I went out into the street, saw that Plovak was badly hurt and ran to telephone the police. I went into the nearest drug store and phoned."

"Are you sure you phoned?" said Mr. Yistle.

"Positive—so did a lot of other people."

"How do you know they phoned?"

"I made sure of it. Didn't you read the papers after the accident? There wasn't any cop around. A cop didn't show up until McArthur came back. Then there was a big crowd there."

"That's a pretty good piece of testimony," said Mr. Yistle. "Where were you actually when the accident happened?"

"Does it make very much difference, so long as nobody saw where I was?"

Mr. Yistle looked at him approvingly. "I suppose you know what would happen to you if you gave this testimony and somebody proved that you weren't telling the truth."

"Certainly! I would be sent up for perjury."

The new district attorney looked thoughtfully out of the window. He needed witnesses badly for the McArthur case. So far he had found no one who had seen the accident happen; and he needed a strong case; it couldn't be too strong.

"How much do you want for going on the stand and giving this piece of testimony?" he asked.

"A thousand dollars," said Willie Applegate.

"I will think it over," said Mr. Yistle. "You understand, I will have to look you up. What is your occupation?"

"I am an artist's model. I have worked a little in the pictures, too."

"That isn't so good," said Mr. Yistle.

"As a matter of fact, I am studying law," said Willie Applegate.

"That is much better. You are a law student. The accident took place about ten o'clock at night. You had been studying law and were out taking a little stroll before going to bed. Come around in a week. Let me have your phone number. Mr. Applegate, did you, by any chance, pick up anything that McArthur threw from the car?"

"I might have," said the obliging Mr. Applegate.

"To prove that the man was drunk, it would be pretty convincing if you had seen him throw, let's say, a pocket flask from the car just after he had run Plovak down."

"It seems to me," said the artist's model, "that I did see him throw a flask from the car, since you mention it. It was a pretty expensive silver flask, and it was half full of gin. Didn't I bring it right down here and leave it?"

"That's just what you did," Mr. Yistle agreed, "and I immediately had a chemist analyze its contents to ascertain whether it was alcoholic or not."

The district attorney pressed one of a row of pearl buttons and Mr. Bullock appeared. Mr. Yistle gazed at his assistant with wide, innocent eyes.

"This young man," he said, "was a witness, it seems, to the killing of Jake Plovak. He is the only person who saw the accident."

"You don't tell me," said Mr. Bullock.

"He saw McArthur throw a silver flask away after he had run Plovak down. He picked up the flask, and next morning he brought the flask down here and left it with you. You were here then, weren't you, Mr. Bullock?"

"Why! I don't recall his bringing a flask and leaving it here," said Mr. Bullock.

"In case you have mislaid it," said Mr, Yistle, "I think the best thing to do would be to go out immediately and buy a plain silver flask, pint size, at some second hand store. I will fill it half full with gin, and we will have the gin analyzed to make sure that it is gin."

"I see," said Mr. Bullock, his eyes shining with admiration.

"That will be all for to-day, Mr. Applegate," said the district attorney. "Keep in touch with me—and don't talk."

"Oh, I know my onions," said the artist's model.

When he was gone, Mr. Yistle said to Mr. Bullock: "Here is that fellow"s address. Have him carefully looked up. If there's anything wrong with his character, we can't use him. Otherwise, I think he will make a fine witness. Now trot out and buy that flask. Be careful. Don't get an ornate one, and don't get one with a monogram."

Mr. Bullock departed for the silver flask. When he returned, Mr. Yistle had mysteriously acquired a bottle of gin.

He half-filled the flask, screwed on the cap, and put in a telephone call for Harry Zarrow, the analytical chemist. Harry and he were old friends.

"Can you come up to my office right away, Harry?" Mr. Yistle wanted to know. "There's a hundred in it for you."

"I'll be right over," Harry promised.

Harry Zarrow was a sallow-faced young man, prematurely bald. He wore thick, gold-rimmed spectacles which gave him a scientific look. His demeanor was exceedingly calm.

Mr. Yistle handed him the flask.

"I want you to analyze a sample of the contents of that flask," said Mr. Yistle, "and be prepared to testify in court just what it is."

Harry Zarrow unscrewed the cap and sniffed.

"I don't have to analyze it," he said with a pale grin. "A child would know that it's raw, new bathtub gin. It was made from reclaimed alcohol, and the denaturant was probably formaldehyde."

"Analyze it, anyhow," said the district attorney. "This flask was thrown from the automobile driven by Compton McArthur on the night when he killed Jake Plovak. That was on the night of June 20, if you will count back. The 20th of June was a Sunday. On Monday morning shortly before noon, Mr. Bullock, took this flask over to your laboratory, you poured off a sample and analyzed it. By the way, where were you on that Monday?"

"I was in my laboratory," said Harry Zarrow, "but I will not get up on the witness stand and swear that Mr. Bullock brought this flask to me on that Monday morning. That would be perjury, and you know it. I never saw this flask until this minute. You are going to give McArthur a black character—proving him to be the kind of fellow who would drive recklessly and drunkenly. Nothing doing."

"He is absolutely guilty, Harry," said Mr. Yistle. "I know he is guilty. You know he is guilty. Everybody knows he is guilty. I am simply interpreting justice broadly. I hate to have you call it by that nasty name—perjury—when all I want is a little harmless fibbing to convict a man who certainly deserves it.

"Don't tell me you haven't done it before. How about that beer case when you took your oath and said that the sample of beer submitted to you contained less than one-half of one per cent of alcohol, when you know damned well it contained at least twelve per cent if not fifteen? If you didn't perjure yourself then, what did you do?"

"That was harmless fibbing," Harry Zarrow replied with his pallid smile. "It contained seventeen per cent alcohol by volume, if you must know the truth, and after I got through giving my testimony, my pockets contained something more than a piffling hundred dollars. Chew on that for awhile, will you?"

"You are nothing but a low-down bum and a he-gold digger," growled Mr. Yistle. "I used to think you were a gentleman, Harry, but now I know that you have the instincts of a man who would trample orphans and widows to death while you were stealing pennies from a one-armed blind man with wooden legs. How much do you want for this practically worthless testimony you are going to give?"

"One thousand bucks," said the calm chemist.

"It's too much."

"You need me or I wouldn't be here. I am not going to get up on that witness stand and perjure myself black in the face and risk my professional standing for any less. Take it or leave it."

"All right, Harry. Now, give me a careful, honest analysis of the sample you are going to take from this flask. Take it and get out of here."

Harry Zarrow withdrew with the sample of gin and Mr. Yistle pressed the pearl button which summoned Mr. Bullock. His assistant entered with his customary fawning smile.

"There's an extremely pretty young lady out here—" he began.

"She can wait," said Mr. Yistle crisply. "Shut that door, Mr. Bullock, and sit down here. I want to have a talk with you. I hope you already have an inkling of which way the wind is blowing in this McArthur case. I understand that you are a perfect wonder at keeping your mouth shut?"

"Yes, sir," said the perfect yes-man.

"Well, you might as well know exactly what is going on. So far this morning we have acquired two excellent witnesses for the McArthur case. Of course, Willie Applegate wasn't anywhere near that accident when it happened, but he has a good appearance and he is a gifted liar. In brief, he will get upon the stand and state that he saw McArthur, driving drunkenly, run down Jake Plovak, whereupon he threw overboard a flask half full of gin.

"Harry Zarrow will take the stand and swear that you brought the flask to him on the morning after the accident, and that it contained pretty poor, but powerful gin. So far these are our only witnesses. If we can comb up a few more who will be as convincing on the witness stand, we will be in luck.

"I only wish we had some real witnesses, but inasmuch as we haven't, we will have to do the best we can with these perjurers. We can win the case without them, but with them we are certain to win it. I hate to start off my term as district attorney using such methods, Mr. Bullock, but, as

I told you before, it has always been my principle to inter-
pret justice broadly. We know McArthur is guilty, and we
have got to win this case."

"Yes, sir!" said Mr. Bullock enthusiastically. "Shall I send
in this girl now? She's a dream, Mr. Yistle."

"What does she want?"

"She says you're an old friend of her father's. Her name
is Joy Halliday."

"Send her right in."

3

MR. YISTLE WAS standing when Joy Halliday entered. The name was strangely incongruous for the girl who timidly crossed the threshold and permitted Mr. Yistle to shake her hand.

She was in mourning, in black that looked cheap, but her face would have lent dignity to rags. It was oval, white and exquisitely beautiful.

Miss Halliday's eyes were large and dark and lustrous, and they were shaded by extremely long, thick lashes. She was slender; on the verge of being thin. The dreaminess of her eyes bespoke suffering; she was a Madonna.

Mr. Yistle deferentially drew out a chair for her, and she occupied it, folding her hands in her lap and looking up at him with a sweet, rather sad smile.

"It was so nice of you to come to the funeral."

The new district attorney cleared his throat.

"Your father and I were very warm friends, my dear. We went through public school together. We played on the same ball team. For years we were closer than brothers. Then we drifted apart, as men do. I am sorry that we saw so little of each other in later years. I feel guilty because I did not come to see him oftener during his illness."

"He was very fond of you," the girl said. "And he told me to come to you if I was ever in trouble."

"Don't tell me you are in trouble!" Mr. Yistle exclaimed with an attempt at a jollying manner.

"I am in great trouble," Miss Halliday confessed. "Gillian Hazeltine was, as you know, my father's lawyer. Mr. Hazeltine drew my father's last will. To make a long story short, my father left my sister and me penniless. We have scarcely enough to last us through the summer.

"Of course, I have said nothing of this to any one else, but the fact is, Mr. Yistle, I have heard so much of Mr. Hazeltine's methods that I wondered—" Her sweet, low, cultured voice came to a stop, but her lustrous eyes were expressive of the rest.

Mr. Yistle slowly and regretfully shook his head.

"As one of your father's oldest friends, my dear, I took the liberty to look into that thoroughly after the will was read. Mr. Hazeltine, I regret to say, has been absolutely honest in his handling of your father's affairs. Your father made the mistake that so many of us make when we grow a little advanced in years. In his youth and middle years he was a shrewd business man; a careful investor; but as he grew older, he seemed to lose his acumen. He made unwise investments. He speculated. I warned him. All his old friends warned him. Even Mr. Hazeltine warned him.

"Much as I disapprove of Mr. Hazeltine's legal tactics, I must admit that he did everything within his power to save your father from a crash. Your father was stubborn. He would listen to no one. There is nothing left of your father's estate but a few worthless scraps of paper. But certainly you can realize a few thousand on the house."

The exquisite daughter of Horatio Halliday slowly shook her head.

"It is mortgaged to within a dollar of its value. Even the furniture, I find, is mortgaged. My sister and I have nothing in the world, and what are we to do, Mr. Yistle? I am twenty-four years old. For the past seven years I have nursed my father. But even that I cannot put to account.

"I cannot go to work as a nurse because I have no certificate, and practical nursing does not pay well enough. I must find work. My sister is only ten. The doctors say that she has a spot on one lung, and that I must take her West. What am I going to do, Mr. Yistle?"

"I will lend you all you need," said the district attorney.

Joy Halliday shook her head in an emphatic refusal.

"I cannot accept that. I must find work. I must find something to do so that, by the end of the summer, I can save enough to take my sister West. I don't want charity. I have my own way to make, my own battle to fight, and I must do it alone. I realize that."

"You could marry," Mr. Yistle suggested. "A girl as attractive as you are ought to marry a man worth millions."

She smiled.

"That's a pleasant and practical suggestion. It would be perfect if I happened to know millionaires. But I don't. I don't know any men. Nothing but doctors. And I don't like doctors. I've grown so afraid of their saying: 'I'm sorry, Miss Halliday, there really isn't any hope.' Day and night for seven years I've been nursing my father. What chance have I had to meet men?"

"You might go into the movies," Mr. Yistle suggested.

"How does one get in?"

"I don't know."

"I must have money, Mr. Yistle. I must have a thousand dollars at least by the end of the summer."

"Let me think," said Mr. Yistle.

He placed the tips of his fingers together and thought. His handsome forehead grew furrowed. His iron-gray brows became furry and flat. His eyes roved hither and yon as a man's eyes will, when he is pursuing ideas.

They stopped presently, having come to rest upon the gleaming side of the gin flask—the spurious gin flask that would soon be used in the McArthur trial as exhibit A for the State.

The words, "I must have a thousand dollars," flitted through Mr. Yistle's busy mind and flitted back again.

What a witness this girl would make! So refined! So appealing! So cultured! How a jury would eat her up!

Mr. Yistle unfurrowed his brow, unbristled his eyebrows. He smiled.

"Look here," he said, "did you read anything in the papers about the McArthur case? Compton McArthur is the dissolute son of Jeremiah McArthur, the man who makes McArthur Paints and Varnishes. D'you remember reading in the papers about two months ago of Compton McArthur's killing a workman named Jake Plovak, by running him down in his roadster?"

"I think I do—faintly. Father had one of his bad attacks at that time and—"

"Don't you live near the corner where the accident happened?" Mr. Yistle interrupted. "Maple and Market?"

"Our house is, or was, about half a block above Market on Maple, the north side of the street."

"You didn't, by any chance, see that accident, did you?" he asked eagerly.

"No; I heard nothing about it until next morning. I was with father all that evening."

"Where was your sister?"

"Oh, she was in bed. I always put her to bed at eight."

"I see," said Mr. Yistle, and to himself he said: "Now, shall I or shan't I?" After a brief pause he went on:

"This fellow Compton McArthur is a bad sort. His brother, Kenneth, who died some few weeks ago, was a very decent fellow. There were only the two sons, you know. Compton has a pretty bad record. He drinks, gambles, goes with a fast crowd and so on. He was certain to come to a bad end. And he must be punished, Miss Halliday. We can't permit loose, fast men of his sort to drive cars and menace the safety of the public. We must make an example of him."

"I fully agree with you," Joy Halliday said earnestly. "A man like that ought to be punished."

"He ought to be sent up for life!" Mr. Yistle exclaimed. "But the extreme limit in this State for manslaughter is twenty years. He certainly ought to get that, Miss Halliday. Killling a poor, innocent workingman like that! Did you know that Jake Plovak left a widow and five little ones?"

"Compton McArthur deserves to be hanged!" Joy Halliday cried.

"I agree with you," said Mr. Yistle, and sadly shook his head. "And would you believe it, I am going to have the fight of my life even to convict him? Gillian Hazeltine is handling the case, and Hazeltine will stoop to anything—perjury, bribery, the lowest trickery, to get that fellow off."

Joy Halliday's eyes were bright with indignation, and her cheeks were rosy with the same emotion.

"Why don't you fight him with his own weapons?" she demanded.

Mr. Yistle gazed at her with surprise. "You can't mean that, Miss Halliday."

"Indeed, I can, and do," said the girl firmly. "Justice is a farce. No matter what crime a man commits nowadays, he only needs a smart lawyer to get him off. It seems to me you are fully entitled to stoop to anything to convict that man."

"I believe in interpreting justice pretty broadly," Mr. Yistle agreed, "but, of course, I shrink from doing anything that is not ethical."

"The Germans used poison gas during the war," Miss Halliday pointed out, "and the Allies had to use poison gas, too. It does seem to me that you have a right to arm yourself with the same weapons your enemy uses. I don't know a thing about law; I've never been in a court room in my life; but I do think that that is plain common sense. If Mr. Hazeltine is going to use trickery to try to get McArthur off; you ought to use trickery to convict him. That may not be ethical, but it's only fair. It's your public duty, Mr. Yistle!"

"But, Miss Halliday, Hazeltine is just as apt as not to ring in witnesses who weren't within miles of the accident!"

"Then why don't you?" she cried.

Mr. Yistle, looking at her, shook his head. Her beautiful eyes were sparkling. Her face was flushed. Her breast was rising and falling with emotion.

"Take yourself as an example," he said. "You wouldn't appear as one of my witnesses, and you know' you wouldn't. You wouldn't get up on the witness stand, for instance, and swear you had seen Compton McArthur, driving recklessly, strike down and kill poor Jake Plovak. That's what I mean, my dear. It is easy to sit here in this office and demand justice, by fair or foul means, but it is quite another thing to get up on the witness stand—"

"But I would! Indeed, I would, Mr. Yistle! I would consider it my public duty to lie myself black in the face to help punish a man as guilty as Compton McArthur is!"

Mr. Yistle seemed more and more astonished. "Of course, even if I were to make it worth your while—say, a thousand dollars—a fine, cultured girl like you wouldn't actually do such a thing. You know very well you would be afraid to, anyway."

"I would not be in the least afraid. As I say, I'd consider it my public duty. Could I really earn a thousand dollars, Mr. Yistle, by doing a thing that is really my public duty?"

"You could if you wanted to, my dear."

"Then I will!" she cried dramatically. "I will! Not because of the money, although I do need a thousand dollars badly, but because I do want to see that man punished! It's high time that this crime wave was stopped, and if we decent people cannot stop it with honorable methods, we will have to use dishonorable ones!"

"You almost take my breath away," said the new district attorney. "It really startles me to hear a refined, cultured girl like you offering to perjure yourself, even in the cause of justice. Besides, what story could you tell?"

"I'd say—why, I'd simply say I had left my father's bedside to go to the drug store for medicine, and that I saw McArthur's car strike down Jake Plovak just as I was nearing the corner."

"Well," said Mr. Yistle, "of course, if you insist—"

"I do insist!"

"Very well, my dear. I may not need your services, but if I do I will certainly call upon you."

4

JOY HALLIDAY SAT in the front row of chairs reserved for witnesses and visiting attorneys. She had never been in court before, and she was thrilled even by the minor processes of legal machinery. She was a little disappointed, however, in the court room itself and in the character of the court attendants. The room was old and shabby and dusty, and most of the attendants were crusty-looking old men.

She had not been present the day before when the final members of the jury were impaneled. The preparations for the trial of Compton McArthur now went forward smoothly, and Joy Halliday enjoyed thrill upon thrill.

There were two long tables a few feet apart in front of the bench, and at one were the district attorney and his assistants, and at the other were Gillian Hazeltine and his assistants.

Joy Halliday looked at Gillian Hazeltine in a new light. Heretofore he had been a friend of her father's and his lawyer; now he was her natural enemy, inasmuch as he was the enemy of that for which she was prepared to perjure herself—justice!

He was a small, rather stout man, but his face was lean and shrewd. His black hair was speckled with silver.

There was a murmur of interest in the court room as two sheriffs appeared at a door near the bench with a tall young man walking between them. He was conducted to the prisoner's pen, and Miss Halliday studied him with the greatest interest.

Compton McArthur was much younger and nicer-looking than she had expected him to be. He had rough blond hair, frank blue eyes, and the complexion of a man who had spent much of his time outdoors.

Compton McArthur had been in jail since the accident, but he did not have the pallor which men in jail are supposed to acquire. Nor did he strike Joy Halliday as dissipated-looking. He really looked like a clean-living, clean-acting young American business man.

She liked his dark gray suit. It fitted him perfectly, and he had fine shoulders.

She wondered if he had perhaps not suffered enough already for the accidental killing of Jake Plovak. It seemed a shame to send such a fine-looking young man to the penitentiary for twenty years. Even if he had been a little bit drunk. He did not look like a drunkard, and perhaps he had reformed.

After all, drinking was no longer a crime. Almost all men had a cocktail or a highball now and then these days.

The eyes of the prisoner had been roving about the court room, and now they came to rest on Joy Halliday. She shivered a little. Never before had she looked into the eyes of a man who had killed a fellow man.

No! She would not think of him as a killer. He had accidentally struck a man, and the man had died. His fine blue eyes seemed to want sympathy.

Joy smiled very faintly, and he smiled wanly in return. It

was, that smile, a sort of communion. If he had not smiled, perhaps Joy would later have behaved differently.

It is hard to say. Perhaps she was convinced, the instant she laid eyes on him, that it would be wrong and cruel to keep him behind bars until he was middle-aged.

Mr. Yistle had sent a messenger to inform the judge that he was ready. A door behind the bench opened, and Judge Manning came in.

Everybody in the court room stood up as the judge took his place on the bench. He was, Joy thought, a very distinguished man. He had white hair and a coppery complexion, which he had probably acquired at golf, and a very pleasant smile. He looked exceedingly well fed.

A bailiff was droning:

"Oyez! Oyez! Oyez! The Superior Court within and for Greenfield County, criminal term, is open and in session at this place. All persons having cause or action who are summoned to appear herein will give attention according to law."

The judge said, "You may call the jury," and a sheriff hastened to obey him. And presently twelve good men and true filed in and took their seats in the jury box.

The names of the jurors were called, and the jurors answered the roll call until all twelve were accounted for. Joy thought they were a dull and stupid-looking lot of old men, but most of them were frowning, as if fully conscious of the responsibility resting upon their shoulders, and that pleased her.

The clerk now read the charge, and it alone, Joy thought, was sufficient to condemn Compton McArthur to twenty years in prison.

"Number eight thousand seven hundred and twenty-four," read the clerk in a ringing voice. "To the Superior Court for Greenfield County comes Adelbert Yistle, attorney for the State in said county, and on his oath of office complaint and information makes that on the twentieth day of June Compton McArthur, of the town of Greenfield, in said county, with force and arms did operate a certain motor vehicle, a more particular description of which is to said attorney unknown, upon Maple Street, in the said town of Greenfield, at a reckless, dangerous and unlawful rate of speed and upon the wrong side of the street, and while under the influence of intoxicating liquor, by the immoderate use of which he became incapable of properly managing and steering said motor vehicle, and while with his right hand he was petting and caressing a woman, and while so operating said motor vehicle he did run into and upon and against Jake Plovak, who was then lawfully crossing said street, and did him beat, bruise, maim, injure and crush so that the said Jake Plovak did languish and suffer and did, within a lapse of minutes, die, so that the said Compton McArthur did then and there commit the crime of manslaughter against the peace of the people of the State and their dignity and contrary to the form of the statute in such case made and provided."

The ringing voice stopped. Mr. Hazeltine was on his feet pleading not guilty to the charge, and Joy Halliday was looking at the man in the prisoner's pen. Compton McArthur was again looking into her eyes, once more smiling that tired smile.

The prisoner was now taken from the pen and seated with his lawyers.

"If he had been petting and caressing a girl then," she said to herself, "he would not dare look me in the eye now. And he would not smile like that. I don't care what Mr. Yistle says. Compton McArthur is not guilty."

She thought it was rather foolish to have to prove that Jake Plovak was dead, but apparently it had to be done, and Mr. Yistle's first witness was Dr. Cutler, the coroner of Greenfield. He stated briefly, in response to Mr. Yistle's questions, that Jake Plovak died almost instantly, his skull having been fractured and one kidney pierced by a broken rib.

The coroner's testimony had only one interesting feature. All of the dead man's injuries indicated that he had been struck from in front; that is, he had been facing the automobile when it hit him.

Gillian Hazeltine, in his cross-examination, tried to make something of this; tried to prove that Jake Plovak had walked into the car; that the accident had been his own fault quite as much as Compton McArthur's.

The next witness was a chubby young Irish policeman with tight red curls. He had arrested Compton McArthur. He was on his beat, he said, near Market and Chestnut, when a man came running to him with the information that a man had been struck down by a roadster.

"Did you go at once to where the killing occurred?" Mr. Yistle asked him.

"Yes, sir; I ran."

"Describe what you found when you arrived at the scene."

"Well, there was a crowd gathered, and they had carried Plovak to the grass at the side of the street. A lot of people were standing around. I made inquiries, but no one seemed to know who had run him down. Whoever had done it had made his get-away."

"You mean," said Mr. Yistle, "the driver of the car had killed Jake Plovak and then run away?"

"Well, it looked that way. While I was asking questions, a roadster drove up and Mr. McArthur got out. He came over and told me he guessed he was the fellow I was looking for."

"Kindly describe his condition, officer. Had he been drinking?"

"There was liquor on his breath. I smelled it. And he sort of staggered. We got into his car and he drove us down to the station house."

Mr. Yistle indicated that he was through with the examination and Gillian Hazeltine cross-examined him.

"Do you know just how drunk the accused was when he came up to you and surrendered himself?"

"Well, I smelled liquor on his breath," the policeman said resentfully.

"Did you ever see a man with liquor on his breath who wasn't drunk?" Mr. Hazeltine wanted to know.

"Yes, sir, I have."

"Yet you say that the accused was drunk?"

"That's what I said."

"Could he walk?"

"Why—yes, I guess he could walk."

"Did he stagger?"

"Yes, he staggered a little."

"In the course of your duties, officer, have you ever seen a man in an extremely excited condition?"

"Sure, I've seen lots of them."

"Have you ever seen a man so excited that he seemed, at first glance, to be drunk?"

"Well, I've seen enough excited men and drunk men to tell 'em apart."

There was a titter in the court room. A bailiff banged a desk with a gavel.

"You insist that Mr. McArthur was drunk?"

"I do," said the defiant policeman.

"Yet you say he drove you down to the station house."

"Why—"

"Do you or don't you? Will the stenographer kindly read the officer's reply to Mr. Yistle's question from the record?"

The stenographer obliged: " 'We got into his car and he drove us down to the station house.'"

Mr. Hazeltine smiled coldly at the witness. "Is that correct?"

"That's correct."

"Then the accused couldn't have been drunk, or you would not have permitted him to drive his own car. In other words, he wasn't drunk at all. Do you know that it is an extremely serious offense, officer, to get up on that stand and tell lies?"

"I object," Mr. Yistle shouted. "Officer Kilpatrick has testified that, in his opinion, the accused was drunk. He might have been sufficiently sobered by the excitement to drive his own car with safety."

"A man cannot be drunk and sober at the same time," Mr. Hazeltine countered. "First the witness declares that the accused was drunk, then he states that the accused was sober enough to drive a car. Officer, why did you permit Mr. McArthur to drive that car if you considered him drunk?"

"It's just like Mr. Yistle says," replied the policeman. "The shock of it all must have sobered him up."

"Did he drive the car as if he were drunk?"

"Nope. He drove it all right."

"You mean, he drove the car as if he were perfectly sober?"

"I said he drove it all right."

Mr. Hazeltine smiled at the jury.

"That will be all," he said.

Joy Halliday was left with the impression that the policeman was not telling the whole truth; that he was prejudiced, and that his testimony, if not untrue, was unfair. She did not know that Mr. Hazeltine had caused that impression to be created.

Whenever she caught Compton McArthur's eye, he seemed to be looking in her direction, sometimes dreamily, sometimes sadly, and sometimes with a faint smile at his lips, as if she understood, and she alone. And as the trial progressed, Joy Halliday realized that she wanted this nice looking young man acquitted more than she had ever wanted anything in her life.

He did not look like the kind of man who would deliberately harm anybody. Under different conditions, he was, in fact, the kind of man with whom she might readily have fallen in love; for he was the kind of man for whom she had always dimly associated ideas of love and marriage.

What Willie Applegate tried to be, this man was. Clear-eyed. Clean cut. Manly. Best of all, she liked his brave, smiling eyes, eyes that told her again and again, "You must trust me. All this is a frightful farce. They can't send me up for twenty years."

By the time Willie Applegate was called to the witness stand she positively hated that too-handsome youth. He was so sure of himself.

Willie Applegate was, indeed, a convincing witness. He was serious and attentive. He seemed to be trying his best to tell nothing but the truth.

He pondered the questions Mr. Yistle put to him. He frowned. Occasionally he asked Mr. Yistle to state his questions more clearly. His whole attitude was one of admirable truthfulness.

"You say you saw a young woman in this car that the accused was driving?" asked Mr. Yistle.

"Yes, sir," said Willie Applegate.

"What was she doing?"

"She seemed to be cuddled against him."

"This was just before he struck down Jake Plovak?"

"Yes, sir."

"What did she do when the car struck Jake Plovak?"

"She screamed."

"What happened then?"

"I saw something shiny thrown from the car."

"Did the car stop after Jake Plovak had been run over?"

"No, sir."

"What was this shiny thing you saw thrown from the car?"

"It was a pocket flask; a silver pocket flask."

"A flask such as is used nowadays for carrying liquor on the hip?"

"Yes, sir, that kind of flask."

"Was this the flask?"

Mr. Yistle picked up the silver flask from the table and held it up. Willie Applegate bent forward.

Gillian Hazeltine stared at the flask. So did the accused. He turned pale.

When Joy Halliday next caught his eye he seemed bewildered, but distinctly she saw his lips form the word, "Lie!"

She fumed. It must be a lie.

Willie Applegate was examining the flask, turning it over and over in his hand.

"Yes," he said presently, "this is the flask."

"How do you identify it, Mr. Applegate?" said Mr. Yistle.

"By three equally spaced nicks along one bottom edge."

"I see. What did you do with the flask?"

"I put it in my pocket. Next morning I took it to the district attorney's office and left it with that young man sitting over here."

"You mean Mr. Bullock? This man?" And Mr. Yistle touched the back of Mr. Bullock's chair.

"Yes, sir, that one. He wasn't your assistant then. He was a clerk, I think, in the old district attorney's office. I left the flask with him and explained how it came into my possession."

"I see. You are perfectly sure, are you, Mr. Applegate, that the defendant was driving the car in a dangerous manner, and that he was doing so because he was intoxicated?"

"Yes, sir; I am positive."

"Tell the jury why you are positive, Mr. Applegate."

"The car was veering from one side of the street to the other," said the obliging witness. "And it was coming at a terrific rate of speed. At least forty miles an hour. I was hoping there wouldn't be another car coming down Market Street toward the intersection, because a serious smash-up would have resulted. Then Jake Plovak stepped out to cross the street and the car struck him."

"Then the girl screamed and, shortly after that, the flask was thrown out of the car?"

"Yes, sir."

"Did the car stop?"

"No, sir; it went right on."

"That will be all, Mr. Applegate. Thank you." And Mr. Yistle bowed, with an ironical smile, to Gillian Hazeltine.

Mr. Bullock had wandered over to Joy Halliday. He slipped into an empty seat beside her.

"Do you still wish to testify?" he asked.

"I do not," said Miss Halliday in an indignant whisper.

"Very well," said Mr. Bullock. "I guess we won't require your testimony after all."

Mr. Hazeltine was cross-examining Willie Applegate.

"You say you are a law student?"

"Yes, sir."

"How long have you been studying law?"

"About two years, sir."

"You are fairly well acquainted with legal procedure, I take it?"

"Well, I'm only a student, Mr. Hazeltine."

"Will you kindly define the word 'tort'?"

"I object," snapped Mr. Yistle.

"On what grounds?" said Judge Manning.

"The question is inconsequential, irrelevant, and immaterial, your honor."

"I merely wished to prove to my own satisfaction that

the witness is what he claims to be," Mr. Hazeltine said apologetically.

"Objection is overruled. You may answer Mr. Hazeltine's question, Mr. Applegate."

Mr. Yistle looked worried, but Willie Applegate only smiled pleasantly.

"A tort," he said, "is any private or civil wrong by act or omission giving rise to a remedy which is not an action of contract."

"Thank you," said Gillian Hazeltine. "You are a very smart young man. Something you said a minute ago puzzles me, Mr. Applegate. You said, in answer to one of Mr. Yistle's questions, that a young lady was cuddled up beside the accused when the accident happened."

"Yes, sir."

"Was she blonde or brunette?"

"I didn't see her clearly enough for that, sir."

"Was she dressed in light or dark material?"

Applegate hesitated. "It was dark."

"It was dark. At the beginning of your testimony you stated that the accused's arm was around this young lady; that he was hugging her or petting her."

"Yes, sir."

"Did you see the accused's hand?"

Again the witness hesitated. "No, sir."

"But you are sure his arm was around her?"

"Yes, sir."

"Now wait a minute. You have said that the girl was dressed in a dark material. We already know that the accused was dressed in a dark material. The street light was some distance away. You could not readily have seen a dark arm around a dark body, and you did not see the accused's hand. Why do you say that his arm was around her, when you did not, could not have, seen it around her?"

Willie Applegate's face was slightly pink. "I have seen enough spooning couples to know how they look when their arms are around each other. Her arm was around his neck, and his arm was around her waist."

"I see. You know all about spooning, eh?"

"I bet he thinks he's a lady killer!" said Joy indignantly to herself.

"After Jake Plovak was struck down, what did you do?" asked Gillian Hazeltine.

"I ran to the drug store on the corner and telephoned for a policeman."

"You didn't go over and examine Jake Plovak, did you, to find out whether there was anything you could do for him?"

"No, sir."

"Why didn't you?"

"I object, your honor," said Mr. Yistle indignantly. "This young man was doing what he thought was the wisest thing when he ran to phone the police. I must take exception to Mr. Hazeltine's constant insinuations against his character."

"The objection is sustained," said Judge Manning. "Kindly confine your questions to the issue, Mr. Hazeltine. I don't want this trial to drag on forever."

"Very well, your honor," said Gillian Hazeltine. "Mr. Applegate, why didn't you give that flask to the first policeman you saw?"

"I have some knowledge of the law," answered Willie Applegate. "When I knew that Plovak was dead, I knew that this would be a matter for the district attorney's office. I took the flask directly there."

"What was in the flask?"

"Gin."

"Did you taste it?"

"No, sir, but I smelled it."

"You aren't a chemist, are you?"

"No, sir."

"Then you can't swear it was gin, can you?"

"No, sir."

"That will be all."

Gillian Hazeltine sat down promptly beside Compton McArthur, and the two of them put their heads together. The introduction of the silver flask evidently worried them.

Joy Halliday was now furious. She was sure that Willie Applegate was lying.

She had met him at Mr. Yistle's office on her second visit. She had heard him agree to change certain features of his testimony. She was sure that he was selling himself, and she was sure that, on the strength of his evidence, Compton McArthur would be sent to prison!

Harry Zarrow, the chemist, was now on the stand, driving the final nails into Compton McArthur's fate. He testified that on the morning of June 21, Mr. Bullock had brought him the flask of gin, that he had poured off a sample and analyzed it, and found it to consist of forty per cent of alcohol by volume. It was ordinary synthetic gin.

"I have no more witnesses," Mr. Yistle said when he had finished questioning the chemist. "I placed this qualified chemist on the stand because I anticipated some such question as my distinguished adversary has raised. The liquid in that flask, gentlemen, was gin. Compton McArthur was drunk on that gin. He was driving his car drunkenly. He was disobeying the law when he struck down Jake Plovak, not only by driving at a lawless rate of speed and by driving on the wrong side of the street, but by being under the influence of intoxicating liquors. The State rests."

The court room hummed with excitement. The public had anticipated a long, wordy trial, and the State was already finished!

Mr. Yistle had slipped into the empty seat beside Joy Halliday.

"I decided not to use you after all, Miss Halliday," he said. "McArthur hasn't a chance. Gillian Hazeltine is clever, but he might as well throw up the sponge now. With my few witnesses I have proved what he can't disprove with as many dozen. Compton McArthur is going to prison!"

He jumped up and left her before Joy could frame a rejoinder. She wanted to tell Mr. Yistle that he had done a cruel, unjust thing.

She heard Gillian Hazeltine pleading for a little time; he had not expected the State to finish so soon. Court was adjourned until the following morning.

Joy Halliday slipped into the hall after the prisoner was taken back to jail by the two bailiffs. An old man with white hair and a drawn, gray face hastened past her shouldering her out of the way. She heard a young fellow say: "There goes his old man."

And she looked again. She recognized him then, from newspaper photographs, as Compton McArthur's father.

The papers had called Compton the black sheep of the family, and it was common knowledge that, because of this latest escapade, his father had washed his hands of him. He had permitted his son to remain in jail until the trial; would not go his bond.

One newspaper had boldly said that Mr. McArthur was grieving because his older son, Kenneth, had died instead of this young wastrel.

Joy now resented that. Compton McArthur did not look like a young wastrel to her. She knew that he had suffered; she knew that he had been taught a lesson. And she wondered what his defense would be. What *could* Mr. Hazeltine say to clear him of the charge?

She heard a man making a bet of three to one that Compton McArthur would be convicted. She shuddered. They must not convict him!

Gillian Hazeltine came bustling out. She hastened to him.

"Mr. Hazeltine!" she said breathlessly.

"Joy Halliday," he growled, "what were you doing in that court room? A criminal court while a manslaughter trial is going on is no place for a nice girl like you."

"I was interested," she said. "You see, Mr. Hazeltine, I saw the accident."

His polite smile had faded. He looked at her keenly.

"You did?"

"If you can use me as a witness, I'll gladly testify," she rushed on. "Willie Applegate is nothing but a liar! I think it's a shame to send that fine-looking young man to prison. It's positively vicious to cheat justice the way Mr. Yistle is doing!"

Gillian Hazeltine took her firmly by the arm.

"Have lunch with me," he said. "I want to hear the whole

story. My dear girl, do you realize that you may save that young man from the penitentiary?"

"That's just what I want to do," said Joy.

"You're an angel, Joy Halliday, that's what you are!"

5

MR. HAZELTINE HELD a long, bright-red pencil in his right hand between the tips of his thumb and forefinger, and this he waved slowly and gracefully as if it were a wand. The court room was packed, and hundreds of people were crowded in the corridor outside.

Joy Halliday watched Compton McArthur's attorney with bright, fascinated eyes. He was no longer her natural enemy, but a dear old friend; he was the man who would save that splendid young man if any one could save him.

She listened eagerly to his opening address to the jury.

"The crime of manslaughter," said Mr. Hazeltine slowly, as if he were selecting his words with the greatest care, "is committed when a man is responsible for the death of another through carelessness or negligence in carrying out a lawful action, and he is likewise guilty of the crime of manslaughter when he is responsible for the death of another while committing an illegal act.

"An example of the first kind of manslaughter would be that of a contractor who had a gang of men at work under a building. If the contractor specified two by four underpinning instead of, say, six by eights, and the building collapsed and killed a man, the contractor would be guilty of manslaughter, because he had not exercised due care.

That is the first kind of manslaughter, and the contractor would be liable to a prison sentence.

"The crime of which Compton McArthur is charged is the second kind of manslaughter. You gentlemen of the jury are to decide whether Compton McArthur was actually committing an illegal act—without extenuating circumstances—when the car he was driving ran down and killed Jake Plovak.

"Mr. Yistle, the State's attorney, has set forth and has endeavored to prove by his witnesses that Compton McArthur was guilty of committing sundry illegal acts while he was driving the car which killed Jake Plovak.

"He has endeavored to prove that Compton McArthur was, firstly, driving on the wrong side of the street; secondly, that he was driving faster than the legal speed limit; thirdly, that he was not managing the car in a proper and legal way because he was at the time petting or hugging a girl who sat beside him; fourthly, that he was intoxicated while driving the car.

"The committing of any one of these illegal acts when Jake Plovak was killed is sufficient to convict Compton McArthur of the crime of manslaughter. If I cannot satisfy you that Compton McArthur is innocent of these four separate charges, it is, of course, your duty to return a verdict in his disfavor.

"The law always permits, as I have intimated, extenuating circumstances within reasonable limits in the violation of certain laws without the penalties becoming operable against the violator. As an illustration, let us suppose that Compton McArthur, in exceeding the speed limit, was driving his car on a matter involving life or death. While he was breaking the speed law, it would be unfair and unjust to punish him for so doing.

"I will endeavor to prove to your complete satisfaction that Compton McArthur did not violate the laws of which he has been accused, or that he did so with good and sufficient reason, and that he should not be held responsible for the death of Jake Plovak, or be punished for having brought it about. My first witness will be Compton McArthur."

There was an audible ripple of excitement in the court room while Compton McArthur, grave and unsmiling, walked to the witness stand and seated himself in the gray light that filtered through the dusty windows.

Gillian Hazeltine was reputed to be a fighting lawyer and a brilliant one, but the consensus of opinion was that, this time, he had bitten off more than he could chew. How could he possibly clear Compton McArthur of these four separate charges? How could he prove extenuating circumstances in the case of any of them?

Compton McArthur sat down and bent forward with his lips slightly parted his clear blue eyes fixed upon his lawyer.

Gillian Hazeltine allowed a number of seconds to pass before he walked slowly over and faced his first witness.

Mr. Yistle was smiling good naturedly. Mr. Bullock was grinning quite frankly. The Silver Fox was in a trap, and there wasn't any way for him to wriggle out of it.

Even some of the jurors were faintly smiling. The court room was not unfriendly; it was simply derisive. Gillian Hazeltine was going to entertain them, but Compton McArthur's fate was already sealed. Nothing he, nor

Gillian Hazeltine, nor any witness could say would alter that fate.

"Mr. McArthur," the lawyer began in a gentle voice, "will you describe to this court just what happened on the evening of the 20th of June?"

"I was dining that evening with my brother Kenneth and his wife Geraldine," the young man with the clear blue eyes answered. "We had a late dinner and afterward went out into the garden behind the house to smoke after-dinner cigars." He hesitated.

"Did you have anything to drink that evening?" Mr. Hazeltine asked.

"I had one cocktail before dinner," the accused answered.

"Did you have a highball during dinner?"

"No, I had nothing more to drink."

"Did you have a liqueur in the garden?"

"No, I drank nothing but one cocktail."

"Go on with your story."

"The three of us sat in the garden, talking. It was about half past nine when my sister-in-law complained of pains in her heart. At first we were not concerned, thinking that she was perhaps suffering a little from indigestion.

"My brother, Kenneth, went into the house and brought her a drink of bicarbonate of soda and water, but that did not relieve the pain. It suddenly became worse and we realized she was having a heart attack. She had had two the year before.

"We laid her out on a swing, and my brother ran into the house to bring a phial of nitroglycerine supposed to be in the medicine chest in the bathroom. He came running back, yelling at me that the phial was gone and to go and get Dr. Osborne, who lived three doors down the street.

"I ran to get Dr. Osborne. He came back with me, but he had no nitroglycerine. He wrote a prescription hurriedly. I ran out and got into my brother's roadster, which was parked on the street in front, and drove as fast as I could to Sillinger's drug store, where I got the nitroglycerine.

"When I was running out the door I almost collided with the nurse my sister-in-law had had during her two previous heart attacks. Her name is Miss Mary Glissen. I told Miss Glissen what had happened, and she jumped into the car with me and we drove back to the house.

"I was driving about thirty-five miles an hour when we approached the intersection of Market and Maple. I slowed to about thirty for the crossing and blew the horn a number of times. I was driving at no more than that speed, between twenty-five and thirty, when a man lurched out from the trees on the right hand side of Maple. I twisted the wheel to avoid him and jammed on the brakes. He seemed to run right into the right front mudguard.

"I knew I had knocked him down, but I was sure that a few minutes would make no difference in his condition, while it might mean the life or death of my sister-in-law. I hurried on to the house and gave the nitroglycerine to Miss Glissen. She jumped out and ran into the house, and I turned around and came back to where Jake Plovak was lying and gave myself up to the policeman."

There were grins and whisperings all over the court room as Compton McArthur finished. Some one tittered, and Judge Manning glared in his direction.

Joy Halliday's heart sank. It sounded *so* unconvincing.

Gillian Hazeltine waited until the rustling of whispers had subsided.

"You say you had but the one drink all evening?"

"That is all. Just the cocktail."

"Do you consider that you were intoxicated?"

For the first time Compton McArthur smiled.

"I didn't even feel it," he said.

"But you were excited when you delivered yourself up to the policeman?"

"I hardly knew what I was doing, I was so excited."

"I want you to tell the court what you and Miss Glissen were doing when you drove her to the house. I mean, did you have an arm around her? And did she have an arm around you?"

"No, sir. I had both hands on the wheel."

"Was she cuddled against you?"

"If she was, I don't remember it. We were both excited about my sister-in-law. She may have huddled against me, but I am sure she was not cuddling. It was not a petting party. How could it have been?"

"That is all," said Gillian Hazeltine.

Mr. Yistle arose, wearing a broad grin. Mr. Bullock was grinning too. And at least half the jurors wore grins.

"You say you were not drunk that night?" Mr. Yistle asked.

"No, sir, I was not."

"You didn't even have a glow?"

"No, sir, I didn't feel the effects of that cocktail at all."

"You're pretty accustomed to drink, aren't you?"

"Yes, sir, I am."

"You've done a good deal of drinking."

"I suppose I have."

"You're generally known as a pretty fast young fellow, aren't you?"

"I don't hear what people say about me."

Mr. Yistle chuckled softly.

"Kindly tell this court where you were on the night of December 31."

"I object," said Mr. Hazeltine promptly. "The question is irrelevant, your honor. The accident did not take place until six months later."

"I am merely endeavoring to ascertain certain features of the accused's character," Mr. Yistle explained.

"The objection is overruled," said Judge Manning. "Mr. Yistle has a right to produce as much evidence as he wishes bearing upon the accused's character as it applies to the subject at issue."

"Will the witness answer my question?" said Mr. Yistle.

"Where was I on the night of December 31?" said the young man. "I spent the evening at a roadhouse between here and Mill town."

"The Black Swan?"

"Yes, sir, I believe that's the name of the place."

"It's a very notorious roadhouse, isn't it?"

"I—I believe it is said to be."

"What were you doing there?"

"I was with a party, celebrating New Year's Eve."

"Who was in the party?"

"There were eight or nine of us, as I remember. Five men and four girls. I would prefer not to mention the names of those who attended the party."

"You mean you don't want to subject them to notoriety?"

"I'd prefer not to drag their names into this, if you don't mind."

"Well, I do mind. Was one of them Harry Larson, the bootlegger, who is now spending two years in the penitentiary?"

"Yes."

"Were the other men Billy Jamieson, Larson's side-kick, and Wally Van Heusen, who spends most of his time at the race track?"

"Yes, they were there."

"Were the four girls members of the chorus of the Qui Vive Burlesque Company?"

"I believe they were."

"That was the sort of company you chose to spend New Year's Eve with, instead of at home with your family?"

"That's where I spent it," the young man said stonily.

"Did you have anything to drink at that party?"

"Yes, we had plenty to drink."

"Did you have gin cocktails?"

"Yes, we did."

"Gin is a favorite drink of yours, isn't it?"

"I used to like it."

"Oh, you've reformed, have you?"

"I don't drink any more, if that's what you mean."

"Hard to get liquor in jail, isn't it?"

The crowded court room rustled with laughter. The bailiff brought down his gavel. The judge smiled.

"Well," the smiling and confident Mr. Yistle went on, "back in the dear old days when you did drink gin you liked it, didn't you?"

"I drank it," said the accused wearily.

"Very well," went on the State's attorney crisply. "In those days when you used to drink gin did you carry it upon your person?"

"In a flask."

"What kind of a flask?"

"A hip flask."

"A silver one?"

"I suppose it was silver."

"Like this one?" Mr. Yistle held up above his head Exhibit A.

"Something like that one."

"This one?"

"No, not that one."

"Are you sure this is not your flask?"

"I certainly am."

"Where is your flask?"

The witness had grown paler and paler. "I don't know. I lost it some time during the week preceding the accident."

Mr. Yistle looked at him with dumfounded amazement. He had not supposed that he was leading the witness into this trap; he had merely wished to establish a circumstantial relationship between the accused and the flask in his hand. This was an unlooked-for triumph. An artist would have called it "an accidental."

The State's attorney quickly turned the accident to his advantage.

"You mean to tell me, Mr. McArthur, that you were so unfortunate as to lose your own flask just a day or two before this one was found beside the dead body of Jake Plovak?"

"That is not my flask," stated the young man.

Mr. Yistle shrugged and grinned at the jury. He shook his head in little jerks.

"Well," he proceeded, "let's drop the painful subject of the flask. I don't blame you for blushing, Mr. McArthur. Let's get on to the question of what became of the gin that was in this flask. It was half full when you dropped it from your car—"

"I didn't drop it from my car!"

"Very well. I know how distressing it is to mention the subject, Mr. McArthur. It's what came out of that flask, not only on the night when you brutally killed Jake Plovak, but on other nights, that interests us. That flask was a well that never went dry, no matter how often the pitcher came to it, wasn't it? A magical spring, that flask. You say you drank heavily—before the reform wave set in."

"I used to drink frequently."

"Were you ever arrested on a charge of reckless driving?"

"I was."

"How many times, Mr. McArthur?"

"Five, I think."

"Were you ever fined for being under the influence of intoxicating liquor when you were arrested for speeding?"

"I was. Three times."

"Getting drunk and breaking the speed limit is one of the best things you do, isn't it?"

The defendant only glared at him and licked his pale lips.

"Let's go back for a moment now to that New Year's Eve party," said Mr. Yistle pleasantly. "The nine of you got pretty drunk, didn't you?"

"I think we were all feeling pretty good."

"There was a lot of love making and general carrying on, wasn't there?"

"I suppose there was."

"Did you indulge in it?"

"I don't remember."

"What started the fight?"

"I don't know."

"Didn't Harry Larson get sore at Billy Jamieson for kissing his girl, and didn't Billy hit Harry on the face with a dishful of lobster Newburg? Wasn't that what started the free-for-all fight that ended in all nine of you being kicked bodily out of the Black Swan?"

"Perhaps it did. I don't remember."

"You were drunk that night, weren't you?"

"I suppose I was."

"Yes, you were! You bet your life you were! Out on a drunken party with bootleggers and chorus girls! Arrested five times for speeding, and three out of those five times you were fined for drunken driving! Yet you were not on the night when you brutally ran down and killed that harmless workingman, under the influence of liquor?"

"I was not."

Mr. Yistle dramatically doubled his fists. He appeared to be very angry.

"You expect this jury of intelligent men to believe that?"

"I hope they believe that."

"You certainly do! After a life of wastefulness and dissipation, so that now your, poor old father is sitting with bowed head in this court room, you expect us to believe that cock-and-bull story!"

"I object," roared Gillian Hazeltine.

"On what grounds?" asked the court.

"It has not yet been proved that the witness is telling a cock-and-bull story, your, honor,"

"It hasn't been proved that he isn't!" snapped Mr. Yistle.

"Finish your cross-examination," shouted Gillian Hazeltine. "Go on and blacken this young man's character all you wish! Do your worst!"

The two lawyers glared at each other.

"Proceed with your cross-examination," the judge curtly directed.

"I am through," said Mr. Yistle. "I have proved my point to my full satisfaction. This man would naturally lie himself black in the face to save himself. The mysteriously missing silver flask! Drunken, reckless driving, time after time. That is all."

"Call your next witness, Mr. Hazeltine."

"The next witness is Mrs. Geraldine McArthur," said Mr. Hazeltine, mopping his brow.

Joy Halliday looked at her keenly as the widow of the late Kenneth McArthur moved to the stand. She was a slender girl in deepest mourning. Her eyes were faded blue. Her blond hair was lifeless.

She had a tremulous, rather full underlip. She seemed embarrassed and inexpressibly sad. Automatically she held up her hand to be sworn in. The court room murmured.

She, they knew, was the widow of the admirable son. Where the accused man had been the black sheep, Kenneth had been his father's greatest hope. He had gone into the McArthur Paint and Varnish Company when he finished college. He had worked hard and honestly earned a responsible executive position.

He would step into his father's shoes when the old gentleman retired. His death had been a blow from which his father had almost succumbed himself.

Much as the curious crowd sympathized with this gentle, pale girl's recent bereavement, they were hostile. It was only natural that she would say the things that would clear her wild young brother-in-law of the cloud over him.

She told her story simply, in a low, cultured voice.

"We had finished dinner and were sitting in the garden when my heart suddenly began to hurt. My husband went into the house and brought me a tumbler of water and some bicarbonate of soda. Then the pains increased. I don't remember much after that, until I opened my eyes and saw Dr. Osborne and Miss Glissen bending over me."

Mr. Hazeltine turned her over to Mr. Yistle for cross-examination without questioning her. The district attorney's manner was gentle and considerate.

"You say you don't remember what happened after your husband brought you the bicarbonate and water?"

"Everything was very confused," she answered.

"You do not know that your brother-in-law, the accused, went out to fetch Dr. Osborne?"

"Yes, I vaguely remember that."

"Do you remember his going for nitroglycerine?"

"I seem to, but it is very dim."

"You cannot swear positively that Compton McArthur went for the nitroglycerine and returned with Miss Glissen?"

"Not positively. I understood that he had gone."

"Do you think, Mrs. McArthur, that you can rely very

dependably upon your memory when you are suffering as you were then?"

"It is true. Everything does become very confused to me."

"It might have been your husband who went for the nitroglycerine and Miss Glissen, mightn't it?"

"Yes, it might have been, but I understood—"

She seemed bewildered. She glanced quickly at Gillian Hazeltine. There were beads of perspiration on the lawyer's brow.

Here was a witness who must be prompted! Mr. Hazeltine turned his back quickly and blew his nose.

"You can't swear that it was Compton McArthur who went to the drug store, can you?"

"I—I'm afraid I can't."

"That will be all, thank you," said Mr. Yistle promptly.

Joy Halliday felt sorry for the pretty, pale widow. Mrs. Geraldine McArthur had done her best to save her wild young brother-in-law, but her testimony was questionable.

She had faltered. She had been frightened. The jury, Joy knew, was not impressed.

She caught Compton McArthur's eye again. He was looking at her gravely, but not hopefully. She wondered if he had made love to a chorus girl that night at the Black Swan.

No, no; he wasn't the kind of man who would make love to cheap girls. He was too clean; too wholesome. There was something about him—

"Next witness!"

6

THE NEXT WITNESS was Dr. Osborne. He was an elderly man with a fine gray beard and sparkling brown eyes. He was a cynical looking man. There was about him the competent, brisk air of a successful professional man.

He sat down with a brisk air, after being sworn in. He was the soul of self-confidence. He was even smiling a little as his shrewd, bright brown eyes darted about the court room.

He was dressed in dark gray. A heavy gold chain stretched across his ample stomach. You knew he was reliable. He was the man you called when you were sick. He was the man who, with a grave smile, assured you that it was not appendicitis, but a stomach ache.

"What is your full name?" Mr. Hazeltine asked him.

"John Murray Osborne," said the physician.

"How long have you practiced medicine in this town?"

"Twenty-four years."

"Do you specialize in malfunctions of the heart?"

"I do, yes."

"Are you considered an expert on heart diseases?"

"Not by my enemies."

The smiling court room broke into laughter. The bailiff banged his desk with the gavel.

"We will concede," Mr. Hazeltine, smilingly went on,

"that you are excessively modest. Your reputation in this town, I believe, will bear out my assertion that you are considered an authority on heart troubles. In other words, doctor, you are generally called into consultations concerning heart diseases."

"I am frequently called upon for such diagnoses," Dr. Osborne admitted gravely.

"You have been called upon at various times, have you not, to treat the witness who just left the stand—Mrs. Geraldine McArthur?"

"Yes, I have attended that young lady four or five times."

"Can you give us an idea of the nature of her malady?"

"She has suffered from time to time from mild attacks of angina pectoris."

"Is this a dangerous disease?"

"Extremely dangerous."

"If an attack is not corrected in time, is the victim apt to die?"

"The victim is, indeed. A corrective cannot be administered too promptly."

"What medicine do you commonly prescribe for an attack of angina pectoris?"

"Nitroglycerine—or amyl nitrate."

"Did you ever leave a supply of this medicine with Mrs. Geraldine McArthur, with instructions that she take it in case of a subsequent attack of angina pectoris?"

"I did. I left a bottle of nitroglycerine with her and also a supply of amyl nitrate ampules after an attack she had last September."

"Were you called upon in your home by any member of the McArthur family on the night of June 20?"

"I was. Compton McArthur, the accused, called at my house at about nine thirty or a little later that evening in a state of great excitement and requested me to come at once to his sister-in-law."

"What did he tell you?"

"The young man said that she was suffering from a sudden heart attack and that the supply of nitroglycerine I had left was missing from the medicine cabinet."

"Tell us what you did then, doctor."

"I picked up my medicine bag and hurried over to Kenneth McArthur's house and found Mrs. McArthur stretched out on a swing in the garden. She was partly unconscious and was suffering greatly."

"Describe what you did then."

"Why, I opened my bag to administer morphine, and I found that I had no morphine, nor any nitroglycerine, either. It was necessary to obtain some corrective in a great hurry. Compton McArthur was standing near by. I told him to jump into a car and go down to the drug store and bring some nitroglycerine."

"Do you recall your exact conversation with him, doctor?"

Dr. Osborne smiled. "I believe I said just about that. 'Jump into your car and break your neck getting down to the drug store and getting back with some nitroglycerine.'"

"Didn't you tell him that her heart was much more valuable than his neck?"

"I think I did."

"Do you recall his reply?"

"I do. He said: 'Can I get the stuff without a prescription?'"

"What happened then?"

"I wrote out a prescription, tore it from the pad, and he dashed away."

"It was he who went?"

"Of course, it was he who went."

"It wasn't his brother, the late Kenneth McArthur?"

"It was not. Kenneth McArthur stayed with me all the time Compton McArthur was gone."

"How long was he gone?"

"I don't know. He didn't return himself. Miss Mary Glissen, the nurse who attended Mrs. McArthur on previous attacks, came in shortly with a bottle of nitroglycerine and whispered to me that Compton McArthur had struck down a man and had gone to see how seriously hurt the man was."

"Why did she whisper to you?"

"Because, I suppose, she did not want to upset the patient."

"You are convinced, are you, doctor, that Compton McArthur went to the drug store with the prescription blank you wrote, and that he procured the nitroglycerine, picked up Miss Glissen and drove her to the house?"

"Of course I am convinced. Why shouldn't I be?"

"That will be all, doctor. Mr. Yistle, you may cross-examine the witness."

Mr. Yistle arose. His confident smile was shaken. He was still smiling, but the testimony of this witness had dealt his cause a decided blow.

He looked at Dr. Osborne for some seconds before he framed a question. Behind her, Joy Halliday heard two people whispering:

"That may be all well and good," said one girl to another,

"but how're you goin' to get around that Willie Applegate's testimony? He said he seen McArthur throw a flask out of the car, and he seen McArthur pettin' a girl."

"I believe Willie," her companion replied. "He's certainly some sheik, Willie is."

"And that's *all* he is," said Joy to herself as she turned about and stared at the two whisperers. Wait until *she* got on the witness stand! She'd show them!

"You say," Mr. Yistle was saying to Dr. Osborne, "that when you reached the swing where Mrs. McArthur was lying, you opened your bag and found that it contained neither nitroglycerine, amyl nitrate ampules nor morphine?"

"It contained neither," affirmed the doctor.

Mr. Yistle looked meaningly at the jury before he framed his next question:

"Isn't it a little irregular, doctor, for a physician to go out on a case—especially a heart case—and not carry in his bag the particular medicines he will require?"

"It may seem irregular to a member of the bar," Dr. Osborne answered, "but it may readily happen. My house, you see, is not my office. And I am not a general practitioner. I am a diagnostician. Diagnosticians seldom administer medicines. Many diagnosticians do not even prescribe medicines, but merely attempt to diagnose an ailment."

"Yet you did, on that and on prior occasions, not only prescribe, but administered nitroglycerine to Mrs. McArthur."

"That is true."

"Why, if I may ask, did you depart in that particular case from your usual practice?"

"Because the case particularly interested me. Angina pectoris is not common in women as young as Mrs. McArthur. I was greatly interested in the underlying causes. Her nervous system, you see, has for years—"

"We are not interested in her symptoms," said Mr. Yistle curtly. "What does interest us, Dr. Osborne, is why you would prescribe and administer medicine when it is admittedly not your custom. Did you have a particular interest in the patient aside from a professional one?"

"I don't know what you mean," snapped Dr. Osborne.

"Isn't it true, doctor, that you have been on the friendliest of terms with the McArthur family for years?"

"It is true, yes. We have been great friends."

"Isn't it true that your interest in the McArthur boys, Kenneth and Compton, dates back to their birth?"

"Yes!"

"Isn't it true that you were the attending physician when both of the boys were born?"

"Yes, I delivered both children."

"Isn't it true that you are Compton McArthur's godfather?"

Dr. Osborne glared at him. "I am his godfather. Yes!"

"Would you like to see him go to prison, doctor?"

"Of course I would not!"

Mr. Yistle again sent a meaning glance toward the jury box.

"You are very fond of him, are you not?"

"I am. Yes."

"You have no sons of your own, have you?"

"No, I have no children."

"Isn't it true that you have said you wished Compton McArthur were your son?"

"I object!" Mr. Hazeltine shouted. "These insinuations against the integrity of the witness are absolutely uncalled for, your honor."

"I am not aware," said Judge Manning, "that insinuations are being made against the witness's character, Mr. Hazeltine. You may proceed with your examination, Mr. Yistle. Objection is overruled."

"Will the witness answer my last question?" said the State's attorney.

"I may have stated that I wished Compton McArthur was my son," said the doctor.

"And you don't want to see him sent to prison?"

"I do not think he deserves to go to prison. I believe he is innocent of this crime."

"And you love him like a son! Of course you do not want to see him go to prison! You are an old friend of the family. You are an old friend of his father's. You wish to spare him further disgrace!"

"Please stop shouting at me," said Dr. Osborne, testily.

"Do you believe, doctor," Mr. Yistle went on in lower, more patient tones, "that a man should be punished for the crime he commits, the evil he does?"

"I think that there are times—"

"Will you answer my question?"

"Yes," Dr. Osborne snapped. "I do."

"Thank you," said Mr. Yistle sarcastically. "I value your opinion highly, Dr. Osborne. I, too, think that a man should be punished for the crimes he commits. That is why I am here representing the State in this trial. My function is

to see that evildoers are punished. I am here in this court
room to-day to see that an evildoer is punished.

"Friendship and paternal feeling must stand aside for
justice. Compton McArthur is indeed fortunate in having
such a loving friend, such a godfather, as you are, doctor.
But friendship can go too far. Friendship must stand aside
for justice, my dear doctor. That is all."

Joy Halliday felt a little ill. Somehow, Mr. Yistle had
cast a cloud of doubt upon all of Dr. Osborne's testimony.
Would any boy's godfather want to see him go to prison
for twenty years? Certainly not!

The whisper of public opinion behind her echoed her
thoughts:

"Gee," said one girl, "at first I thought Compton had
a real chance, but, say, I wonder if the doc *was* telling the
truth. Mr. Yistle made it all look kinda fishy, didn't he?"

"He sure did," her companion agreed. "Who wouldn't
tell lies for somebody they loved? I would!"

"He isn't lying! It's the truth!" Joy wanted to shriek at the
two girls. "It's Willie Applegate who was lying. What Mrs.
McArthur said was gospel truth, and what Dr. Osborne
said was gospel truth. People like that wouldn't lie!"

But she kept her counsel. A man behind her said:

"Hazeltine is trying to build up a clever wall of defense,
but he can't drive past what that Applegate fellow testified.
Compton McArthur is going up the road. I'll bet anybody
five to one the jury brings in a verdict of guilty—and no
recommendation for mercy."

"You want something for nothing, don't you?" another
whisperer said with a low chuckle.

"They mustn't bring in a verdict of guilty!" Joy said frantically to herself.

Another witness had taken the stand. He was a worried looking little man with weak eyes, that he blinked constantly, and a codfish mouth.

He had buck teeth and a frightened air. His hand trembled visibly when he raised it to take the oath to tell the truth, the whole truth, and nothing but the truth.

Gillian Hazeltine smiled at him reassuringly.

"What is your full name?"

"Anthony G. Silinger," said the witness in a scared voice.

"What is your occupation?"

"D-druggist!"

"Where is your store?"

"On the n-n-northeast corner of Maple Street and Fourteenth Street."

"Was a prescription filed in your drug store on the evening of June 20 at approximately nine fifty o'clock for two ounces of nitroglycerine?"

"It was, yes, sir."

"By whom was it filed?"

"By Compton McArthur."

"Who wrote out that prescription?"

"Dr. Osborne, sir."

"Is this the prescription?"

Mr. Hazeltine handed to the witness a small square sheet of white paper. The druggist examined it and bobbed his head vigorously.

"Yes, sir, this is it."

"I wish to submit this as material evidence," said Gillian Hazeltine. "This is the prescription which Dr. Osborne wrote out and gave to Compton McArthur; which Compton McArthur took to Silinger's drug store and had filled. The date is June 20. The prescription calls for two ounces of nitroglycerine."

Joy Halliday could have clapped her hands. Inch by inch, that wall of defense was rising between Compton McArthur and twenty years in the penitentiary.

Mr. Hazeltine concluded his questioning and Mr. Yistle, wearing his good-natured and self-assured smile, began the cross-examination.

He fixed his gray eyes almost fiercely upon the shrinking witness. Joy had the sinking feeling that all was not well; that something unpleasant was going to happen, the lawyer was so confident the witness so frightened.

"Mr. Silinger," began the State's attorney in a vigorous, accusing voice, "did you personally wait upon Compton McArthur when he brought in the prescription blank, as has been alleged?"

The druggist looked more scared than ever.

"Why, no," he faltered. "My assistant waited on him."

"Where were you at the time, Mr. Silinger?"

"I—I was at the movies with my wife."

"You weren't in the store, then, when the accused came in, as has been alleged, for the nitroglycerine?"

"No, sir, I was at the movies. My assistant filled the prescription."

"I see. What is your assistant's name?"

"His name—well, you see, Mr. Yistle, I haven't the same assistant I had then. The name of my old assistant was Terence Conway."

"Where is he?" Mr. Yistle snapped.

"Why, he—he isn't living, sir. He was killed in that automobile smash-up near Steel City a couple of months ago."

"Ah! I see! He can't testify in this trial that Compton McArthur actually came to this drug store of yours for nitroglycerine, so you are testifying in his place, eh? Just what are you so anxious to prove to me, Mr. Silinger?"

"Why! That Compton McArthur came to my store on the night of June 20, with a prescription and bought two ounces of nitroglycerine!"

"Yet you didn't sell it yourself, and you didn't see Compton McArthur!"

"No, sir, I didn't."

"Then what makes you so sure that he did enter your store with the prescription blank, got the nitroglycerine and went out?"

"Why! The blank proves it, doesn't it? There it is, in plain writing!" said the shivering witness.

Mr. Yistle glowered threateningly at him.

"When did you find this prescription blank, Mr. Silinger?"

"The other day, sir, when a lawyer from Mr. Hazeltine's office came out and asked if I could locate it."

"Could you locate it?"

"Certainly, sir. It was right there on the spindle with the other prescriptions I had filled during the month of June!"

"Now pay close attention to me, Mr. Silinger. Does any one aside from yourself have access to the back of your pharmacy besides yourself and your assistant?"

"Why—why—yes, sir. Customers occasionally come back there."

"Isn't it true that you were arrested and fined for selling grain alcohol about a year ago?"

"Yes, sir, I was fined for that."

"I thought so. You let people come back into the pharmacy and you sold them grain alcohol by the quart."

"I—I regret to say I did, sir."

"Very well. Now give your sharpest attention to this question, Mr. Silinger. Would it not have been possible for some one to have come into the back of your store and have slipped a forged prescription blank upon one of those spindles?"

"I object!" roared Gillian Hazeltine, leaping to his feet. "Your honor, I must request you to have my distinguished adversary refrain from casting aspersions, as he has so openly been doing, upon the integrity of my witnesses. This man has told a straight, honest story, and I insist—"

"I cannot see," interrupted Judge Manning, "that the State's attorney is casting aspersions upon the integrity of this witness. It is permissible for him to state a hypothetical proposition. This court and this jury have enough intelligence to recognize it as a hypothetical proposition. The witness may deny the reasonableness of the hypothesis or not as he sees fit. Go on, Mr. Yistle."

Mr. Yistle was fairly marching on to triumph. His lost smile had returned. Joy hated him.

"Will the witness answer the question?" he fairly cooed.

"I suppose so," said Mr. Silinger in a very frail voice.

"That is all I wished to prove," said Mr. Yistle happily. "You did not see the accused enter your store; you did not wait upon him; the man who is alleged to have waited on him cannot be produced to give testimony; and it is well within the bounds of probability that this prescription was forged and placed upon that file for the purpose of strengthening Mr. Hazeltine's extremely interesting line of evidence."

Mr. Hazeltine took a step toward him with clenched fists.

"Are you intimating that the witnesses I am producing are liars?"

"Oh, dear me, no," said Mr. Yistle with mock contrition. "I would not dream of such tactics, Mr. Hazeltine. I am simply satisfying my curiosity. I am trying to convince myself that Compton McArthur did take a prescription written by Dr. Osborne to Silinger's drug store and have it filled. But I am not at all certain that this happened, and I am sure that the jury sides with me. Why not? They know that all I seek is justice! Justice, Mr. Hazeltine! Bring on your witnesses!"

Judge Manning ordered a recess for luncheon.

7

GILLIAN HAZELTINE "BROUGHT on" his first witness after luncheon to the tune of murmurous voices all over the court room. Joy Halliday heard those voices. They formed the one word "Guilty!"

Willie Applegate it was, who had sealed Compton McArthur's fate. What a travesty of justice. Willie Applegate was a liar, a deliberate perjurer! Yet what he had said on the witness stand discountenanced all that Mr. Hazeltine's witnesses had said or could say.

One after another, Mr. Yistle took the wind out of their sails, ridiculed them, made them seem either unreliable or strongly prejudiced. Something must be done for Compton McArthur, and soon, or the tide against him would be sweeping so strongly that nothing could check it.

She gnawed her nether lip with impatience. As far as the people in the court room were concerned, the trial was over. They were staying simply to be entertained and amused.

All the jurors had the patient look of men whose minds were already made up. Gillian Hazeltine was flushed, and Compton McArthur looked dismal. The looks he occasionally dispatched in Joy's direction were discouraged. For the first time since the trial began, hopelessness sat upon him.

The next witness who undertook to add another inch to

that wall of defense was the nurse, Miss Mary Glissen. She was a pretty, pert little thing, a little too loudly dressed, a little too aware of the fact that her picture would appear in the evening tabloids.

She was bright-eyed, rouged, mascaraed and lip-sticked to within an inch of her life, Joy thought. It was too bad she wasn't an elderly woman, homely and fat.

This girl matched a little too closely Willie Applegate's lying testimony about the girl whom Compton had been riding with. Miss Glissen was the kind, she knew, who would love to cuddle and hug and pet.

She answered the routine questions glibly, almost impertinently; smiled ravishingly at the judge and upon the jurors. She was nothing but a cheap little girl.

Her testimony, pertly given, upheld Compton McArthur's story. Yes; she had been standing in front of Silinger's drug store at approximately nine fifty on the night of June 20 when Compton McArthur came hurtling out, almost colliding with her.

"He grabbed me and hustled me into the car before I hardly knew what was happening. I don't like to be hurried, because I have one of those meditative natures." She smiled impudently.

Joy Halliday heard cameras clicking all over the court room.

"If one more picture is taken without my permission," Judge Manning interrupted the testimony, "photographers will be excluded from this room. Go on, Mr. Hazeltine."

"When we were approaching Market Street," the dimpled brunette took up her story, "we weren't going faster than thirty. And when we crossed the intersection, a man sort of staggered out, and I shut my eyes and I almost climbed up on top of Mr. McArthur, I was so scared! I heard the thump as the mudguard struck him, and when I opened my eyes again we were pulling up in front of the Kenneth McArthur home. I got right out and took the nitroglycerine into Dr. Osborne, and Compton went on back to see how much the fellow he hit was hurt."

"Was Mr. Compton McArthur drunk?" Mr. Hazeltine asked her.

"My land, no! When he's drunk, I know it. No, he wasn't drunk that night. There wasn't a drop on his breath."

"That will be all," said Mr. Hazeltine wearily.

Mr. Yistle leaped up, smiling. Joy knew that he was simply delighted at having another witness to slaughter.

"How long have you known Compton McArthur?" he shot at her.

Miss Glissen promptly became defiant, holding her chin haughtily in the air and looking at him down her nose as she had perhaps seen "ladies" in the movies register disdain.

"Five years," she said snippily.

"How well have you known him?" the State's attorney snapped.

"I've known him well enough to know that he's a perfect gentleman—just as much a gentleman as anybody in this court room, including you!" she cried in one breath.

Judge Manning frowned at her. "You will kindly answer his questions and omit personalities," he said.

"I won't have him snapping at me that way!" she exclaimed. "I'm a lady, and I expect to be treated like a lady!"

Gillian Hazeltine groaned audibly. He was perspiring

more copiously than before. The trial of Compton McArthur was practically out of his hands.

Inwardly, Joy Halliday raged. What a mistake he had made in putting this cheap little girl on the stand!

"You say you've known the accused for five years?"

"Yes," she said haughtily—"that's what I said."

"In your previous testimony, Miss Glissen, you stated that you knew when Mr. Compton McArthur was drunk and when he wasn't. You mean, you've seen him when he was drunk?"

"I have."

"What was the occasion?"

"He took me out to dance one night. It was when I was nursing his sister-in-law last September. It was my night off, and Compton asked me if I wouldn't like to take a little ride and do a little Charlestoning."

"Did you?"

"You bet I did. We had a lovely time. We drove out to Chestnut Park and we danced all evening. He's a perfectly wonderful dancer."

Mr. Hazeltine had seated himself. He had placed his head in his hands. He was whipped and he looked whipped.

"And did Compton get drunk during the evening?"

"Well, he had a flask and he took a few drinks."

"A silver flask?"

"I don't know what it was made of. I only know what it was full of."

"What was it full of?"

"Gin."

"So he got drunk on that gin?"

"Well, he acquired a glow. And pretty soon I told him

he had had enough and it was late and I must be getting back. So he drove me home."

"Did he—er—become familiar during that drive home?"

"I should say not! I told you he was always a perfect gentleman!"

"Thank God!" groaned Joy.

Here was a ray of hope. The girl's very freshness was in her favor now; it stood for a certain kind of sincerity. She was frank about everything. Cheap but honest!

"Does this look like the flask he carried?" asked Mr. Yistle, holding up Exhibit A.

"One flask looks like every other flask to me," said the nurse.

"But this may have been the flask?"

"It may and it may not. You can't prove it by me, mister!"

"But he was drunk."

"He was feeling pretty good."

"Did he manage the car properly?"

"He's a swell driver, drunk or sober. He keeps his eyes on the road every minute. I mean he attends to his own business."

"And he didn't make love to you, hug you or pet you in any way on that drive?"

"I told you he was a gentleman, did I not?"

"I think you did," said Mr. Yistle, with a humorous look at the smiling jury. "And you can't say for sure, can you, that this is the flask he threw from the car the night he picked you up and took you to the McArthur's?"

"I don't know what flask he threw from the car. I tell you, one flask looks just like another, as far as I'm concerned."

Joy heard the hiss of indrawn breaths all over the court-room. A flask *had* been thrown from the car!

"All you know," said Mr. Yistle, prompt to follow his advantage, "was that a flask was thrown from the car right after Jake Plovak was struck down. That's all I want to know."

"You're crazy!" cried the girl on the stand. "I didn't say a flask was thrown from the car. It was you who said it."

"But you admitted it."

"I did not! It's you who've been throwing a flask from that car all day long—yes, and all yesterday morning, too. You have got me so I almost believe a flask was thrown from the car. I didn't see any flask thrown out of that car. No, sir-ee! You're just trying to make a liar out of me. Go right ahead and enjoy yourself!"

Joy Halliday fumed. That impertinent young thing on the stand had spoiled everything. What good she might have done had been undone by the hasty admission that a flask *had* been thrown from the car after Jake Plovak had been struck down. And that admission weakened every word of the preceding testimony, in spite of the girl's prompt retraction.

Miss Glissen retired from the witness stand with the air of a wronged heroine in a cheap movie melodrama, cheap hat high, impudent nose high. A titter followed her, and she bowed as though she were leaving an appreciative audience. Well, she was. She was the brightest spot in an exciting day.

"Next witness!"

Joy sat back and relaxed. A tall, dignified man was walking toward the witness box. He had smooth ivory hair and bushy, dark eyebrows, and smooth, clear, ruddy skin.

Mr. Yistle looked at him with amazement. What was John Wharton Ames doing in this court room? John Wharton Ames was president of the Ames Products Company; one of the wealthiest men in town; a public benefactor; a leading citizen; a pillar of the community.

He seated himself and faced the court room with the assurance of a man of large affairs. He was alert, dignified, and calm.

"You were, I believe," Mr. Hazeltine began his examination, "the employer of Jake Plovak at the time he was killed?"

"I was," said Mr. Ames in a deep voice.

"Were you acquainted with the deceased?"

"I was. I knew him well. The condition of his family was brought to my attention frequently."

"Will you kindly elaborate on that, Mr. Ames?"

"I will, gladly. Jake Plovak was a slovenly, careless man. He was a hard drinker and an unreliable workman. It was repeatedly brought to my attention that he spent his wages on drink instead of turning them over to his wife. When I learned that he had been killed—"

"I object!" shouted Mr. Yistle. "With all due respect to Mr. Ames, your honor, this testimony he is giving is absolutely irrelevant to the issue. The past of Jake Plovak is of no concern to this court."

"I must exclude this evidence," the judge ruled. "If Mr. Ames has testimony to offer bearing directly upon the issue, he must produce it."

Mr. Hazeltine seemed disappointed.

"I merely wished to prove to you, on the testimony of Jake Plovak's employer, that Jake Plovak was an undesirable citizen; a hard drinker, a slacker, a wife beater—"

"Excluded!" snapped Judge Manning.

Mr. Yistle was grinning. Gillian Hazeltine mopped his moist forehead.

"Very well," he said. "Will you tell the court, Mr. Ames, whether or not Jake Plovak carried insurance, as most of your employees do?"

"He did not," stated Mr. Ames.

"I object!" snarled Mr. Yistle.

"Objection is sustained," ruled the court. "I must ask you again, Mr. Hazeltine, to confine your questioning to the issue."

"I wish to proceed on the grounds, your honor, that the world and Jake Plovak's family is much better off with Jake Plovak dead than with Jake Plovak living."

His honor smiled. "You ought to know better than to ask permission to proceed on those grounds, Mr. Hazeltine. We are conducting the trial of Compton McArthur, not the memory of Jake Plovak."

Mr. Yistle looked a little worried. What Gillian Hazeltine was doing was cleverer than it appeared.

"Very well," said the famous criminal lawyer. "I will proceed to use this witness for purposes of establishing a clearer idea of the accused's character. Is that permissible?"

"It is quite permissible," said the smiling judge.

And Mr. Yistle looked uneasier than before.

"Kindly tell this court, Mr. Ames," Mr. Hazeltine took up the thread, "whether or not Compton McArthur sent for you on the day after he was put in jail—that is, on the afternoon of June 21?"

"Yes, he sent for me," said Mr. Ames.

"Kindly tell us what took place on your visit, Mr. Ames."

"It seems," said the obliging Mr. Ames, "that a month or two prior to that date, Compton McArthur inherited a sum of about fifty thousand dollars from an aunt. He sent for me to give me the authority to liquidate the securities he had received, the proceeds to be invested in an annuity for Plovak's widow and children."

"I object!" Mr. Yistle roared.

"On what grounds, Mr. Yistle?" asked the bench.

"The evidence is irrelevant to the issue!"

"The issue," cried Mr. Hazeltine, "is the accused's character."

"The character of the accused after the act has no bearing upon this case," Mr. Yistle shouted.

"Objection is sustained," said Judge Manning.

"The seed of that impulse was certainly in the heart of the accused before the death of Jake Plovak," Mr. Hazeltine argued. "The accused did not want to see the family of the worthless, shiftless, drunken sot suffer for his loss. The accused turned over his entire personal fortune to that end, your honor. The family of Jake Plovak is in better circumstances by far than before the death of Jake Plovak. They are eating three meals a day now. They are properly clothed. That income will be paid to them until the death of Mrs. Plovak, when the principal will be divided among the children."

"Excluded!" snapped Judge Manning.

Mr. Hazeltine seemed cast down by this ruling, but Mr. Yistle was red with fury.

"Perhaps my distinguished opponent wishes to cross-examine this witness, all of whose testimony is excluded," said Mr. Hazeltine ironically.

"Cross-examination is waived," snapped the district attorney.

"My next witness," said Mr. Hazeltine, "is Miss Joy Halliday? Will you take the stand, please, Miss Halliday?"

8

SHAKING AT THE knees, guiltily conscious of the surprised and accusing stare that Mr. Yistle was directing at her, Joy crossed the room and entered the witness box. She swore to tell the truth, the whole truth, and nothing but the truth, fully aware that every word about to leave her lips was a lie of the blackest sort.

But she was doing it so that justice might not be thwarted. The defense built up by Mr. Hazeltine was a frail structure. Each of his witnesses had, in some way, failed. Above their testimony the lies of Willie Applegate stood out as clear, unsullied truths.

What a burlesque of justice! The words of the only witness who had lied carried more weight than the words of a succession of truthful men and women! If the case were to go to the jury now, Compton McArthur would be adjudged guilty!

Joy, in the light of all this, felt no qualms in entering the witness box and perjuring herself. All she wanted was justice. Compton McArthur had fully paid the penalty for killing Jake Plovak. How unjust it would be to make him suffer more!

Mr. Yistle was glaring at her. Mr. Bullock was staring at her with bewildered surprise. And Gillian Hazeltine was smiling upon her benevolently.

Joy knew that she had created a stir when she went upon the stand; knew that the whispers now buzzing the air were questions concerning her. She knew, too, that she was attractive; in his turn, Mr. Yistle and Mr. Hazeltine had each complimented her upon her desirability as a witness, she was so beautiful, so refined.

Compton McArthur was looking at her with the expression of a man who grasps a last straw. Upon her testimony his fate hinged.

Could she withstand the cruel lashing of Mr. Yistle, knowing that he knew her to be perjuring herself? She must keep her wits about her, not be tricked or blustered into saying the wrong thing.

She focused her faculties. Mr. Hazeltine was beginning the examination.

"Where were you on the night of June twentieth?" he asked.

She was aware that the jurors were bending forward, in order not to miss a word of her testimony.

"I was, most of the time, at the bedside of my father," she answered in a low but full voice.

She did not want them to strain to hear her; she wanted to be as perfect a witness as Willie Applegate had been. She wanted to be the extreme opposite of the impudent little Glissen girl.

By commanding their respect she would enlist their belief. And she wanted them to believe those stark lies she was about to tell!

"Your father was ill?" asked Mr. Hazeltine.

"He was dying of cancer."

So far it was all true—a background of truth upon which to place the elaborate embroidery of lies.

"He did, eventually, die?" said Mr. Hazeltine.

"He died ten days ago. He was buried last week."

"Will you kindly describe, Miss Halliday, the events that took place on the evening of June the twentieth?" Gillian Hazeltine's voice was the respectful one commonly used in conversing with recently bereaved widows and orphans.

"I put my young sister to bed at eight o'clock," Joy replied, "and I went in to sit with my father and to read the evening papers to him. It was a little after nine thirty when he asked for a drink of grape-juice. I went out to the ice box and found that there was no grape-juice in the house, so I put on my hat and started for the corner, where there is a little Greek fruit stand."

"Let us get this very clear," Mr. Hazeltine interrupted. "Your house is situated midway down the block from the corner of Maple and Market, where the accident took place?"

"Yes, midway down the block from Market, on Maple."

"When you say it *is* your house, you really mean it *was* your house, don't you, Miss Halliday?"

She nodded, "Yes. The mortgage was foreclosed only a few days after my father died," she said in a low voice.

"You and your sister were driven out of your home?"

"We were."

Mr. Hazeltine permitted this poignant fact to sink into the minds of the jurors before he asked his next question.

"Did you buy the grape-juice?"

"Not at once."

"Kindly explain why you did not."

"I was halfway to the corner when a drunken man came lurching into sight. He was so drunk he could hardly walk. He staggered from tree to tree. At least three times he sat down heavily in the grass, and once he fell to the sidewalk as I was approaching. I was a little frightened."

"Did this drunken man accost you?"

"He did," said Joy, emphatically. "He made insulting overtures to me, too."

"What did he say?"

Joy hung her head. "He said—he said, 'Come on, kid and let's stage a little party.'"

"Were those his exact words?"

"Yes, sir; he said just that."

"What did you say?"

"I simply avoided him. I darted out of his way, but he lurched after me. He tried to grab me."

"One moment, Miss Halliday. Did you see this man's face?"

"I did, indeed. I saw it clearly in the light from the street lamp."

"Was he a young man?"

"Yes, sir. About twenty-three or four, I should say."

"How was he dressed?"

"Very flashily."

"Go on with your account. Miss Halliday."

"He wouldn't let me pass. He glared at me with bleary eyes. He held onto me. I screamed, but there was no one in sight. Then he pulled something out of his hip-pocket. It was a flask."

"What kind of a flask?"

"It was a silver flask."

"Would you be able to identify it if you saw it again?"

"I think I could."

Mr. Hazeltine picked up the silver flask, Exhibit A, and handed it to her.

"Yes, this is the flask."

"Are you sure it is?"

"I am positive it is."

"How do you identify it?"

"By the three little equally-spaced nicks along the bottom edge. He took it out of his pocket and thrust it into my hand, and he said, 'Come on, sweetie, and join me in a drink.' I said, 'No, thank you, I don't drink.' And he said, 'Oh, don't be such a spoil-sport. You are drinking out of a solid silver flask.' Then he seized it again and turned it up to show me the sterling mark on the bottom. It was then that I saw the three nicks. I can remember that the street light glittered on them."

"What happened then, Miss Halliday?"

"Why, he—he thrust it into my hand again and commanded me to drink. By that time I was desperate. I thought rapidly. The only way I could get rid of him, I knew, was by getting rid of the flask. So I threw it. I threw it as far as I could!"

"Then what did he do?"

"He cursed at me!"

There was a murmur of indignation in the court room.

"I want you to tell this court room just what he called you."

"He—he called me a damned little prig!"

"Then what happened?"

"I started again to go past him, but again he seized me.

He tried to take me into his arms. I—fought him off. I felt his hot breath in my face. I screamed again. Out of the corner of my eye I saw a man start across the street. He was coming to my assistance.

"Then a car came down the street, and the man who was coming to help me was struck down. The car hesitated, and went on, and the man lay there in the street."

"You saw all this—clearly?"

"Quite clearly. The car was going pretty rapidly, and poor Mr. Plovak was running over to help me, when the car struck him."

"Was the car on the right side of the street?"

"Yes, it was."

"Was it going from side to side, as if the driver were drunk?"

"Oh, no, it was going perfectly straight. And the driver was blowing the horn repeatedly."

"How fast do you estimate that the car was going?"

"I only know that it traveled from the big elm tree on the corner to the big elm in front of Mr. Waters' house between two strokes of the bell in the tower of the town hall."

"Let me get this straight," said Mr. Hazeltine. "Two bell strokes elapsed from the time the accused's car passed the elm on the corner until it was abreast of the second elm?"

"Yes sir, the town clock was striking ten."

Mr. Hazeltine turned to the jury and drew a slip of paper from his vest pocket as he did so.

"Gentlemen," he said, "I have had the distance between the two elm trees measured off by competent surveyors and I have had the elapsed time between the strokes of the town hall clock timed. My measurements can be checked and my figures can be gone over by expert mathematicians.

"The distance between the two elms referred to is approximately eighty feet. The time between bell strokes is two seconds. It took the accused's car two seconds to cover those eighty feet. In other words, the car was moving at the rate of forty feet a second. If you will reduce this speed to miles, you will find that the accused's car was being driven at a speed of between twenty-five and thirty miles an hour—not fifty miles an hour as one witness testified. Now, Miss Halliday, when you saw Jake Plovak struck down by the automobile, what did you do?"

"I cried to the drunken man who had accosted me, 'Oh, see what you've done!' By that time, he was aware that an accident had happened and he was staggering toward the spot where I had thrown the flask."

"Now, Miss Halliday, I wish you would describe to me the occupants of the car that struck down Jake Plovak as he was hastening to your assistance. Did you see the occupants clearly?"

"Quite clearly."

"Who were they?"

"The man at the wheel was the man who is sitting over there."

Mr. Hazeltine crossed the room and placed his hand on the back of the chair in which sat Compton McArthur.

"You mean this young man?"

"Yes, sir."

"Did he have both hands on the wheel?"

"He did. He had both hands at the top of the wheel, and he was bending forward."

"Was there some one in the car with him?"

"There was. Miss Glissen was in the car. I recognized her when she took the witness stand a little while ago."

"Did he appear to be hugging or petting her?"

"He did not! She was huddled against him, but both his hands were on the wheel."

Mr. Hazeltine faced the jury again, with his head thrown back a little.

"Now, Miss Halliday, I wish you would tell us who the man was who insulted you, tried to force you to drink gin from his flask, and, indirectly caused the death of Jake Plovak to occur."

"His name is Willie Applegate!" said Joy in a firm, ringing voice.

9

THE COURT ROOM burst into a hubbub. The bailiff banged on his desk with the gavel time and again, and finally order was restored.

Mr. Yistle was staring at her venomously. Mr. Bullock was staring at her open-mouthed. Only Gillian Hazeltine appeared to be calm.

"Tell us what happened, Miss Halliday, after Jake Plovak was struck down as he was coming so gallantly to your rescue."

"I was uncertain just what to do, but I hurried, after a moment, to the fallen man. I remember thinking at the time that the man who had run over him was cruel to go on without ascertaining if he were hurt, but I did not know then, of course, that he was racing to save a woman's life.

"A number of men came, and I went on down to get the grape-juice for my father. Just before I left I saw Mr. Applegate pick up the flask, and he was muttering to himself."

Joy looked across the court room to where Willie Applegate had been sitting. His pale, distressed face was no longer visible. He had left the court room.

"I got the grape-juice and hurried, home to my father."

"Did you see a policeman?"

"No, I did not. I believe a policeman came later."

"That will be all, Miss Halliday." Gillian Hazeltine

bowed deferentially to Mr. Yistle, who was gnawing his lip and suffering as, perhaps, he had never in his legal life suffered.

The look in his eyes as he faced Joy was little short of murderous, but she knew she had saved the day for Compton McArthur, and nothing Mr. Yistle could say to her would shake her. She was no longer afraid of the man.

Justice had triumphed. Perhaps its weapons had been stark lies, but, after all, Willie Applegate had dealt only in lies.

"Do you realize," said Mr. Yistle in a deadly cold voice, "that the testimony you have just given might readily send Willie Applegate to prison for twenty years? Do you realize that you have, with your evidence, Miss Halliday, shifted the blame for this killing from the shoulders of one man to the shoulders of another?"

"I am not aware that I have done anything wrong," said Joy sweetly. "I have only told what happened and what was actually said in my presence. I do not want to see an innocent man suffer for the crime of another. If Mr. Applegate is responsible for the death of poor Mr. Plovak, then he should suffer."

Heads all about the room were craning. Where was Mr. Applegate? Mr. Applegate, it was later learned, had taken advantage of an excellent opportunity to visit the Far West.

He had always longed to travel to those sun-kissed, wind-bitten areas where men are reputed to be men. He was a little sick of court rooms, anyway. He was traveling on a fast train, and he intended to continue in one direction.

It was useless for Mr. Yistle to carry the cross-examination further, Joy Halliday had bolstered every weak spot in Compton McArthur's wall of defense. The enemy was routed.

Mr. Yistle's rebuttal was aimless and unconvincing. He tried in vain to pick flaws in Joy Halliday's testimony. But her testimony was bullet-proof.

For perhaps a half hour he floundered about with legal technicalities. Then Mr. Hazeltine took the floor and, in simple, eloquent language summed up his evidence. Mr. Yistle's closing argument was hardly more than the profanity of a defeated man angrily couched in long legal expressions.

Judge Manning's summing up of the case was brief and concise. In fewest possible words, he practically urged the jury to bring in a verdict of not guilty with the slightest possible delay.

The jury had gone less than five minutes. Twelve good men and true returned from the jury room with a verdict of acquittal.

Tears of happiness filled Joy's beautiful eyes as she saw Compton McArthur's father seize the young man in his arms. It was a beautiful scene—those two men united again, after all these months of bitterness and misunderstanding.

And Joy could well say: "It was my black lies that united this father and son!"

A battery of cameras clicked all about her as she emerged from the courthouse into the late afternoon sunlight. She had been the star witness in Greenfield's most sensational trial in years!

10

SOME SIX MONTHS after the trial and the acquittal of Compton McArthur, Joy Halliday was his guest at a little dinner for two in the Crystal Dining Room of the Greenfield Tavern. Since the trial, she and Compton had become the closest friends, and recently this emotion had given way to one which was much more thrilling and dangerous.

In those passing months, the young man had admirably lived up to the assertions he had made on the night of his arrest. He had completely reformed.

He had gone into the McArthur Paint and Varnish factory; he had taken hold of things with a vim, and it was now common knowledge that he had become his father's right-hand man. It was even said that he was a shrewder and farther-seeing business man than his brother Kenneth had been.

At all events, he was succeeding; he no longer drank; he no longer even kept late hours.

And he loved Joy Halliday. His eyes said so at every meeting and at every parting. She had saved him from twenty years in a noisome prison; he was doing his best to justify and repay her faith in him.

Somehow, as they loafed and chatted over their after-dinner coffee, he possessed himself of her hand. He held it in his, gently, for some time before Joy was aware that he was taking liberties that must not be taken.

She tried to draw her hand away, but the pressure of his own increased. And he bent toward her.

"Joy!" he said softly.

There were only *yesses* in her heart, and only *noes* at the tip of her tongue. She had loved him from the moment their eyes first met across the court room, but it was a love that could not, must not, bear fruit.

She heard his voice, as if from a great distance. It was soothing, caressing. He was asking her to marry him; telling her he loved her, adored her.

"I owe everything to you!"

Joy tried again to pull her hand away, and this time he suffered her to release it.

He looked at her gravely.

"Joy, I can't ask you to pardon the things I did before I got straightened out. I can only ask you to believe me when I tell you that I'm never going back to those things. It's true I drank, I ran around, I was a pretty wild young man; but that's all in the past, honey. You know it's in the past.

"There isn't a thing I want to do, or have tried to do since the trial, but to please you—to make you have some respect for me. It isn't a temporary reformation, Joy. All that sort of thing, the wild days, have lost all appeal for me. I was on the wrong track. Now I'm headed straight and true.

"I've got my father's love and confidence and respect for the first time since I was a kid. He trusts me. He told me just the other day that life had really become good again. Can't you feel that way, too? Isn't life good? Will you ever stop distrusting me?"

"It isn't that," said Joy, quickly, with averted head. "I trust you. Oh, I know you're on the right track, Compton. It's wonderful, what you've done with yourself. I think it's great. No, it isn't that. It's that you—you never can respect me. I want love to last. You'll know the truth some day. No, I'd rather not have you at all than to lose you soon, as I would. You would have to know the truth. I could not live a lie with you."

Compton McArthur had become quite pale. His eyes, full of concern, were fixed on her downcast ones.

"I don't think I know what you're driving at, dear," he said presently.

She flashed a hard glance at him.

"You might as well know now, Compton. I know—I'll always know—that you were guilty of killing Jake Plovak. And you'll always know that I got up on the stand and told lie after lie to clear you. Why pretend any longer, Compton?"

He was staring at her.

"You—lied?"

"I lied," she said, almost in tears. "I wasn't near the scene of that accident. I wasn't out of my father's bedroom all that evening!"

She sat back in her chair and glared at him defiantly.

"Well," he said after a moment, with a queer smile, "that makes it just about unanimous. You lied; I lied; my sister-in-law lied; Dr. Osborne lied; Mr. Silinger lied; Mary Glissen lied."

"What do you mean?" Joy demanded in a low voice.

"It was all done," he explained, "to protect my father from the shock, the real truth, Joy. My sister-in-law did

not have a heart attack that night. I did not run and bring
in Dr. Osborne. Dr. Osborne did not write a prescription
for nitroglycerine. I did not take a prescription to Silinger's
to be filled. Mr. Silinger, or his assistant, did not fill it.
Furthermore, I did not collide with Miss Glissen when I
was leaving the drug store. I did not go to the drug store. I
have never been in Silinger's drug store in my life.

"Don't faint, my dear. As I say, it was all done to protect
my father from the shock, the real truth. My sister-in-law
lied to spare him—brave kid! Dr. Osborne lied to spare
him. That prescription was written by Dr. Osborne three
days before the trial. Mr. Silinger was paid handsomely for
his very poor testimony. Miss Glissen adores my sister-in-
law, and would not only lie but would beg and steal for her,
if necessary.

"In other words, my dear, of all the witnesses who took
the stand that day, only one man was telling the truth, and
he only partly. That was John Ames, the employer of poor
Jake Plovak, and he told the truth only in part. He did
not know Jake Plovak. While it was true that Jake Plovak
worked for him for years, he had never, so far as he knew,
come face to face with the man."

"Was it a lie," Joy demanded in a furious little voice,
"that you turned over your entire personal fortune to Mr.
Plovak?"

"No, that was true, I did."

Joy Halliday knew now that she could never, never love
Compton McArthur. She stared at him through hot, bitter
tears.

"You mean, you had all those witnesses perjure themselves, and those you did not buy you influenced through

their affection for you or your father, in order to clear your-self of a charge for which you should this moment be in prison?"

"Not quite that, dear," he said gently. "What I am going to tell you now must remain a secret to the grave. I am not the man who was driving the car that ran down and killed Jake Plovak!"

Joy could only stare at him.

"No, my dear, not another lie, but the truth. The man who killed Jake Plovak was my brother Kenneth. There was no girl in the car, but there had been one. You see, Joy, this is a secret that ought to go to the grave with me, but you've got to know. Nothing but the truth will help us now.

"My brother Kenneth," he went on earnestly, "never had a fling when he was a young man. He went directly from college into business and also into matrimony. I don't say that a man ought to have a fling, but Kenneth didn't. He went directly into the grind without preparation, and—well, he turned wild almost overnight, so to speak, and secretly.

"I don't want you to think I am criticizing him. Given a little time, Ken would have had his fill of it and he would have straightened up. He began boozing and—oh, there was a woman. Who she was doesn't matter. It was an infat-uation that wouldn't have lasted long. Of course, father didn't know, and he was probably the only one who didn't.

"His wife was mighty fine about it. She knew Kenneth. She knew he would snap out of it, so she gave him all the rope he needed. On the evening of the 20th of June, my dear—the fatal 20th of June—he had been calling on that woman, and when he started for home he was drunk.

Alone, but drunk. He was in that condition when he came to the house. I was there. I had had dinner with Geraldine and Dr. Osborne."

"She didn't have a heart attack then?" Joy interrupted.

"Positively not, although she might well have had one. Kenneth was drunk and terrified. He said he had killed a man. Well, what was there to do? I had already disgraced the family. I was the black sheep. I became the goat. I elected myself, and she and Dr. Osborne gave their very reluctant consent to go through with the scheme. What did I amount to, anyhow?

"Perhaps it would have been better if we had allowed Kenneth to give himself up. The suffering he went through, knowing I was in jail for a crime he had committed, was what really killed Kenneth. A dozen times, Geraldine tells me, he wanted to make a clean breast, but the fat was in the fire then. We had to go through with it."

"Then everybody who testified at the trial, with the possible exception of the coroner, was telling lies for some reason or other," said Joy. "After all, Jake Plovak was killed, wasn't he?"

"Sometimes," said Compton McArthur, "I am skeptical about even that. Oh, yes, poor Jake Plovak was killed."

"Willie Applegate was lying. Harry Zarrow, the chemist, was lying—or was that flask your brother's?"

"My brother's flask was of genuine gold, and it had been full of—Scotch!"

"Then," Joy mused, "the only ones who lied were Willie Applegate, Harry Zarrow, you, your sister-in-law, Dr. Osborne, Mr. Silinger, the druggist, Mary Glissen, the nurse, John Wharton Ames and I. How about the policeman? Was he lying?"

"The policeman was not on his beat when the accident happened," Compton answered. "To save his skin, he said just what Mr. Yistle told him to say."

"I want to know if he was telling the truth when he testified that you were drunk when you gave yourself up."

"I had had one cocktail," said the young man. "Didn't I swear to that at the trial?"

"How many cocktails had you actually had, Compton?"

"Only five," the young man grinned. "Will you kindly answer the question I put to you before this argument started?"

"Do you love me?" Joy answered.

"I adore you," he said. "Do you love me?"

"I adore you," said Joy. "Are you lying to me, Compton?"

"No," said Compton. "Are you lying to me, Joy?"

"Not guilty!" said Joy.

THE LOVE BANDIT

1

ELMER ON THE JOB

ELMER WIRPLE WAS afraid of his job. He was afraid of many things, but his job will do to start with.

Although he worked diligently, loyally, faithfully, giving the best that was in him, he lived in constant fear that the job would be taken away from him.

He was but twenty-four; yet he already saw himself in his middle years—the years between forty and fifty—being displaced by a younger man. He had seen all this so often; older men being pushed out for younger men; younger men being shoved aside for better men.

It sometimes seemed to him miraculous that he was employed at all, and because he was in such constant terror of losing his job, he worked harder perhaps than any other man in the office.

All day long, from nine in the morning until five in the afternoon, and often later, Elmer Wirple sat at his desk in the great outer office of the Purity Pulverized Egg Corporation, doing his little best by the firm's slogan:

WHEN BETTER EGGS ARE PULVERIZED
PURITY WILL PULVERIZE THEM

So anxious was he to impress his superiors with his earnestness that he frequently stayed at his desk during lunch hour, having a sandwich and a glass of milk brought in by an office boy from the soda fountain on the ground floor; and, actuated by the same anxiety, he frequently worked overtime.

It was not at all uncommon for Elmer Wirple to be the last man out of the office, not because he was so overwhelmed with work, but because he thought that Mr. Wainright, the president of the Purity Pulverized Egg Corporation, might notice him and be impressed by his earnestness.

If Elmer Wirple lived in daily fear of his job, he lived in even greater fear of Mr. Wainright. Whenever he saw Mr. Wainright bearing down upon him, whether the president was frowning or smiling, Elmer's spine became a race track for cold chills.

Mr. Wainright never stopped at Elmer's desk, however. He always walked on past. In the four years that Elmer had been in his employ, Mr. Wainright had not once stopped or even paused at Elmer's neat, orderly desk.

Elmer often wished that Mr. Wainright would stop and give that desk of his just a glance. It would have convinced Mr. Wainright that Elmer was a kind of employee who deserved never—no matter how bad the pulverized egg market became—to be fired.

That desk top was always dustless and orderly. The ink-pot was always neat. Beside it there was always a tidy little row of nicely sharpened pencils and clean pens.

It did not occur to Elmer to wish for promotion. Other

men all about him were constantly sliding up into better jobs; but Elmer was satisfied with the one he had.

He was earning twenty-eight dollars a week, and he found this sufficient for his needs. On twenty-eight dollars a week he lived comfortably, dressed according to his modest tastes, and was even able to put a little something by.

His ambition was to own a little home of his own, with room enough in the back yard to raise chickens, to sail out upon the placid and uneventful sea of matrimony with the young lady of his heart's fondest fancy—and not to lose his job.

Perhaps it would be stretching the facts a little to say that a shrinking violet in a bosky woodland dell was a charging lion in comparison to Elmer Wirple.

Perhaps it would be fairer to say that Elmer Wirple combined the traits of meekness, humility, and self-effacement to such a degree that, in comparison, an immature rabbit resembled an insulted bull elephant.

On a certain evening in spring the Western Union clock on the south wall of the great outer office lacking but one minute of five o'clock, Elmer Wirple sat at his desk, preparing to stay from fifteen to twenty minutes overtime, due to the fact that the pulverized egg market was in a bad way, and that a rumor was in circulation to the effect that a number of clerks were going to be let out.

And inasmuch as this was the last opportunity to glimpse the outstanding figure in this narrative under normal conditions, it will be not inadvisable to watch him rather closely.

All about Elmer trim young men and pretty stenographers were preparing to knock off for the day. The young men were throwing things into drawers and slamming them shut with much gusto; the girls were putting the finishing touches to noses, lips, and cheeks.

Immune to this activity, Elmer Wirple sat at his desk, frowning slightly as he again checked over the items of an invoice. The hands of the Western Union clock suddenly described that popular angle better known as five o'clock, and all about Elmer young men and young women were passing his desk with the orderly haste of people in a theater who were walking to the nearest exit at the outbreak of a fire.

In less than half a minute the great outer office of the Purity Pulverized Egg Corporation was empty of all but the lone, preoccupied figure at the desk.

Elmer frowned diligently over his task of checking over the items, for the fourth time, of the invoice from the Interstate Poultry Products Association. A glimpse, stolen from his occupation, informed him that a light was burning in Mr. Wainright's frosted-glass office.

Ten minutes passed. Then the door of the president's office opened, and the portly figure of the president appeared. He had his derby on, and was struggling into his overcoat as he issued forth.

Elmer Wirple's heart action took on an additional count of fifteen beats. He frowned a little more darkly, and lowered his eyes to the invoice as the heavy footfalls of Mr. Wainright approached.

When the president was about three desks away, Elmer Wirple looked up with an expression on his pale countenance which indicated that he had been surprised—nay, startled—from the fascination of his work by the heavy staccato of Mr. Wainright's heels.

Mr. Wainright was puffing vigorously at a large brunette cigar.

"Hard at it, eh?" said the ruling genius of the Purity Pulverized Egg Corporation; but he did not stop. He did not even hesitate in his stride.

"Yes, sir," Elmer said briskly; "hard at it, Mr. Wainright!"

"Well, good night, Elmer," said Mr. Wainright.

"Good night, Mr. Wainright!"

And Elmer was left to a gratifying glow, and the rich, oily fragrance of his employer's passing perfecto. In his mind's inner ear he could hear Mr. Wainright saying emphatically, to Mr. Ledges, the head clerk:

"No, Ledges, positively no; Wirple is the last man I would consider letting out, no matter how bad business becomes. He is the most faithful man we have. Night after night I've seen him working away there at his desk when the rest of you have gone rushing off. Wirple isn't a clock watcher. Wirple stays!"

Elmer lifted his eyes almost reverently to the large,

boldly lettered sign which hung under the Western Union clock. In large black block letters it inquired:

ARE YOU WORKING FOR THIS CLOCK OR
FOR THE PURITY PULVERIZED EGG CORP.
????

Certainly he had satisfied Mr. Wainright on that point.

Elmer waited long enough for his employer to reach the street and to enter his limousine. Then he locked his desk, obtained his hat and coat in the cloak room, and left the building.

As he walked to the corner for his street car, he attracted attention from no one. A day would come when necks would crane, when crowds would gather wherever Elmer Wirple went, when police escorts were required to preserve him from the curious, and to save his clothing from the scissors of souvenir hunters; but as he walked to the corner this evening to catch the Maple Avenue street car his presence was acknowledged by nothing more than passing glance.

Elmer Wirple, in short, did not stand out in a crowd. He was not homely, nor was he handsome; he was neither too tall nor too short to attract attention, and the clothes he affected were peculiarly adapted to the position he occupied in life. A meek man, he dressed accordingly in neutral browns, inconspicuous grays, and safe blues.

Because it was Wednesday night, he took a bath when he reached his boarding house, rigged himself out in his best suit and newest tie—it was a blue four-in-hand with tiny white polkadots—and ate his dinner.

He was, if not Mrs. Myrtle Gibney's star boarder, at least her model one; and while he was treated with only casual attention by the other boarders, he was at least given the respect due a man who has never missed paying his board and room rent punctually and in advance.

Having carefully avoided the onions on his steak and the hearts of lettuce—the latter because it was anointed with Roquefort cheese dressing—he repaired to his room for certain finishing touches before going forth upon his evening's errand.

The discerning reader has long before this leaped to the conclusion that Elmer Wirple was soon to gratify his deepest, finest instincts by associating this evening with the young lady of his heart's fondest fancy, and the discerning reader, in so leaping, is well within his rights.

Before setting forth, however, Elmer Wirple consulted his bank book. A light of surprise gleamed in his eyes, for he had unexpectedly discovered that his balance, with interest compounded over the past month, would exceed one thousand dollars!

This was the mark at which Elmer Wirple had been aiming for upward of two years. His face, as the realization dawned, became slightly flushed, and his forehead slightly damp. His heart was, without warning, thumping with excitement, while feelings of terror and delight swept through him in a tumultuous tide.

One thousand dollars! With trembling fingers he placed the bank book in the inner pocket of his coat, examined himself once more in the mirror over his dresser, placed his dark gray felt hat on his head so that it exactly paralleled an imaginary line drawn through the centers of his eyes, and started out.

And to this point, and perhaps a little further, we have seen Elmer Wirple's actions at the close of a normal Wednesday evening in his life. For upward of two years he had not varied this simple routine by as much as a hair.

We have seen him stalling around at the office so that old man Wainright might be suitably impressed by his earnestness; we have accompanied him to his boarding house; through his ablutions and his meal; have even seen him fastidiously avoid such pungent items as onions and Roquefort cheese, so that his breath might remain pure and sweet for reasons of romance. But the discovery that his savings account balance had at last passed the thousand-dollar mark was, in more ways than one, a turning point.

Never again would he dally at the office to impress old man Wainright. Never again— But let us deal with the events in the order with which they struck Elmer Wirple, like knives from the night.

2

"WE SHALL SEE!"

IT WAS ELMER Wirple's custom to walk from his boarding house to the home of Carrol Jameson, timing his arrival so that there should be just comfortable time for them to reach the Alto Theater for the second performance.

Elmer could have combed the world over, he was sure, and not found a girl who suited him the way Carrol Jameson suited him. She was slim and bright and charming; her eyes were large and brown, and she had a most alluring and provocative way of looking at you through the lacy fringe of her long lashes.

Ever since Elmer had been keeping company with Carrol Jameson he had carried in his heart that appealing picture of the little white cottage with a back yard large enough for raising chickens. He had seen Carrol running to the front door to greet him when he returned home from the office. Her cheeks were flushed from dinner preparations, and her lovely eyes were sparkling because of joy at seeing him again.

"Darling!" she crooned in that throaty, honeyed voice of hers.

Then they would kiss, lingeringly, and she would begin chattering in her inimitable way about the pranks of Junior and Suzanne. And then—their dinner, prepared by her own loving hands.

Elmer Wirple could call up that pleasing fancy almost any time of the day or night he wanted to. And it always brought a glow to his heart. He loved her so!

So far, however, he had refrained from admitting her to the delicious secret. He had wanted to be able to come to her manfully and say:

"Carrol, I want you to be my wife. I have a thousand dollars saved up, and I have the house picked out. I love you—will you?"

This last, "I love you—will you?" Elmer had culled from a popular song, and it pleased him.

He made the decision, as he mounted the front steps of the Jamesons' house, that there would be no movies to-night. They would sit in the parlor, and he would relieve his mind and his heart of this load without delay.

It was characteristic of Elmer to press the pearl button set into the front doorjamb once—very lightly. He hated the idea of annoying the Jamesons with long, peremptory ringing.

The door was promptly opened by Carrol herself, prettier than ever in a new black satin dress that came hardly to her knees, revealing to a grateful world a pair of slim, beautiful, golden-silk clad legs.

A small black hat fitted snugly down about her curly brown hair. She carried a pale-blue coat over one arm.

"Hello, there, Elmer!" she greeted him gayly. She was always gay, always bubbling over with pep.

"How are you this evening, Carrol?" he phrased himself. It was the same phrase he had used, Wednesday after

Wednesday, since he had first mustered up enough courage to ask her to go to the movies.

"I'm just fine," said Carrol, and held out her coat for him to hold.

The words were trembling at Elmer's lips: "Listen, Carrol, do you mind if we don't go down to the Alto to-night? I've got something I want to say."

But the chance passed. He was holding her coat for her, and a moment later they were walking down the sidewalk toward the Alto. While they walked she chattered. Now and then, to be sure, she paused, but only to catch her breath.

Elmer, walking along beside her, grew angrier and angrier at himself for missing his opportunity. He would, he promised himself, find it later.

Once or twice during the show he reached out tentatively to take her hand. He had never held her hand, had always lacked the courage; and he still lacked the courage to-night.

The feature picture was the romantic story of a hardy, debonair young horseman of the Western plains who got himself into and out of no end of exciting trouble, all because of a wisp of a thing with great starry eyes and curly golden ringlets. In the end he gathered her into his great hairy arms, and into her eyes came a light never before seen on land or sea.

Elmer wished that he could do things that way, without hesitancy, without fear. He wondered if Carrol would lift one foot and raise it behind her when she was kissed, the way the girls in the movies did.

Perspiration broke out freely all over Elmer as he and

Carrol approached her front porch. He was going to get it out now—if it killed him. Now or never—do or die!

Now they were climbing the porch steps. Now Carrol was holding out her hand and saying good night.

"Good night," said Elmer in a thin voice.

She was gone. The front door closed gently. He had let another chance slip by. Fairly trembling with fury at his cowardice, Elmer slowly descended the steps, but he did not go.

He stood there, in the grass at the edge of the sidewalk, flinging insults at himself, and demanding of himself in no uncertain terms why he had not said to Carrol Jameson what he had intended to say.

Twice he started determinedly toward the steps, but each time he lost heart and returned to the grass at the edge of the sidewalk. Tears of rage burned in his eyes, and with a gesture of despair he dashed them away.

In the confusion which attended his agony he heard, only half awarely, a window being raised. Then, more awarely, he heard a gasp.

"For the love of Mike, Elmer, I thought you were a burglar! I'm coming right down!"

A new layer of fresh, prickling perspiration found its way to Elmer's hot forehead. He frantically wondered what he was going to say to her.

The front door opened, and Carrol came out. Her hat was off, and her hair looked rather wild. His terror grew. She had him cornered now, and there wasn't any way for him to wiggle out of it.

She was on the top step, and he was on the bottom, looking up at her with a hammering heart.

"What is it, Elmer?" she said impatiently.

"Listen, Carrol—" he began, and choked.

"Come on in," said Carrol. "What are you acting so funny about, Elmer? I never saw you act like this before. Why, you're as white as a sheet! Are you sick—or something?"

Elmer grasped at the straw.

"I—I feel kind of funny," he admitted. And he permitted her to lead him into the parlor.

Carrol turned on the lights and stared at him.

"Do you think I'd better get a doctor?"

"Oh, no," he protested; "it isn't anything serious."

"Do you want a drink of water?" she asked, her eyes still fixed penetratingly upon his.

"Yuh—yuh-yes," he gulped.

He seated himself, and tried to bring himself to hand while she was gone. Fury at his cowardice and terror of the task confronting him took possession of Elmer Wirple.

He was sitting there with his head in his hands when Carrol returned with a glass of water. He looked up at her with swimming eyes.

"Good night," the girl exclaimed, "you certainly do look like the last rose of summer, Elmer! You must have eaten something that isn't sitting very pretty."

"I—I guess so," Elmer agreed flabbily.

Carrol sat down on the davenport beside him, and examined him with deep concern. Elmer was fumbling at his inner coat pocket. His eyes flashed.

The girl gazed at the worn cover of the bank book in his shaking hand with round, startled eyes. From it she looked at his face with unvoiced inquiry.

"See?" Elmer got out, and he opened the bank book. Now he was pushing it into her hands.

Carrol looked more and more bewildered.

"Well," said she, "I see you've got about a thousand dollars in the bank. That is fine, but what of it? Is that what you're feeling sick about?"

"No," Elmer breathed; "it isn't that. Can—can't you guess what it is, Carrol?"

"Good night!" Carrol cried. "How in Sam Hill do I know what it is? First you act like a burglar, then you act as if you're going to faint, and now you show me your bank book."

"But haven't you any idea what I've got all this money saved up for?" he bleated.

"Maybe you're going to buy yourself a trip around the world," said Carrol. "If I had a thousand dollars in the bank, I'd knock off work, believe me, and this hick town wouldn't see me for dust. If you're asking my advice on how you ought to spend your thousand, that's it."

"Is that the only way you can think of for spending this thousand dollars?" the young man pleaded.

"Say, listen, Elmer, will you kindly tell me what under the sun you're driving at? Will you please stop all this beating about the bush, and stop looking at me as if you'd just lost your right arm, or something?"

Elmer sucked in his breath. He expelled it in a gush, which consisted of the words:

"I love you—will you?"

Then he seemed about to collapse. The beautiful girl looked at him with growing wonder.

"Elmer," she said sternly, finally, "are you kidding me?"

"I am certainly not kidding you," Elmer returned vigorously, finding his voice at last. "Listen, Carrol. Gee whiz—I mean—aw, say, Carrol, you know what I mean. You know I'm c-cuc-crazy about you!"

"Me?" cried Carrol, indicating her wishbone with her thumb.

"You know I am!"

"Honestly, Elmer, you could knock me over with a pin feather!"

"You know I'm crazy about you!" he repeated grimly.

"What am I, Elmer—a mind reader?"

"Good night! Do you suppose I would have been c-coming around like this all this time if I wasn't?"

"You mean, it didn't come on all of a sudden?"

"No, sir; it came on right along, ever since we started going out together. And I—I've been saving my money, Carrol. I—I— You know how much I'm getting. It—it's a good, steady job, Carrol. We'll be able to put something down on a—a little house I've got my eye on, and we can get the fur-furniture on the easy payment plan. Well—well?"

Carrol did not reply to him at once. She looked at him, though, with the greatest interest, as if she had never seen him before. Then she leaned toward him.

"Elmer," she said gently, "I know you are not kidding me. Anybody who almost fainted dead away the way you did could not be kidding. So there can be only one interpretation of all this. You mean it."

"You bet I mean it!" he declared in a voice which he intended to make gruff and masterful, but which instead emerged thin and squeaky, although his normal voice was a pleasant, deep bass.

"You want me to marry you?" she helped him.

"That—that's it!" Elmer gasped. "When—when will you, Carrol?"

Carrol again fell into a deep, thoughtful silence.

"When?" she repeated. "Just about five minutes later than never, Elmer. That is when!"

His mouth remained open.

"Now you're kidding me," he accused her.

But the lovely girl shook her curly head.

"I never even dreamed that an idea like that ever came into your mind," she told him. "Honestly, Elmer, I was never more astonished in all my life. To think of you—*you* wanting to marry *me!*"

Her face, at first pale, was now quite pink. And now she began to laugh. She tried not to laugh, but the impulse was irresistible. Peal after peal of laughter fell shockingly upon Elmer's eardrums.

"It's—so—fun-ny!" she explained after a time.

"What's so funny?" Elmer demanded suspiciously. "I don't see anything funny about it."

"I know you don't," she choked, "and that makes it funnier. Here you've been acting as if you wouldn't touch me with a ten-foot pole for almost two years. Why! You never even tried to hold my hand—not once! And now—you—"

"I've acted that way because you're pure and innocent," said Elmer stiffly.

Carrol Jameson tried to maintain her gravity, her dignity; but some element in the situation which did not strike Elmer as the least bit funny was making her almost hysterical.

"I don't think it's very polite of you to laugh in a man's face like that," he stuttered, "when I've just got through saying the things I've—"

"Elmer," she stopped him, "I didn't mean to be rude. Honestly, I didn't. But it's all so—so queer or something. First you acting like a burglar, then terrifying me by acting as if you were going to faint, and then—then showing me that bankbook. Talk about an evening of surprises! Gee!"

"I love you," said Elmer grimly, "and I want you to marry me. I mean it. I want to marry you, and—and everything!"

Miss Jameson promptly dropped her face into a convenient cushion, and kept it there until the convulsion had passed. Then she dried her eyes upon a tiny bright-blue handkerchief, and faced him seriously.

"Elmer, I am sorry I acted so rudely. You must remember that, after all, I am only a woman, and all women are apt to get hysterical when something excites them. I guess it was your bankbook that excited me. Anyhow, I will promise not to laugh any more. I will discuss things seriously with you.

"First of all, I will not marry you, and if you want to know why, well, I will reluctantly go into that—if you insist."

"Go ahead," Elmer requested.

"Well, to begin with, Elmer, you are not the kind of man that a girl marries; anyway, not the kind of girl I am. And I am a good girl, too, Elmer, as they say."

"You're in love with somebody else!" he accused her.

"No, Elmer; I'm not in love with anybody, and it isn't that I'm a cold sort of girl, either, because I'm not. I'm awfully affectionate, but I could never give my affections to a man like you, Ebner.

"I don't want to be cruel or anything, but you asked for it, and here it is. Just look at the way you dress, Elmer.

"And look at the way you brush your hair! Right in the middle! And you seem so scared all the time, Elmer. You're always clearing your throat, and begging somebody's pardon or some thing. You—you don't assert yourself."

"Is that all?" Elmer coldly inquired.

"No," said the girl, "that's only the beginning. For your own good somebody ought to tell you this, anyway, and I might as well be a martyr and do it myself.

"You're too good, Elmer, if you want to know the honest truth. By that I mean you're too slow. And this isn't a slow age, either, Elmer. Girls like men with some dash and go to them.

"Girls like men they can be a little afraid of. To be quite frank with you, Elmer, you haven't a particle of sex appeal. You're just sort of colorless, and—and— Say, hasn't anybody ever told you this before?"

"Go on," Elmer urged her.

"Well," she obliged him, "girls like men who are a little bit devilish. I guess you don't see the picture of our married life the way I do.

"A little house. You coming home at night. Cooking and babies. No future. No fun to look forward to. No, thank you, Elmer; I won't have some. I want some excitement. I want to know that the man I marry has had a little of a past.

"I'd hate like mischief to think I was the first girl he ever loved, because if I was he'd soon begin wondering how it felt to love some other girl. He'd wonder if he hadn't missed something, maybe.

"You see, Elmer," she went on, "I'm not urging you to a life of crime or anything like that, and there are probably loads of girls in the world who would simply adore having a nice, steady man like you; but I'm not one of them. I want a man I can respect. And I could never respect you, Elmer. You're too tame. You're a refrigeratin' papa!"

Elmer was slowly beginning to bring order out of chaos. He had an orderly mind, and it was natural for it not to remain in a confused state very long. In spite of the way he was suffering, he contrived to bring a smile to his lips. It was more of a terrifying grimace than a smile, but it became easier as he tested it out.

His pride was aroused, and his imagination was rallying to his rescue.

"So that," he said, finally, coldly, "is what you think of me, is it?" He did not permit her to answer, but went swiftly on: "So you think I'm cold and tame, do you?

"Well, I'm sorry you look at it that way, Miss Jameson. Because you're mistaken."

He had arisen, and now he was starting toward the door. A step at a time, slowly, he backed toward it.

"You think I haven't a past, do you?" he got out hoarsely. "Well, I have a past, only I don't go around bragging about it, the way most men do! I could tell you a lot about girls I've known, but I'm not going to. I thought you'd rather think I was decent and clean, and—wholesome, and—and not just an ordinary rotter."

Step by step, as he retreated from the field of his humiliation, Carrol Jameson followed him. There was a strange, dancing light in her large brown eyes. It was only too evident that she was on the verge of another hysterical attack.

"You—you mean," she whispered, "that, in spite of appearances, you're really a sheik?"

Elmer Wirple found the doorknob. He jerked open the door, and wheeled savagely on the girl with the dancing eyes.

"That's what I am," he snarled. "A sheik!"

Carrol was holding one hand firmly over her heart.

"Furthermore," Elmer went on, "I will cease annoying you with my undesirable attentions! Good night!"

"Good night," came the faint answer from the closing crack of the door.

Retreating, stiffly, haughtily, down the sidewalk, Elmer Wirple heard, muffled, her unrestrained, unrefined, unladylike laughter.

With nails biting into palms, with teeth gritting, he ground out:

"Is that so! We shall see! You bet we shall see! By thunder, we *shall* see!"

3

HUNTING A PAST

ELMER WIRPLE DID not walk toward his boarding house. His footsteps carried him swiftly in another direction. The thought of his neat little room was intolerable. He wanted to walk and walk. He wanted to walk until his brain was cool, until his thoughts had caught up with each other.

He was boiling with rage—the rage of a man who had been unjustly humiliated, and scorned, and ridiculed. And coupled with his rage was a growing self-hatred. She had, he realized, stripped a curtain from his eyes; had revealed to him the ghastly truth about himself.

All that she had said was the horrid truth! He was tame. He was uninteresting. He was a "refrigeratin' papa." He was cautious, timid, dull. He hated her for saying such things, but he hated himself even more, because all she said was true.

What he had said about his past was the product, purely, of hurt pride and inflamed imagination. He had had to say those things to save his face. He had never had a love affair.

He had, in all his life, kissed but one girl, and that had been an accident of fortune. It had happened at a party of high school boys and girls, and there had been a silly game called postoffice. A girl had got him in a dark corner, and somehow, awkwardly, he had kissed the girl.

His only real passion, if it could be called a passion, had been Carrol Jameson. And now that she had spurned him, the future was black and horrible.

He gave way for a few minutes to self-pity, then his rage returned, his rage and the awful baffled feeling that she was right, that girls didn't care for men who were innocent and decent and wholesome.

They wanted sheiks. They didn't want you to put them on pedestals and worship them; they wanted you to treat them rough, and to boast about your previous conquests. That's what they all wanted, damned them!

Elmer stepped into a cigar store, and bought a large, black cigar. He never smoked, except an occasional cigarette. Now he wanted the feel of a strong cigar between his teeth.

With a gray plume of smoke trailing along behind him, he started down the street again. He was approaching the business center, the theatrical district. The theaters were dark, but crowds of people were still moving here and there, heaven only knew where they were going to or coming from!

Elmer Wirple strode down the sidewalk, with the cigar clutched fiercely in his teeth, his head jutted forward, his hands deep in his pockets.

"The man without a past, eh?" said the suffering young man to himself. "A dead one, eh? A refrigeratin' papa, eh? We'll see about that! We'll see who's a dead one or not! By thunder!"

Never had Elmer felt this way. He was a public menace,

and he knew it. In his present smoldering mood, he was a dangerous character. He wished somebody would come up to him and start a fight. How he would love to lash out with both fists, let the consequences be what they might!

A girl was coming toward him, a girl with painted lips and mascarraed eyes and tinted cheeks. She wore a black-and-white-checked coat, and a tight-fitting, black hat trimmed with white. There were glittering things, like diamonds, on her patent leather pumps, and she wore stockings of a striking lemon color.

"There," said Elmer Wirple to himself, "is a wild woman."

The idea fashioned itself in his brain while she was nearing him. It came into full flower when they were abreast.

"Hello, there, girlie," he said distinctly, and stopped, with heart suddenly hammering furiously in his throat.

He turned about.

"What's the hurry?" he called.

The girl stopped.

"Are you addressing me?" she asked, icily.

"Sure, I'm addressing you, girlie. How about droppin' in some place and havin' a little drink?"

"Roll your hoop, Insipid!" the girl snorted.

"Well," Elmer remarked philosophically, "no lives lost."

The girl edged away from him, started off at a brisk walk; and Elmer went on. Another girl was coming toward him, and it seemed to Elmer that she was even more of a wild woman than the other had been. This girl was short, rather plump, and big-eyed. She was a brunette. She was, in a way, beautiful.

Elmer slowed as she neared, and when she was abreast of him, he wheeled and fell into step beside her.

"Good evening, girlie," said Elmer.

The girl stopped. She looked up at him with blazing eyes.

"Say," she inquired, "how do you get that way?"

Elmer was smiling fatuously.

"How about droppin' in some place and havin' a little drink?" he pressed.

"Well, of all the gall!"

"You look good to me, kiddo," said Elmer.

"You let me alone," the girl growled, "or I'll yell."

Elmer felt uncertain. How did one go on from here?"

"No offense meant," he muttered. "Can I take you home, girlie?"

Elmer's next impressions were bewildered and incoherent. From the nowhere two rows of brass buttons against a field of blue and below a square, Irish, fiery-red face materialized.

"Officer," a shrill voice was explaining, "this fellow insulted me!"

"This guy here?" a bull-like voice inquired. And Elmer found himself being looked at by a pair of amazed blue eyes. "Not this guy!"

"Yes, he did!" the girl insisted. "He tried to take my arm. Why! I never laid eyes on him before in my life! He wanted to get me drunk. He said so! And he tried to drag me off to his apartment!"

"That's a lie!" Elmer bleated. "I never said any such thing. I only said—"

"Aw, tell it to the desk sergeant," growled the long arm of the law. "Will you come along and appear against him, miss?"

"Indeed I will!" the girl cried. "I never was so terrified in my life! The big sheik!"

A crowd was gathering about Elmer, the officer, and the girl, and through the crowd Elmer suddenly saw the face of the tall girl in the black-and-white checked coat. She was wedging her way through.

Perspiration broke out freely on Elmer's forehead. All rage and hatred were gone now. He was terrified. The policeman was holding him firmly by the elbow, and people were staring at him as if he were a safe-cracker or a boy bandit.

He felt suddenly sick in the region of his digestive organs. It would come out in the papers! Mr. Wainright would hear of this! His job—he would lose his job!

During the confusing minutes that followed, until Elmer was hustled into the station house, a dim, dreary place, his mind had room for only that one sickening realization. He would lose his job!

Elmer had never been in a police station before in his life. He had always been afraid of the police; they and the sinister people they dealt with represented a side of life that he was utterly unfamiliar with. A phrase popped into his mind from somewhere: durance vile. He was in durance vile!

Firmly gripped by the policeman who had arrested him, Elmer was led into the station house, into a large room at the farther end of which there was a long, golden-oak table, scarred by usage, and innumerable cigarette butts and cigar stumps.

A grim-faced man in uniform, with a cap tilted back from his face and a big book opened before him, sat at the table. The room seemed to be full of idlers. Later, Elmer would learn that they were plainclothes men.

He was almost grateful to the policeman for holding him so firmly. If the policeman relaxed his grip Elmer was sure he would fall.

Out of the tail of his eye he saw that the last girl he had accosted was standing beside him, and that the first girl he had accosted was standing beside her. They were talking.

It occurred to him that they had been talking incessantly since the march to the station house had begun. They had been talking about him, and they had used such expressions as "fiend," "sheik," and "beast."

Elmer licked his lips. He tried to pull himself together, but it was hopeless. He was faced by overwhelming disaster. What would Mr. Wainright think? What would Carrol Jameson think?

"I grabbed this guy, sergeant, up on Spruce Street, doin' his stuff," the policeman was explaining. "You wouldn't think it to look at him, but he was cert'n'y workin' hard and fast.

"He was insultin' one girl after another as fast as they come along. Here's two and Lawd only knows how many others he tried to drag off to his lair. I guess it's a technical charge of disorderly conduct," he concluded.

The sergeant, who had snow-white hair and eyes like bits of ice, which seemed to penetrate to the uttermost recesses and niches of Elmer's soul, wrote something in the book.

"What's your name?" he growled.

Elmer hesitated before answering. Heretofore, he had always done his thinking first, and his acting afterward. Now he reversed the process.

How he would get out of this mess was still a baffling mystery; but it was certain that embarrassment would be spared him if his real name did not leak out. Where the name came from, he would never know. It simply sprang, full-formed, in his mind.

"Eric Vardon," he said.

"Where do you live?" snapped the sergeant.

Again Elmer hesitated before answering. His thoughts floundered about for a moment, then they came to rest on a huge new apartment building—a swagger place—on the corner of Myrtle and Beechnut Avenues. It was a large apartment, and to live there was a distinction.

"The Herendon Arms," he answered.

Then doubt assailed him. How easily they could prove that that was a lie! Elmer gave a moment's frantic consideration to the tangled webs we weave when we first inaugurate the practice of deception.

"How old are you?"

Elmer answered that question truthfully. Why not?

"Well, young lady, tell me just what happened."

The excited girl began to talk. Her voice seemed, to Elmer, to come from remote distances.

"I was walking home from work. I'm the telephone operator at the Witz-Raldorf, and I was walking along Spruce Street when this sheik came up to me and insulted me.

"Honest, I never was so mortified in my life! I'm a decent girl, and I never talk to men I'm not properly introduced to. This fellow grabbed me by the arm, and he said he wanted me to get drunk with him—"

"Why, I did not!" Elmer bleated. "All I—"

"Shut up," snapped the sergeant. "Go on, young lady."

"I tried to pull away from him, but he hung on—and he leered at me. He leered at me, and he said he was going to take me up to his apartment, and—"

"Listen," Elmer feebly interrupted, "all I said—"

"Shut up!" said the sergeant. "What happened then, young lady?"

"I—I told him I'd yell if he didn't stop terrifying me with his improper proposals, and just then this nice big officer came along and grabbed him.

"And I've never been so humiliated in all my life, and I think you ought to do something with these dangerous men who prowl about our streets at night, threatening the lives of us working girls."

"Yes, ma'am," the sergeant grimly agreed, "something certainly ought to be done about it. Will you appear against him in court?"

"I most certainly will. My name is Minnie Schwartz, and I'll certainly come to court any time you say."

"Well, this wolf will come up for a hearing to-morrow in the city magistrate's court." The sergeant now addressed himself to the tall girl in the black-and-white-checked coat. "Did this fellow insult you, too, miss?"

"I'll say he insulted me!" cried the tall girl grievously. "I've got a solo act on over at Keith's—Charmaine's Charming Chatter—and I was out for a little ozone after the show before going to my hotel, and this menace tried to do the same thing to me he tried to pull on Miss Schwartz here.

"My Lawd, isn't a lady safe anywhere? Do I look like the kind of dame who lets every Tom, Dick, and Harry pick her up? I'm a refined girl, and I've got a refined act."

"What's your name, young lady?"

"Charmaine Dulcimer," said the tall girl tremulously.

"Did this bird say the same thing to you?"

"Yes, sir! He wanted to get me drunk, and he wanted to take me to his apartment!"

"Say, listen," Elmer broke in feebly, "I never said any such—"

"Bottle it!" snapped the sergeant.

The room was fairly crowded with curious onlookers who had followed Elmer, the policeman, Miss Schwartz, and Miss Dulcimer to the station house.

People were crowding in to get a better look at him, and Elmer was sure that if he only pinched himself hard enough he would wake up and find that he had been having a dreadful nightmare, that he was really nowhere but in his hard little bed at Mrs. Gibney's.

"Will you appear against him in court, Miss Dulcimer?"

"You bet I will, sergeant!"

"I'm going to hold you without bail," the sergeant gruffly told Elmer. "Take him away, boys. Jim and Mike, I guess you better ask him a couple of questions about that love nest he's got up at the Herendon Arms."

Elmer was spirited down a long, dark hallway, and into a room that was barren of furniture except for a small, battered table, three battered oak chairs, and a cuspidor.

He had always thought that cells were small affairs with grilled windows and barred doors, but he was in no condition now to think clearly, or at all. His brain felt numb. He had become, in a twinkling, a creature of chance, a plaything of fate. He could only take things as they came.

His two captors were broad-shouldered men who wore derbies, and blue serge suits, and shoes with very square toes. One of them also wore a stubby mustache, and it suddenly occurred to Elmer's dazed mind that Mike and Jim were detectives. And he wondered, dazedly, what they were going to do with him. As he wondered, his terror grew.

"Sit down," growled the man with the mustache.

Elmer Wirple obediently seated himself. There was a lamp stand with a large cone-shaped reflector at the top near the table.

The man with the mustache dragged this across the room until the reflector was only a foot or so from Elmer's face. Then he switched on the light.

It was a blinding, white light, and its beams were focused full upon Elmer's pale, harassed face. The detective with the mustache said jovially:

"We want to have a good look at you. It ain't often that somebody lifts up a stone and one of you crawls out."

"That light hurts my eyes," Elmer complained.

"Listen, fella; you'll learn to love that light. That light ain't only a fraction of what's goin' to happen to you if you don't talk, and talk fast."

An icy chill struck at Elmer Wirple's laboring heart. He had heard of the phrase "the third degree," which officers of the law employed in forcing desired information from suspects, and it struck him with devastating force that he was about to be introduced to the terrifying mysteries of that hideous process.

"Feel like tellin' us somethin' about that love nest of yours?"

"I don't know what you're talking about," said the prisoner.

Mike and Jim exchanged a meaning glance, and Mike pulled up a chair close to Elmer's and seated himself. His back was to the light, and in its dazzling rays Elmer could not see his face; but he sensed a menace to himself in the detective's attitude. Physical violence was somehow implied by it, and Elmer's terror grew and grew.

The door opened, and another detective came in. He paused at the threshold and said, in a jarring voice:

"There ain't anybody registered at the Herendon Arms by the name of Eric Vardon. He must have it in somebody else's name."

Then the door closed, and the detective who sat close to Elmer tapped him on the knee with a stiff forefinger.

"What name is it registered under?" he growled.

"Listen," Elmer whimpered, "I was only kidding about that apartment. I haven't got any apartment at the Herendon Arms. I live in a boarding house. My—my name isn't Eric Vardon. I—I just thought that up on the spur of the moment. My real name is Elmer Wirple."

"I don't believe it," stated the detective. "There never was any such name as Wirple, and there never will be. Take my advice, fella, and tell your story, and tell it straight. I have a big heart and I am chuck full of sympathy for you, but it happens to be past my bedtime, and I haven't any time to waste on the likes of you."

"Tell your bedtime story," the other detective urged.

Elmer remained mute. The light was blinding him. He closed his eyes, but opened them sharply as something icy splashed into his face. He mopped his face with a handkerchief. One of them had thrown a glass of ice water at him.

"You better talk," advised the ogre beside him. "Come on, baby, spill the beans before you get hurt."

"I've told you the truth," Elmer wailed. "My name is Elmer Wirple, and I work for the Purity Pulverized Egg Corporation as a clerk. I'm telling you the honest truth. I live in Mrs. Gibney's boarding house on Chestnut Street—"

"Light me that cigar," the man with the mustache interrupted him.

Elmer heard a match being struck, then he smelled the odor of a cheap cigar. The smell came closer. He had heard of the cigar trick—how these brutes pressed the burning end of a cigar against the flesh of a man who wouldn't squeal.

"Are you goin' to talk, or ain't you?" the man beside him snarled.

"Listen," cried Elmer, "I'll tell you anything you want me to, but I've told you the honest truth. I gave the wrong name to the sergeant out there, because I thought if I gave my right name, I'd lose my job with the Purity Pulverized Egg Corporation. Honest," he whimpered. "I'm telling the truth."

Through the glare of the spotlight, he saw, coming toward him, the glowing red disk of the cigar end. His hands were suddenly caught in a viselike grip from behind, and his head was jammed between a pair of hard, unyielding elbows.

They were going to burn his face with the cigar end!

"You goin' to talk?" urged the man beside him.

The hot ruby disk of the cigar end was now only inches

from his face. He could already feel the heat of it. They were going to apply it to his left cheek.

"Listen, I'm telling you the truth," he babbled. "I never spoke to a girl like that before in my life. I must have been crazy. I didn't mean any harm to her. I was only joking. I wouldn't hurt any girl! I'm telling—"

"Tell us," grated a voice that seemed to come from afar, "what name you've got that love nest of yours in."

Nearer and nearer came the hot end of the cheap cigar. Now it was almost touching Elmer's cheek. He could all but feel the pain of that contact in his left cheek. He writhed. He tried to free himself from the viselike grip, but he could not move.

Elmer kicked out with his right foot. His toe caught the seated detective sharply in the left shin. He uttered a yelp of pain.

Then a queer buzzing filled the room. A great wave of blackness rose up inside of Elmer and engulfed him.

4

BACK TO LIFE

WHEN ELMER RECOVERED consciousness he was lying on a hard, narrow little cot in a tiny cubicle. At one end of this cubicle was a small window covered with steel grating, and at the other end was a door consisting of bars.

Elmer sat up. He was soaking wet. Evidently a pail of water had been thrown in his face; he had been tossed into the cell, and left there unattended to recover.

His first thought was for the wound on his left cheek. He rubbed an exploring finger over his left cheek, but it produced no sensation of pain. The detective had not, after all, burned him with the cigar.

The prisoner sat up and swung his feet to the floor of the cell. He tried to marshal his thoughts, but he found that he had no thoughts to marshal. He had been caught up in a net of strange circumstance. How was he, Elmer Wirple, to go about unmeshing himself?

For five minutes, at the most, he had stepped out of the role of meekness and humility which he had played for twenty-four years on life's great stage. How was he going to step back? What would Carrol say? What would Mr. Wainright say? In those five foolish abandoned minutes, he had ruined his life.

The few friends he had would forever eschew him, as one tainted. After to-night no reputable business house would employ him. He could see the look of utter horror and repugnance on Mrs. Gibney's face when next she saw him. He would be a pariah. He would have to leave town, and he would never dare return.

The thought of leaving town, a striking out into some new, fairer land, where perhaps adventure beckoned, terrified him. Anyway, adventure did not beckon to Elmer. He didn't want adventure. What he wanted was peace. He wanted to be let alone.

An old memory was beginning to stir awake in Elmer. It became fully awake when he asked himself pointblank to whom he could turn for counsel and guidance in his hour of need. A name, finally, leaped from the confusion of churning thoughts: Gillian Hazeltine!

Elmer began to grow calm the moment that name came into his mind. Gillian Hazeltine was reputed to be the most brilliant criminal lawyer in this section of the country. Gillian Hazeltine had been a boyhood friend of Elmer's father.

Elmer's father, a few days before his death, had told his only son, "If you should ever get yourself into trouble, call on Gillian Hazeltine."

That old, forgotten memory, now so vividly recalled, cheered Elmer immensely. A great weight slipped from his shoulders, and was taken up by the shoulders of the famous criminal lawyer. Gillian Hazeltine would know what to do. Gillian Hazeltine would know how to hush this matter up; would know how to help him keep his job.

So great was his relief from the strain of the past hour

that Elmer laughed a little, and cried a little. Presently he heard a step in the corridor. A warden, or a guard, or some one was about to pass his cell.

Elmer sprang up, and grasped two bars of his cell door. An old man in blue uniform was slowly limping past.

"Hey!" Elmer called.

The old man stopped. He had rheumy blue eyes, and a large nose covered with a network of little purple veins. He peered sourly through the bars at Elmer.

"Oh, ya've come to, have ya?"

"Look here," said Elmer pleadingly, "will you do something for me? I want to get hold of my lawyer. Will you let me get out of here long enough to phone him?" The old man snorted. "You ain't been in jail much, to ask a dumb question like that. No, of course ya can't use no telephone."

"But I've got to get a message through to him."

"Well, all I can do for ya is to ask the desk sergeant, and if he says it's all right I'll phone the message for ya."

"It's to Gillian Hazeltine," Elmer panted. "Get him on the phone, please, and tell him that Geoffrey Wirple's son is down here in jail and wants him to come right down. Tell him not to waste a minute. Tell him it's a matter of life and death."

"I'll see what kin be done," the old man promised, and he limped away.

Elmer sat down and waited. He wondered what time it was. He looked at his watch, but it had stopped. Probably it was full of water. He was soaked to the skin, and the jail was cold.

Presently the old man returned.

"I got Mr. Hazeltine out of bed. He didn't seem to know

who you was at first, and when he did realize who ya was, he wasn't any too crazy to come down, but I told him you said it was a matter of life and death. Who did ya bump off?"

"I didn't bump off anybody."

"You didn't?" The old man seemed disappointed. "Well, what they got ya in here fer?"

"It's a mistake," said Elmer.

The old man waited. He waited with right hand outstretched, as if he wished to shake Elmer's hand. The palm, however, was upward.

"One buck," he growled.

"What for?" Elmer wanted to know.

"Fer the phone call."

"But a local call is only a nickel," the prisoner protested.

"The other ninety-five cents is fer service charge," said the crusty old man.

Elmer paid him and waited. He waited with growing anxiety. Perhaps Gillian Hazeltine wasn't coming, after all. Perhaps he'd had a smash-up on the way down town. Perhaps he had stopped at the sergeant's desk, learned what a fiend in human form Elmer Wirple was, and had gone away, shocked and disgusted.

But presently footfalls echoed along the corridor, and a man stopped at his cell, looked in at him, and confidence flowed back into Elmer in a great wave; for the man he saw was the kind of man who would inspire confidence in anybody.

He was a small, rather stout man, but his face was keen and shrewd. His black hair was speckled with silver. But not for his hair alone was Gillian Hazeltine known in these parts as the Silver Fox. He was reputed to be the smartest lawyer in the State. He had the brightest pair of blue eyes Elmer had ever seen.

These eyes were giving Elmer a very thorough overhauling. And presently Mr. Hazeltine said:

"So you're Geoffrey Wirple's son."

"Yes, sir," said Elmer eagerly, trying to smile. "My father told me to call on you if I ever got myself into trouble; so the first thing I did when I came to was to send for you. They gave me the third degree, and I guess I fainted."

"You don't say!" breathed the lawyer.

"Yes, sir! They were going to shove the hot end of a cigar in my face, and I fainted dead away. And when I came to, here I was!"

Elmer, in his relief, was trying to be a little humorous; but not a trace of a smile appeared in Mr. Hazeltine's face.

"What's the charge against you?"

"Disorderly conduct," said Elmer.

"What?" said Mr. Hazeltine, as if he had not heard aright.

"Disorderly conduct. You see, Mr. Hazeltine, I—I was walking down Spruce Street, and I—well, I spoke to two girls. I don't know what made me do such a crazy thing; but I did, all right, and then a cop came up and arrested me."

The Silver Fox looked at him for a long time before he said anything. He gave Elmer an even more thorough overhauling with those sharp blue eyes than he had before.

"What's your given name?" he finally asked.

"Elmer," said Elmer.

"Elmer," said Mr. Hazeltine, "do you mean to tell me that you got me out of bed and had me come racing all the way down here to help you out of a charge of disorderly conduct?"

"But—but," Elmer stuttered, "if Mr. Wainright finds it out, I'll lose my job."

Mr. Hazeltine opened his mouth to say something, closed it again firmly, and then said:

"How much does your job pay?"

"Twenty-eight dollars a week, Mr. Hazeltine."

"Twenty-eight dollars a week. You got me out of bed at three o'clock in the morning to save a job that pays you twenty-eight dollars a week. With your nerve, you ought to be getting a minimum of ten thousand dollars a year."

Elmer blushed.

"I—I thought," he stammered, "that considering that my father was one of your best friends—"

"Oh, I'm not going to walk out on you," the lawyer interrupted. "Your father was one of my best friends, and I am going to stand by you, Elmer.

"But, at the same time, I do think you have a hell of a lot of nerve getting me out of bed at three in the morning because you accosted a couple of girls. Is this your usual practice, to accost girls you don't know?"

"No, sir!" Elmer cried. "Absolutely not, Mr. Hazeltine. I never did a thing like that before in my life."

"Well, you ought to stop drinking the kind of stuff they're selling nowadays. This ought to be a lesson to you, Elmer."

"But I wasn't drunk," Elmer protested. "I hadn't had a drop to drink, Mr. Hazeltine."

The Silver Fox half lowered his lids.

"Look here, Elmer," he said sternly, "if you want me to

help you, you have got to come clean. I am not going to raise a hand to help you if you don't come clean."

"I have come clean," Elmer said earnestly.

"You weren't drunk, and you'd never done anything like this before?" the lawyer asked.

"No, sir; I hadn't had a drop, and I never in my life spoke to a girl I didn't know."

Once more Mr. Hazeltine gave him a thorough overhauling with his bright blue eyes; then he shook his head.

"There's a mystery here," he said. "I am going out and have a little chat with the desk sergeant. I'll be back in a few minutes."

Elmer waited.

Gillian Hazeltine returned presently, and he was wearing a dark frown.

"Why," he wanted to know, "did you give your name as Eric Vardon?"

"Because," Elmer answered, "if I'd given my right name, Mr. Wainright would have heard about it, and I'd have lost my job."

"Is that why you gave your address as the Herendon Arms?"

Elmer nodded. "Yes, sir. I thought maybe I'd pay a fine and nobody would ever find out."

"I see," said Gillian Hazeltine thoughtfully. "Now, Elmer, I want you to come absolutely clean with me. From your looks, I'd say you were not the kind of young man to accost strange young women on the street at midnight. Why did you do it?"

"I—I was sore."

"Who were you sore at?"

"A—a girl."

"Why were you sore at her? Come clean, Elmer."

Elmer hesitated. He executed a diagram on the floor of his cell with the toe of his left foot. He began to talk. He talked slowly, in a low, muffled sort of voice at first, but soon he was talking rapidly and with deep feeling.

He told the Silver Fox all about Carrol Jameson: how he'd fallen in love with her two years ago; how he'd been taking her to the Alto every Wednesday night; how he'd been saving his money; and how finally he had screwed up enough courage to ask her to marry him. At this point Elmer came to a full stop.

"And she turned you down?" said Mr. Hazeltine helpfully.

"She called me a refrigeratin' papa," Elmer stated hoarsely. "She said I was dead and slow, and that I wasn't the kind of man a girl wants to marry. She said I didn't have a past."

"The ladies do seem to prefer men with pasts," the famous lawyer murmured.

"I should think they would prefer clean, decent, wholesome men," said Elmer warmly.

Mr. Hazeltine shook his head.

"From the ladies' point of view—and their point of view, I am sad to confess, Elmer, is, on this subject, a correct one—a man without a past is a coward. It is a normal impulse of youth, Elmer, for a man to raise a little hell. Some of us raise more hell in our youth than others.

"It is, I say, a perfectly normal impulse. Hence, if a man has never raised a little hell, the ladies are correct in assum-

ing that he is, as the young lady called you, a refrigeratin'
papa."

"Do you mean to tell me—" Elmer began indignantly.

"We won't argue that point," the lawyer stopped him.
"Miss Jameson is right. I will confess, however, that your
case is beginning to interest me, Elmer. You may be relieved
to know that I am no longer peeved at being yanked out
of bed at three in the morning. Your character interests
me greatly. Did any one ever tell you that you are the spit
image of your father?"

"It seems to me that people have mentioned that," Elmer
admitted, wondering what it was all about.

"Your father," the lawyer went on, "was a man, Elmer.
I will never forget the time we went West together, and
stayed a month on Bert Heffelfinger's ranch in Wyoming.
Did your father ever tell you about the whisky race?"

"I don't think he ever did," said Elmer.

"We rode mustangs," said the lawyer, "that were hardly
broken to the saddle. We rode them in relays. That is, each
of us started with six mustangs, all saddled. At each end of
the half-mile course were three mustangs and three pints
of one-hundred-and-eighty-proof rye whisky. Whoever
got through riding all the horses and drinking all the rye
first, won the race.

"If you could have known your father, there would have
been no doubt in your mind as to who won that race, Elmer.
And having won the race, do you suppose he retired to his
downy couch and slept for thirty-six hours, as I did? Not
at all, Elmer. Your father picked the freshest horse of the
six, and rode into the neighboring town of Gold Nugget,

which he proceeded thoroughly and expeditiously to shoot up.

"The town of Gold Nugget," Mr. Hazeltine went on, "is nothing but a scattered handful of shacks now. Like all the other good things, the old Gold Nugget has gone. But there are still a few of the old settlers left, and I can assure you, Elmer, that the name Wirple is spoken of to this day with the greatest respect.

"I have told you this true story for a purpose, Elmer. I want you to take all the time you need to think it over, and then I want you to tell me just what you think of that episode."

"I don't need any time to think it over," was Elmer's prompt answer. "I think it was pretty disgraceful—that's what I think about it."

"You do, Elmer?"

"I certainly do, Mr. Hazeltine."

The Silver Fox nodded thoughtfully.

"I am going to ask you a few more questions, and I want you to answer them just as freely and frankly and honestly. Supposing I were to exert pressure in certain quarters and got you off scot-free. I mean, supposing I fixed things here and there so that you were permitted to go away from this jail without Mr. Wainright or any one else ever learning of your strange behavior on Spruce Street to-night. What would you do?"

"I—I guess I don't know just what you mean, Mr. Hazeltine."

"I'll be more specific. If you were to walk out of here, let's say in ten minutes, a free man, would you ever again be as wild and wanton as you were to-night? Think that over carefully before you answer it, Elmer. And remember, I am not a moralist."

"The answer is too easy," Elmer cried. "I would certainly do nothing like that again as long as I lived."

"You'd go back to your job at the Purity Pulverized Egg Corporation and be perfectly content?"

"You bet I would. I certainly would, Mr. Hazeltine."

"H-m," said Mr. Hazeltine. "What do you do there?"

"I'm a clerk."

"How long have you been a clerk?"

"About five years."

"Ever had a promotion?"

"No, sir."

"Ever asked for one?"

"No, sir."

"Ever asked for a raise?"

"No, sir. They raised me two dollars a week last Christmas, and two dollars a week the Christmas before."

"With all the other clerks?"

"Yes, sir. Most of them got raises then, too."

"I see," said the Silver Fox thoughtfully. "All you want in the world is to go back to that job and stay there forever."

"That's all." Elmer affirmed.

"Perfectly satisfied?"

"Perfectly."

Gillian Hazeltine nibbled reflectively at his thin lower lip. He was pondering.

"Elmer," he said briskly, "can you recall, looking back as far as possible into your youth, that any one ever scared you? I mean, did any one ever tell you ghost stories, or threaten you with the bogy man when you were naughty?"

"No, sir; I was always a model child."

"Did any one ever tell you, or keep on telling you, that the traits worth developing were those of prudence, meekness, and humility?"

"No, sir; quite the contrary. Both my father and my mother, as far back as I can remember, were all the time harping on the necessity for boldness, audacity, fearlessness, and such things."

"Those lectures didn't make much impression, did they?"

"I guess they didn't, Mr. Hazeltine. I can't see the use of being bold and audacious and so on, because, it seems to me, they're always getting you into hot water. All I want out of life is peace."

"You gave your age to the sergeant as twenty-four."

"Yes, sir; I'm twenty-four."

The Silver Fox fell silent again. He seemed to be thinking. A cloud passed over his eyes. He scowled. Then the frown cleared. He smiled faintly. Then he fell to gnawing at his lower lip. All this time he was looking at Elmer, at his face, at his hair, at his shirt, at his coat, at his trousers.

Under this strange, persistent scrutiny Elmer grew more and more nervous.

"You—you can get me out all right, can't you, Mr. Hazeltine?" he said in a tremulous voice. "I mean, so Mr. Wainright won't find out about it, and so—so I won't lose my job?"

"Elmer," the great criminal lawyer answered gravely, "I'm afraid it would be useless trying to bring pressure to bear. I'm afraid we'll have to see this thing through.

"I'll be on hand in the City Magistrate's Court in the morning when your case comes up. You are in hot water,

Elmer Wirple, and the chances are it will be hotter before it becomes any cooler. Good night, Elmer."

On this depressing note Gillian Hazeltine left Elmer. He left the station house, saying good night cheerily to the sergeant at the desk, and to several of the detectives he knew, and entered his Lincoln roadster, which was parked in front of the green light at the curb.

He did not at once start the engine. He lighted a cigar and sat in deep thought until the cigar was almost finished.

Inasmuch as Gillian Hazeltine was justly reputed to be one of the fastest thinkers in the State, it is fairly safe to say that, during the time it took him to smoke the cigar, he did a vast amount of pondering, cogitating, and cerebrating. He had once worked out an entire successful gubernatorial campaign for his State in less time than that.

The crystal-clear mind of the Silver Fox reached out over many miles; it tested this, discarded that. He peopled a stage with actors and actresses, and in those few minutes he saw the play through to its logical conclusion.

He was going to bring about a great many sweeping changes in the lives of a great many people, not among the least of whom was Elmer Wirple. Elmer Wirple, to put it another way, would presently become a whirling leaf before the gust of an onrushing destiny.

When Gillian Hazeltine started his engine, finally, a great, complex procedure was worked out in his mind to the finest details.

He drove to Spruce Street and down Spruce to Seventh Street, where the massive masonry of the Witz-Raldorf Hotel went up to scrape the stars.

The lawyer entered a lobby that was all but deserted.

His overcoat was pulled up about his ears, and his hat was pulled down over his eyes.

He walked casually to the row of telephone booths, which by daytime were presided over by Miss Minnie Schwartz. After midnight they were ordinary pay stations, each one a little pay station unto itself.

He entered booth No. 5 and, closing the door after him, dropped a nickel into the proper slot.

"Highridge 4-7-6-3," he presently said to an operator.

He heard the rhythmic burring on the wire as the bell of No. 4-7-6-3 Highridge was rung.

After a considerable wait, a man's sleepy voice answered.

"Is this the prosecutin' attorney?" he asked, pitching his voice to a deep, rough bass and employing the accent of the underworld.

The man at the other end growled:

"Yes, this is Mr. Yistle. What do you want?"

"Listen," the Silver Fox bade him. "I got somethin' good fer you, see? There was a guy pinched around midnight tonight fer tryin' to make a couple o' dames on Spruce Street, see? This bimbo gave his name to the desk sergeant down at the Third Precinct Station as Eric Vardon, see?

"Well, his real name ain't Eric Vardon, or anything that sounds like it. His real name is Elmer Wirple, do you get me? If you want a hot tip, you'll look him over good.

"What I'm tellin' you is that mebbe he knows somethin' about the disappearance o' Dorothy Murphy. That's up to your office to find out.

"If you think I ain't spillin' the dope right, I'll tip you off to somethin' else you can check me up on. This guy Wirple has retained Gillian Hazeltine, get me? He wouldn't retain

Hazeltine if he was nothin' but an ordinary disorderly conduct case, would he?"

Mr. Hazeltine stopped and waited.

"Did this man you're talking about abduct Dorothy Murphy?" the prosecuting attorney snapped.

"That's fer you to figure out," said Mr. Hazeltine.

There was another silence. Then:

"Who is this talking?"

"Well," said the famous criminal lawyer, "mebbe it's Santy Claus." And he hung up the receiver.

He retreated from the lobby of the Witz-Raldorf as casually as he had entered. He knew that, within five minutes, policemen would be combing these premises for the sender of that mysterious information.

Mr. Hazeltine reentered his roadster and drove swiftly up Spruce Street to the Rittenhouse Building, where his offices were located. A night watchman took him up in an elevator to the seventeenth floor. The Hazeltine offices occupied the entire floor.

He let himself into the imposing walnut reception room, strode down a corridor, and entered a door at the farther end. This led, through a small room, into his private office.

The Silver Fox worked swiftly. He switched on the great, cream-colored bulb which hung on bronze chains from the ceiling, and knelt on the thick gray carpet before a small safe.

This safe was—or was advertised to be—positively burglar-proof. In it Mr. Hazeltine hid those tangible bits of evidence which he did not permit even those coworkers closest to him to know about.

He spun the dial, and presently the heavy little patent-steel door swung open. Mr. Hazeltine removed a small drawer. From this he extracted a small, square manila envelope.

He tore open the envelope, and removed from it a gold bracelet; rather a bizarre, oriental-looking gold bracelet. The inner surface of it was flat. The periphery was studded with semiprecious stones—tourmalines, garnets, and amethysts.

The bracelet he placed in his inner coat pocket. He closed the safe, spun the dial, switched off the light, and made his way out to the elevator again.

Presently Mr. Hazeltine was driving swiftly south on Spruce Street. As he neared Water Street he slowed and turned. Halfway down the block he threw out his clutch and applied the brakes.

A gloomy, dark building was on his right. At the foot of Water Street lights were mirrored on the unhurrying black surface of the Sangamo River.

Mr. Hazeltine debouched, and briskly entered the dark, gloomy building. It was the city morgue.

A night watchman sat in the office, drowsing over an old corncob pipe. A copy of a late tabloid newspaper lay neglected on his lap.

He sprang up, fully awake.

"Mr. Hazeltine!" he exclaimed, and doffed his cap.

"I'm interested," the Silver Fox explained his presence, "in that stiff that was brought in here this afternoon. How old would you say she was, Jake?"

"I'd say she was about twenty, Mr. Hazeltine."

"Is she in pretty bad shape?"

"Yes, Mr. Hazeltine; I reckon she's been in the water at least two weeks."

"Nobody been around to identify her yet?"

"No, sir; not yet."

"What color hair has she got?" the lawyer wanted to know.

"She was a brunette."

"How tall, would you say?"

"Oh, I'd say she was about five feet two, Mr. Hazeltine. Do you want to take a look at her?"

Mr. Hazeltine shuddered slightly. "No," he said emphatically. It was one of the famous criminal lawyer's few weak spots—this aversion he had for looking at dead people.

He had built up a great fortune because of the propensity that people have, now and then, of taking each other's lives in violence; yet the sight of a dead face terrified Mr. Hazeltine.

"No," he repeated, "I don't want to look at her. I want you to do something for me, though. Do you want to do me a great big favor, Jake?"

"Mr. Hazeltine," the night watchman said huskily, "you ought to know that, after the way you got my son out of hot water that time, there's nothin' I wouldn't do for you. Just you tell me what it is, and I'll do it."

"First," said Mr. Hazeltine, "I want to know just who has seen this body."

"Nobody, sir, but me and Al. Al and I were on duty when a cop came in, and said they'd found a floater down by the iron ore docks, and Al and I both went down in the wagon and fetched her up here.

"I don't think Al got a very good look at her. He ain't

used to handlin' 'em yet, Mr. Hazeltine, and when we got her here, I had him phone your office right away, and I put her in the big room myself."

"I see," said the lawyer. "Now let me check you once more on the measurements. You say she's about five feet three. She's about twenty years old. And she's a brunette."

"Yes, sir. That's right, Mr. Hazeltine."

"Very well, Jake. What I want you to do is to take this bracelet, and place it on her left wrist. It's a big bracelet, and you won't have any trouble slipping it on, no matter how much the wrist may be swollen. Put it on by force if you must.

"All I want you to do is to swear on the witness stand, if necessary, that that bracelet you have was on her wrist when you found her.

"All I can tell you, Jake, is that this is only one part of a plan of mine that will do certain people a great deal of good. You will be perjuring yourself, but it will be good perjury."

"Hell's bells, Mr. Hazeltine; you ought to know I'd lie myself black in the face for you. Anything else, sir?"

"Nothing else. Just forget that you've seen me to-night. Remember that the bracelet was on the wrist—the left wrist—of the body when found.

"Some people in this town," Mr. Hazeltine added, "are pretty dumb. If nobody happens to examine the inner side of that bracelet, you might find some natural and easy way of calling the coroner's attention to it.

"It isn't particularly valuable, but don't let anybody steal it. Make sure, if you can, that it gets into the possession of the prosecuting attorney. But that isn't absolutely important.

"All I really want you to do is to put it on now; and to swear, at any time, that it was on the body when found. You may be called on to testify in a case for the prosecuting attorney. I will probably be representing the other side.

"But don't let that bother you. I may have to be pretty nasty to you, Jake, when you're on the stand; but don't let that worry you.

"Have a cigar, Jake, but throw away the band before you put it in your pocket. It won't do to let people know I've been here. How's your son making out now?"

"He's doin' just fine, Mr. Hazeltine. He's got a good job in the Ford factory in Detroit. We hear from him regular. He likes the work, and he's in line for promotion. My old lady never speaks your name but what she gives up thanks to heaven for you. I'll put this bracelet right on, Mr. Hazeltine."

Again the Silver Fox shuddered slightly. He went to the door.

"Good night, Jake."

"Good night, Mr Hazeltine."

Gillian Hazeltine turned his car around, and drove rapidly to his mansion in the new Riverside Heights Development; he entered his kitchen and brewed himself a pot of coffee. He drank three great cups. Then he ascended to his bedroom, undressed, and climbed into bed.

Two minutes later he was asleep with the innocent conscience of a two-months old baby.

There were many excellent authorities who held that Mr. Hazeltine did not possess a conscience.

5

AT THE HEARING

THE ORDEAL OF that morning in the City Magistrate's Court was one that Elmer Wirple would never forget. He had slept only by fits and starts.

Mr. Hazeltine's parting words had been so many barbs to his harassed soul. And by morning, when he was taken over in a patrol wagon to the jail adjoining the City Magistrate's Court, there were dark depressions under Elmer's eyes and, if you had looked at him in the morning's batch of miscreants and evildoers, you would have said that he looked like the most hardened criminal of them all.

His shirt was soiled and rumpled because of the drenching he had received when he fainted; his collar was wilted down to hardly more than a rag, and his suit looked as if it had never known the refining pressure of a tailor's sad-iron.

The City Magistrate's Court was a dreary place to Elmer. Dusty high windows behind the justice's bench faced north, and permitted a gray cold light to sift in. There was an oak rail which extended from one side of the room to the other.

An aisle and the judge's bench were on one side of the rail, and on the other side were rows of benches where spectators and witnesses sat. They were a scrubby, raffish looking lot, women with hard faces, and men with hard or shifty eyes.

Elmer was brought in, with a bailiff on either side of him, in time to hear a girl accused of throwing milk bottles into the court of her apartment at unseemingly hours of the night sentenced to ten days in the workhouse.

She looked like the kind of girl who would throw milk bottles into empty courts, but Elmer was too busy looking for Gillian Hazeltine to pay much attention to her.

His heart beat alternately fast and slow. He was filled with dread of the future, terror of the present, and hopelessness for the past. All three were going to be ground to a pulp by the legal machinery through which he would presently pass.

A man in uniform, who looked like a policeman, was standing in the aisle below the judge's desk. Elmer heard him say, in a clear, ringing voice: "Elmer Wirple"; and Elmer winced. Then he heard the words "disorderly conduct." There were a great many more words.

Everything to Elmer was confused. He felt sicker and sicker. It was already past ten o'clock; he should have been at his desk in the great outer office of the Purity Pulverized Egg Corporation for an hour.

Never before had he been late or absent, except on vacations, since he had gone to work. And after his disgrace was aired to the world, he would, in all likelihood, never sit at Desk Twenty-Four again.

Elmer looked desperately about him for the lean, capable face of Gillian Hazeltine. Was his father's oldest friend going to desert him in his hour of greatest need?

A pink-cheeked young man stepped up to him.

"You Elmer Wirple?" he asked crisply.

Elmer nodded speechlessly, searching his face as if to ascertain from his eyes, his nose, his mouth, if this healthy looking young man was friend or foe.

"I'm Mr. Hoyle, from Mr. Hazeltine's office," the young man said. "Mr. Hazeltine was too busy to come over. He sent me to handle your case."

A fresh tide of doubt and despair welled up in Elmer. Mr. Hoyle looked too young, too inexperienced to be of much help at a critical time like this.

"I guess there isn't much hope for you," Mr. Hoyle remarked cheerfully. "Are you going to plead guilty, or not guilty?"

"I'll do whatever you think is best," Elmer groaned. "Oh, why didn't Mr. Hazeltine come?"

"Well, this routine stuff he usually turns over to us beginners," the young man explained. "He doesn't bother with unimportant cases."

"Unimportant!" Elmer wailed.

"Sure! The most you'll get is ten days—or a hundred dollars fine. Were there any extenuating circumstances? I mean, were you drunk, or did these girls try to flirt with you?"

"N-n-no!"

"Oh, well, we'll plead not guilty, anyhow, and if there's a chance we'll ask to have it remanded to General Sessions. Then we'll get a jury trial. I've never taken a case before a jury, and I'm dying' to do it!"

"But I've got to get back to my job," Elmer moaned. "That is, if there's any job for me to get back to. I don't want a jury trial."

The judge snapped a question.

"W-whuh-what?" Elmer blurted.

"The defendant pleads not guilty, your honor, to the charge as read."

"Hustle this thing through," growled the judge. "I've got a jail full of bums out there to attend to. Where are the witnesses in this case? Bailiff, call for the witnesses again in this Wirple case."

There was a gate in the oak rail, and a bailiff stood there, a bailiff who had the appearance of a mastiff, and the voice of a healthy, full grown bull.

"Witnesses in the case of Elmer Wirple!" he roared. "Step this way, please."

He opened the gate, and admitted a tall, hard looking young man with a fiery-red face, whom Elmer identified as the policeman who had arrested him last night. Behind him came two girls whom he recognized respectively as Minnie Schwartz and Charmaine Dulcimer.

Elmer looked fearfully at the judge. He had black eyes, and they were, without a doubt, the coldest eyes in the world. They were circles of black ice. His face was the color of underdone pie crust, and he was bald, except for a fringe of coarse black hair.

Minnie Schwartz seated herself in a chair elevated on a platform beside the bench. Her big, bold eyes were defiant, and she snapped out her answers to the questions the judge put to her.

Yes; she identified the accused as the man who had accosted her on Spruce Street last night as she was going home from work. Yes; she was the public switchboard operator at the Witz-Raldorf.

"Yes, sir; he wanted to get me drunk. He said so. I was never so mortified in my life. I think something ought to be done—"

"Young lady, will you take the stand?"

Minnie Schwartz got down, and Charmaine Dulcimer took the stand. There were more questions. More spiteful answers. More bewildered terror for the quaking prisoner.

"What has the prisoner to say for himself?"

"Your honor," spoke up Mr. Hoyle, "it is the prisoner's first offense. He is a young man of sober and industrious habits. He is a conscientious employee. One look at him, your honor, should convince you that he is not the kind of man who habitually does this sort of thing."

"He looks like a thug to me," the judge growled.

"Yes, he has suffered enough, your honor. The experience has taught him a lesson."

"And you let him plead not guilty?"

"I did, your honor."

"Well, if you want my advice, you'll go back to law school and learn your legal terminology. I find the prisoner guilty of the charge as read. I—"

"One moment, your honor," the flustered Mr. Hoyle interrupted, "I respectfully petition that, in view of the circumstances, this case be remanded to General Sessions."

"In view of what circumstances?" the judge snapped.

"The prisoner's record of sober and industrious application."

"Petition denied. This case doesn't have to go out of this court room."

The judge bent down, and fixed cold and baleful black eyes upon the cringing Elmer.

"I am going to make an example of you, Wirple. There has been too much of this sort of thing going on. You are a menace to the community.

"Because of scoundrels like you, decent girls need armed escorts when they venture out upon the streets of this city after sundown. I am going to give you the maximum penalty. One hundred dollars fine and costs or ten days in jail. Next case!"

6

MRS. PERKINS'S PLACE

GILLIAN HAZELTINE AWOKE that morning punctually at five thirty. He needed no alarm clock, other than the one with which an all-seeing Providence had equipped him. The mechanism of it was a mystery to Mr. Hazeltine, but he had always found it to be infallible. Always, when he went to bed, he told himself the exact hour at which he wished to awaken; and at that exact hour he would awaken.

A man of enormous energy, he required very little sleep. He had slept but an hour and a half, yet his affairs would not suffer because of that, and to-night he might make it up by having six long, sweet hours of slumber.

He shaved, took a cold shower, and dressed. It was too early for the servants to be about. He tiptoed down into the kitchen, and prepared himself breakfast. Mr. Hazeltine, being a hard worker, was, accordingly, a hard eater.

He fried himself a half dozen eggs, a quantity of bacon, and toasted himself a dozen slices of toast. These items, with four large cups of coffee, constituted his breakfast.

The first heliotrope luster of dawn was shining against the eastern sky when he let himself out of the house. Overhead the sky was clear, and of a deep, divine blue. It was going to be a beautiful morning.

Mr. Hazeltine loved beautiful mornings. He had a most affectionate disposition which embraced almost everything, but first of all, it embraced Gillian Hazeltine.

He lighted a large, expensive blond cigar, and puffed away at it with the deepest pleasure as he made his way down the gravel drive to the garage. The mists of sleep were already gone from his eyes; they were clear, bright and sparkling.

He loved intrigue; nothing appealed to him more than knotty problems and complicated situations. He was faced by both. Consequently, he was as happy as a lark.

He was whistling softly as he entered his powerful roadster; he was humming as he backed the glistening gray monster out into the open; and when he reached the highroad he was singing in a deep, contented voice.

His first wife had left him because of the painful quality of his singing voice; but Gillian Hazeltine had not minded that. One woman more or less in his life did not concern the Silver Fox. He loved them all.

At present he was without a wife; he was keeping, in his handsome house, bachelor hall. There would be a new Mrs. Hazeltine as soon as he got around to it.

The sun came up as he was leaving the outskirts of the city behind him; it came up into a world of silver and gold, and scintillating lavender mist.

There were no cars on the road, and the road was a good one, a concrete one, as smooth as silk, as straight as a die, and wide enough for five cars to pass abreast. And the curves had been well banked by a thoughtful commissioner.

Most of the way it ran beside the Sangamo River, which,

by dawn, was not the unhurrying black stream that it was by night, but a fairyland river of silver and coralpink.

Singing in a louder voice and keeping an eye upon the unfolding beauties of the river, Mr. Hazeltine stepped on it. A flawless fifteen-mile drive lay before him. He settled down into the comfortable upholstery, and pushed his right foot down on the accelerator.

The roadster fled. Handsome houses passed. White, prosperous looking farmhouses, set in fields upon which the faint green of early spring grass was already glowing, fled arear.

Mr. Hazeltine's attention was abruptly distracted from the enchantments of landscape and river by a brisk *pop-pop-popping* which originated at a point not far from the left hind wheel of his car.

He glanced into the rear-view mirror, and slowed down to a comfortable forty-five.

The motor cycle policeman shot up alongside him.

"Say!" he bellowed. "What's the big i—" His scowl departed.

Gillian Hazeltine slowed to twenty miles an hour.

"Morning, Terry!" he greeted the officer. "You're out pretty early. You aren't pinching me, are you?"

"Gee, I didn't know it was you, Mr. Hazeltine," the grinning cop answered. "Didn't recognize the car. New one, ain't she?"

"Got her last week," said the lawyer.

"She's a stepper, Terry."

"I'll say she's a stepper," said Terry. "You was doin' seventy back there if you was doin' an inch. I been followin' you for five miles. Don't let me detain you, Mr. Hazeltine, if you're in a hurry. Sorry for the mistake."

"You ought to know I'm never in too much of a hurry to pass the time of day with you, Terry. How is the missus?"

"Mr. Hazeltine, I'm beginnin' to think she's goin' to pull through all right. It was that case o' port wine you sent down to her that did the trick. She began pickin' up the minute she started takin' that wine.

"She was sayin' just last night: 'If I ever become a healthy, well woman again, Terry McGinnis, you can give all the credit for it to Mr. Hazeltine.' Yes, sir, and nobody knows it better than me.

"Say, Mr. Hazeltine! Did you know the body of that Murphy girl had been found?"

"You don't tell me!" breathed the Silver Fox.

"Yes, sir; found her in the river late yesterday afternoon. They got her down at the morgue now. It changes it from a disappearance case to a possible murder case, and that's goin' to mean hard work for us for awhile, with the way the tabloids've been razzin' the department lately."

"Sure it's the Murphy girl?" asked Mr. Hazeltine.

"Dead positive! Had a bracelet on with her name engraved on the inside of it. They say she must've been in the water a couple of weeks, anyhow."

"Well, well!" murmured the lawyer. "Too bad, too bad. Have a smoke, Terry?"

"Thank you, Mr. Hazeltine, I guess I can snitch a smoke on my ride back to town."

And he accepted the cigar that Mr. Hazeltine held out to him.

"There won't be any cops between here and Cloverdale until nine, Mr. Hazeltine. You can open her wide."

"Thank you, Terry; and if that port wine gives out, don't be bashful. There's plenty more where it came from. So long."

"So long, Mr. Hazeltine."

The famous criminal lawyer proceeded on his way. He drove to a crossroad which was approximately fifteen miles from the city limits. He turned west on this, and drove slowly down a declining clay road toward the river.

The road turned right eventually, and he stopped the car before a brown cottage with a series of coarse wire mesh runs in back, which resembled chicken runs. The runs, however, contained animals. They contained guinea pigs of all sizes, and all colorations.

"Elmer Wirple," mused the lawyer, "belongs in one of those runs. But— Oh, well, we'll see, we'll see."

He turned off his ignition switch, but did not at once dismount. His eyes followed the dirt road, which was now hardly more than a pair of wagon tracks across the grass. The road, at the nearest point, was about one hundred feet from the shabby brown cottage. It disappeared over a rise in the middle distance. The tops of the gnarled branches of an oak tree could be seen beyond.

Mr. Hazeltine climbed down from the car as the front door of the cottage opened, and a slender, elderly woman in a black dress and a blue gingham apron came out on the tipsy porch.

She shaded her eyes against the sun with one hand as the lawyer walked toward her. Then, evidently ascertaining his identity, she came toward him at a run.

It was obvious that she was delighted to see Gillian Hazeltine. She shook his hand effusively; light sprang into her faded blue eyes.

"Gillian!" she exclaimed. "What in the world are you doing up at this unearthly hour?"

"I got to wondering about you, Mrs. Perkins," he explained, "and I thought I'd run out. Besides, maybe there's something you can do for me."

Her eyes were dancing. "You're up to some more of your deviltry, Gillian, but you know there's nothing under the sun I won't do for you. Land sakes, it's been ages since I saw you last! How long ago was it you cleared up the title on this land for me?"

"Must have been ten years," said Gillian.

"And I've never got over being a mite peeved at you, Gillian, for not charging me for your work. You're just a lamb."

"Yes," said the lawyer with a sigh, "I've been called every kind of animal from a river rat to a ravenous Bengal tiger. How's business?"

"Business is bad—mighty bad," said Mrs. Perkins. "People don't seem to buy guinea pigs the way they used to."

"H-m-m-m."

"I'm thinking of switching to chickens. I like guinea pigs, and I hate chickens; but folks don't seem to want guinea pigs any more. Or rabbits either, and I'm not even making ends meet. I was going to come in one of these days and ask your advice what to do, Gillian."

"And I came out here to give it to you," said Mr. Hazeltine. "It came into my head last night that the guinea pig business probably wasn't what it ought to be, and I told myself then that I'd make a trip out here this morning and talk things over with you.

"I've got an idea that would make a barrel of money for you, Mrs. Perkins. Have you got that high-wheeled bicycle of yours still?"

"Oh, yes; it's out there leaning against the side of the house."

"Ever use it?"

"Yes; I ride into Cloverdale on it once a week for things I need."

She was staring at him with wide, curious eyes.

"Why, Gillian?"

"Let's walk on down to the end of this road," the lawyer answered.

The road ran on perhaps an eighth of a mile beyond the cottage. It terminated abruptly under the gnarled old oak tree at the edge of a sheer escarpment perhaps seventy feet in height. At the bottom of this cliff, or bluff, flowed the Sangamo.

The road had been used, years before, by wagons which had hauled stones and rocks from the fields. This field litter had been dumped off the cliff into the river.

Mr. Hazeltine questioned Mrs. Perkins as they walked toward the cliff.

"Do cars still come out here?"

She nodded. "I guess a car comes out here on an average of three or four nights a week."

"Petting parties?"

She chuckled softly. "I reckon so. I never bother them. It's a romantic sort of spot, Gillian, and on a moonlight night it's just beautiful down here. Look at that view you get across the river! And on a real clear day I can see Cloverdale.

"If I was rich I would have the house moved down here, and I'd spend my declining days reclining on a porch."

"There's a fair chance that we can make that possible," was the lawyer's comment. "Does the same car come out on these nightly petting expeditions?"

"No. Sometimes it's a Ford, sometimes a Buick, sometimes some other make."

"Well, you'd be safe in saying that the same couple doesn't use it all the time."

"I'm sure it's different couples, Gillian."

The Silver Fox nodded thoughtfully. Then he inaugurated a careful inspection of the land about the oak tree. He ventured to the edge of the escarpment, looked down and drew back, shivering.

Mr. Hazeltine had no more liking for heights than for corpses. Mrs. Perkins watched him with growing curiosity. He finally returned to her.

"Yes," he said mysteriously, "I think you're going to make a lot of money, Mrs. Perkins.

"How much do you estimate it would cost to put up a fence ten feet high with barbed wire at the top, extending from the edge of the cliff at that point, enclosing this tree, and continuing on to the edge of the cliff over there? Do you think five hundred dollars would cover it? I mean a good, strong fence."

Mrs. Perkins stared at him.

"Gillian, what under the sun are you driving at? You're up to one of your schemes."

"I'll explain it all in a moment," the lawyer answered. "I forget that most people think frontwards, while I do most of my thinking backwards. I start with the effects, or results, and then work back to the causes.

"I'm going to lend you one thousand dollars, and you can pay me back out of the proceeds. I want you to order the material for this fence—it must be strong, and at least ten feet high, with barbed wire at the top, with a strong door in it.

"Another thing I want you to do is to stop selling guinea pigs, and to breed them as fast as you can.

"And another thing," Mr. Hazeltine went on. "All that I am telling you, and am going to tell you, must be kept in the strictest confidence.

"You must buy the materials for this fence very quietly. If any one should ask, you'll tell them you're getting that lumber for new guinea pig houses, or chicken houses. Understand?"

"Gillian," the old woman answered, "if I didn't know how smart you are, I'd say you'd gone daffy."

"One final point," the famous lawyer went on pleasantly. "Are you prepared to go on the witness stand and perjure yourself for me? You have got to answer that question with a flat yes or no."

"Gillian," said Mrs. Perkins, "you know how my female curiosity whetted to the point where I would say yes to any fool thing you wanted me to do.

"You are a queer combination, Gillian. You are the wickedest man I ever knew, and at the same time you are the finest.

"I should think the struggle that's going on inside of you

between God and the devil would tear you apart. Now stop beating about the bush, and tell me what's on your mind."

"Have you any pie in the house?" Mr. Hazeltine shrewdly answered.

The old woman laughed again. "Yes, I've got a nice new lemon meringue pie that hasn't been cut."

"Let's go into the house," the Silver Fox suggested.

7

WHAT THE "PAPERS" SAID

GILLIAN HAZELTINE NEVER appeared to be in a hurry; yet this morning he was in the greatest of hurries. It was essential that all of the irons he had in the fire be heated to the proper temperature for forging at one and the same time.

It was only nine-thirty when he stopped his purring roadster before the chic and exclusive shop of the city's leading modiste. The plate glass window of her shop bore simply the name Madeline Sœurs.

Mr. Hazeltine pushed open the door, and was greeted by a faint yelp of pleasure. The shop was empty except for the proprietor, a tall, handsome, blond girl with fine blue eyes, and the manner of a princess.

"Mr. Hazeltine!" she exclaimed.

The lawyer took her arm companionably.

"Come back here and tune in on my wavelength for ten minutes," he said.

They seated themselves on chairs in her little private office.

"Keep calm, Maggie," said the lawyer. "Last night the body of a girl was found in the river down near the Iron

Ore docks. A bracelet was found on her wrist with the name Dorothy Murphy engraved on it.

"I said, 'Keep calm!' I had that bracelet put there, Maggie. It isn't going to be very pleasant for you, but you're going to do this, anyway. The early editions of the afternoon papers will carry the story.

"You're going to get in touch with the coroner immediately, and go down to the morgue and identify that bracelet as Dorothy Murphy's. You can refuse to look at the body, if you wish."

"I'm not afraid of dead bodies," answered the handsome girl. "Heaven knows I saw enough of them while I was nursing in France. How long has this girl been dead?"

"Over two weeks," said Mr. Hazeltine, shivering slightly. "Later you're going to be called to the witness stand to testify that the bracelet was Dorothy Murphy's. You're going to testify for the State, not for me. If I'm nasty to you on the witness stand, don't let it worry you."

"You want me to perjure myself, do you?"

"I do. Will you?"

"You know darned well I will, Gillian Hazeltine. What else do you want me to say and do?"

"That will be all," answered the Silver Fox pleasantly.

"I suppose I can't ask you a single question?"

"Not one," said Mr. Hazeltine. "How is business?"

"Business will be a great deal better if I can grab off some snappy court-room publicity," the girl laughed.

"I was thinking of that," said the lawyer. "Good-by, Maggie."

"Good-by—Satan," said Maggie.

Mr. Hazeltine reentered his roadster and drove on down

Spruce Street, stopping this time before a very large plate-glass window in the middle of a block which was called, colloquially, Automobile Row. Here the representative cars of America were on display. The salesroom before which the famous lawyer had pulled up was that of the Dulcier Big Eight, Queen of the Highway.

The Dulcier was a new car, and rather a flashy car; it had been placed on the market only a few months before.

A young man with brown eyes and brown skin was standing inside the door, looking out into the street, and his expression, when he saw Mr. Hazeltine, became rather bilious.

He opened the door as if reluctantly.

"Good morning, Harry," said the lawyer genially.

"I suppose," the young man replied, "that you've come around to find out why I haven't paid the interest on that note of mine you're holding."

"You must never jump to conclusions," Mr. Hazeltine told him, "until you are absolutely sure where you're jumping. How is business, Harry?"

"Business," Harry answered, "is rotten. It is so rotten that I'm going to have a long heart-to-heart talk with my landlord on the first of the month. Words cannot express how rotten business is."

"I was afraid so," said Mr, Hazeltine, "but I have an idea that I think would boom business considerably. That is certainly a noisy roadster."

"It is a damned fine car," said the young man, "and if I could only get these cars started I know they would sell like hot cakes."

"That," the lawyer murmured, "was the idea I had in

mind. I have an idea to get them started. I am going to lend you another five thousand dollars to carry you along until the boom starts. In return, you are going to take the witness stand when the time comes and perjure yourself black in the face for me. Are you willing?"

"I'll do anything you want me to do, Mr. Hazeltine."

"The first thing I want you to do," said the lawyer, "is to put that roadster in the paint shop and have it painted lavender. Then I want you to break it in—after dark, Harry, over some back-country dusty roads, so that it will appear to have been used a little.

"When the time comes I want you to testify that you sold it to a man named Elmer Wirple. A month ago. You will testify for the State—that is, against me. My check for five thousand dollars will be mailed to you this afternoon. Have that car painted immediately."

"Very well," said the young man. "I hope I won't get into any trouble."

"You won't if you do exactly what I tell you. As soon as the paint is dry and there is a little dust on the car, I want you to deliver it to the garage of the Herendon Arms.

"You are then to telephone the prosecuting attorney, and tell him that you sold this car to Elmer Wirple on the 1st of March. He paid cash. That's all you have to tell him. Leave the rest to me."

"Very well, Mr. Hazeltine."

The famous criminal lawyer departed. He drove down Spruce to his office. A dozen people, men and women, were waiting for him in his reception room, but he rushed past all of them.

He instructed his secretary to telephone Addison Yover,

the owner of the Herendon Arms, to tell Mr. Yover to come down immediately. Then Mr. Hazeltine sat down at the typewriter in his private office and tapped off a letter that he would not trust even to his highly trusted secretary. He had addressed and was sealing an envelope when Addison Yover was ushered in.

Mr. Yover was a dapper little man in his middle forties. He had snapping blue eyes, and a nervousness of manner which most people found very irritating. He placed his hat, stick, and gloves on the long walnut table in the center of the office, and nervously lighted a cigarette.

"Well, Gillian?" he said in a rasping voice.

The Silver Fox leaned back in his chair, picked up his cigar from the edge of the desk, and looked at Addison Yover. Addison Yover was the final link in the chain he had been forging so busily, and Mr. Yover, he believed, was going to be a hard nut to crack.

"How is business?" he asked.

"Business," rasped Mr. Yover, "is simply terrible."

"The Herendon Arms filling up?"

"Gillian, I am almost frantic. I have advertised and advertised, and people simply come, look at apartments, and go away. They aren't used to such refinements, and they aren't used to paying such rents as I have to ask. I was coming in to see you, and I'm glad you sent for me. I'm pretty nearly up against it, Gillian."

"I have an idea," said Mr. Hazeltine, "that I think would fill up that apartment. It's a pretty daring idea. You may think it's a risky idea, but I have thought it all out. You can take my word that it would fill the Herendon Arms—if you have nerve enough to see me through with it."

"I am desperate enough to try anything," Mr. Yover assured him. "What is the idea?"

"The idea, briefly," Mr. Hazeltine answered, "is this. A young man named Elmer Wirple is going to go on trial pretty soon for the murder of Dorothy Murphy. What I want to establish is that he had a love nest in the Herendon Arms."

"Great guns!" cried Mr. Yover. "Do you think that idea is going to help my business?"

The Silver Fox nodded emphatically. "It will, before we're through, Addison. He has had this love nest in your apartment house for two months. Do you get me?"

"I don't see why you had to pick on me," said Mr. Yover.

"You'll be grateful that I did by the time the trial is over," said Mr. Hazeltine. "That apartment must be filled before tonight with luxurious furniture. I will call up Dan Ferguson, who, as you know, rents all kinds of furniture for all kinds of occasions, and have him send up a couple of truckloads of fancy furniture early this evening. And you will pay the bill."

"I don't get this at all," muttered Mr. Yover.

"You will have to take my word that I am not shooting at the moon," said Mr. Hazeltine. "Everything is going to be for the best in this best of possible worlds. Darkness invariably precedes the dawn, and the silver lining of the cloud will be revealed to you in due course.

"Do as I tell you, Addison. I will have Dan Ferguson send the furniture by men he can trust, and you and I, with our own hands, will arrange it about the apartment.

"I will drop in at the Herendon Arms at about eight this

evening, for the purpose of taking some flashlight photographs. I will take them myself."

Mr. Yover fidgeted.

"It looks to me," he said finally, "as if you're getting both of us into a kettle of trouble. I know you're smart, Gillian. I know you're the smartest lawyer west of New York. Sometimes I think you're too smart.

"But I'll do what you say. I haven't any alternative. Black ruin stares me in the face, anyway, and—yes, I'll do what you tell me to do."

"That's fine," said Mr. Hazeltine. "Now beat it, Addison, because I have ten thousand things to do."

Addison Yover picked up his gloves, his stick, and his hat, and departed. Mr. Hazeltine pressed the pearl button which summoned his secretary.

"Bring me," he instructed her when she entered, "the latest editions of all the afternoon papers, and when Mr. Hoyle comes in with Mr. Wirple, send Mr. Wirple right in. I'm not in to any one else, and I want you to handle all phone calls."

The girl left. She returned in a few minutes with an armful of newspapers, still smelling fragrantly of printer's ink. She was pale with excitement.

"Mr. Hazeltine," she exclaimed, "they have found the body of Dorothy Murphy! It's been in the water two weeks! I thought—"

"A wise old owl," Mr. Hazeltine interrupted, "once lived in an oak. The more he heard, the less he spoke. And the less he spoke, the more he heard. Now, wasn't he a wise old bird?"

The girl flushed, and smiled nervously.

"I understand, Mr. Hazeltine," she said in a low voice.

"It is your gift of understanding," said the lawyer, "that makes you such a valuable secretary. That will be all Miss Waters."

Miss Waters withdrew, and closed the door. Gillian Hazeltine settled back in his chair, and contemplated glaring black headlines. The story in all the afternoon papers was the same.

Mr. Hazeltine glanced at them all, then gave his undivided attention to the *Evening Gazette*, which was the most sensational tabloid newspaper in the city. It set the pace, and the others followed. The more dignified and respectable newspapers hated the *Evening Gazette* with the cold, resentful hatred of the old and dignified for the new and shocking. But they followed whither it led. They had to!

The front page of the *Evening Gazette* was covered with photographs of Dorothy Murphy. They showed her alive, and, with a gruesome lack of feeling, they showed her in death. Mr. Hazeltine shuddered over that photograph, and turned to an inside page.

Another black headline smote him in the eyes, and he read, in the left-hand column:

> The mysterious disappearance of Dorothy Murphy, who vanished from this city three weeks ago, has been solved at last. The body of the unfortunate girl was found late yesterday afternoon floating in the river near the Iron Ore docks. It was identified this morning by a bracelet on the girl's left wrist.

Mr. Hazeltine skipped on down the column until he came to this:

Dorothy Murphy disappeared under the most mystifying circumstances. She was a partner in the business of Madeline Sœurs, one of the city's most exclusive shops.

Dorothy and her sister, Marguerite, owned and ran this shop. They lived together in an apartment on Wakely Place. On the evening of February 28, Dorothy Murphy went out for a walk. It was the last seen of her.

Rumors are rife to the effect that Dorothy was kidnaped. The *Gazette* has learned, on excellent authority, that her death was the result of foul play. The suicide theory is flouted. Police announce that an arrest will be made within twenty-four hours.

The *Gazette* is behind the police to the last ditch. "Stop this crime wave!" is our slogan.

Mr. Hazeltine read on. Now and then he smiled. Occasionally his brows drew together in a mild frown. He grinned broadly when he read:

Adelbert Yistle, the prosecuting attorney, admitted to a reporter from the *Gazette* that his office was already hard at work on the case. He is in possession, he claims, of the name of a man closely identified with the disappearance of Dorothy, and promises to make startling disclosures in a short time.

Mr. Hazeltine was still reading the newspaper when Miss Waters opened the door.

"Mr. Wirple is here," she said.

"Send him right in!" cried Mr. Hazeltine.

8

DESTINY LEADS ON

IT WAS A pale and somewhat belligerent Elmer who entered the private office. In one hand he clutched a copy of the *Evening Gazette.*

"Well," Mr. Hazeltine inquired affably, "how did you make out?"

"Make out!" blurted Elmer. "Look at this! Just look at this!"

He pointed with a shaking forefinger to an item tucked away on page 19. It was headed:

MASHER FINED $100

And under that heading a stick of type informed the reader that Elmer Wirple, arrested on a charge of disorderly conduct for speaking to Miss Minnie Schwartz and Miss Charmaine Dulcimer on Spruce Street at midnight, without being properly introduced, had been found guilty as charged.

"I am ruined!" bleated Elmer. "Mr. Wainright is going to see this. It means my job is gone. I thought you said you were a friend of my father's!"

"I was," replied Mr. Hazeltine. "We were more than friends: we were pals."

Elmer was breathing rapidly.

Elmer drew himself up haughtily.

"All I can say," he growled, "is that you're one—one hell of a pal, to let his son suffer all this disgrace."

Elmer," said Hazeltine with an air of pained surprise, "you swore!"

"I don't care if I did! I said hell. I'll say it again! Hell!"

"You mustn't let yourself get so excited," Mr. Hazeltine reproved him. "Excitement tires the brain cells, and it creates an acid condition in the digestive tract. After all, I did the best I could."

"You didn't even come to court!" Elmer blazed.

"You will have to forgive me. I was working in your interests all morning."

Elmer gazed at him suspiciously.

"My interests!" he snorted.

"Elmer, you must stop fretting over that twenty-eight-dollar-a-week job you've lost. As you so truly said a moment ago, what the hell? The world is full of twenty-eight-dollar-a-week jobs."

"And it's full of men to fill them!" Elmer argued.

"What I'm curious to know," said the lawyer, "is, why aren't you interested in climbing out of the cheapskate class and going on to bigger and more exciting things?"

"I've lost my job," Elmer muttered. "You could have used your influence and saved me all this disgrace, and you didn't."

"I heard you the first time," said Mr. Hazeltine patiently. "I was hoping that your experience in court would jolt you out of your smug satisfaction in a twenty-eight-dollar-a-week job. Don't you know that the world is clamoring for men who can fill ten-thousand-a-year jobs? And more?"

Elmer sniffed.

"In other words," said the Silver Fox sharply, "you're not interested in getting somewhere. And yet you wonder why Miss Jameson turned you down when you asked her to marry you. Elmer, you ought to be ashamed of yourself.

"Now, listen to me. I have been working all morning—since five thirty—in your behalf. The results won't become apparent to you for a day or two, and when they do become apparent you will be sorely tried and bewildered.

"But you must remember that I am standing by you. No matter what betides—I am standing by you—because you are the son of the man I loved more than my own brother. Get that, Elmer?"

"It doesn't mean a thing to me," said Elmer.

"It will, my boy. Now let's go out and have some lunch. Then we are going to my tailor's."

"What for?" said Elmer.

"All of these little mysteries will clear away as does the morning mist before the rising sun, Elmer. Do not forget that I am standing by you to the bitter end, and that, no matter what dreadful things happen to you, everything will come out all right in the end.

"I won't ask you to be grateful to me. Because I am not doing it for you. I am doing it because I loved your father. Remember that."

Elmer mumbled something under his breath, and they went out to lunch. They lunched in Mr. Hazeltine's very exclusive club, where there was excellent beer on draft.

Then they walked around the corner to Mr. Hazeltine's tailor.

Mr. Hazeltine's tailor was a small, pudgy man with beautiful brown eyes and a seraphic smile.

"I want you to measure this young man for six or seven suits," said Mr. Hazeltine.

"What for?" blurted the mystified Elmer.

"You will learn what for in due course. I want you to fashion these suits, Mr. Grand, along the smartest conceivable lines. They are not to be loud and flashy, nor are they to be conservative and dignified.

"I want you to build six or seven suits for this young man as if he were a matinee idol. They must convey the impression that he is extremely worldly-wise, but a gentleman; they must express sophistication. Let's look at samples."

They looked at samples. The samples at which Mr. Hazeltine uttered cries of greatest interest fairly made Elmer's blood run cold. Never would he have selected such clamorous materials. He liked quiet, dark colors. Most of these were loud and light. When the selections had been made, Elmer's measurements were taken.

"I want you to rush this order through. There will probably be no opportunity for you to make alterations or try-ons. They must be perfect the first time, Mr. Grand."

"They will be," simply stated the little man with the seraphic smile and the beautiful eyes.

From the tailor's Mr. Hazeltine and the bewildered Elmer went to a haberdashery. There, Mr. Hazeltine let his imagination run riot in the matter of ties, shirts, colored silk handkerchiefs, and silk socks.

"I won't wear them!" Elmer announced.

"You will do as I tell you when the time comes," said the lawyer, "and be damned glad of the opportunity. I am running this show, Elmer, and you are going to do just what I tell you to do."

Elmer lapsed into moody silence. Last night he had felt that he was a twirling autumn leaf before the gusts of destiny; today he was experiencing that emotion again.

Mr. Hazeltine ushered him into his roadster, and they drove at a fast clip out to the River Road. Mr. Hazeltine drove out to the guinea pig farm much more slowly than he had that morning. He did not want to be apprehended by any mounted policemen now.

All of the irons he was heating were close to the temperature at which they could be removed from the fire, and forged into the intricate pattern on which he had been scheming so diligently.

He parked in the same spot that he had earlier in the day, and Mrs. Perkins, who had been waiting for him, came running out. The old woman looked at Elmer shrewdly. Mr. Hazeltine said nothing. He merely waited while Mrs. Perkins gave Elmer a careful scrutiny.

"Very well, Gillian," she said at length.

"When it happens," said the Silver Fox, "you will telephone the prosecuting attorney at once, won't you?"

"I will, Gillian, I will."

And that was all. Mr. Hazeltine turned the car around, and they started back for the city.

"It certainly is a mystery to me," said Elmer.

"Just have a little patience," Mr. Hazeltine begged.

They drove at a cautious speed back to the city. Before the Dulcier Big Eight salesroom, the same mysterious procedure was gone through with. Harry Benedict, the sales manager of this branch, came to the curb, and looked carefully at Elmer.

"This is he," said the lawyer.

"All right, I'll remember him, Mr. Hazeltine. I've got that roadster in the shop, and they're rushing the paint job. I'm having 'em use a quick dryer, and I ought to be able to take her out by midnight to-night. She'll be ready to deliver first thing in the morning."

"That's fine, Harry. So long."

"So long, Mr. Hazeltine."

Elmer was frowning as they rolled off.

"Gee whiz, Mr. Hazeltine, I wish you would tell me what all this mystery is about. What roadster was he talking about?"

"Your roadster, Elmer."

"My roadster! But I haven't got one."

"You have one now, Elmer."

"Listen, Mr. Hazeltine, won't you tell me what it's all about?"

"I can't, Elmer. The shock would be too great."

"Is—is something terrible going to happen?" Elmer gasped.

"Something terrible," Mr. Hazeltine echoed, "and I'm afraid it's much too late to head it off. I can only repeat what I said before: Put your trust in me. Remember, no matter what happens, I am behind you to the last ditch. Don't worry."

"Where are we going now?"

"To my house, until this evening. There is so much to be done, Elmer."

When they reached the lawyer's handsome home in the Riverside Heights Development, Mr. Hazeltine took Elmer at once up to his luxurious bedroom. He picked up a pair of military brushes from the dresser, and handed them to Elmer.

"Now, Elmer, the first thing I want you to do is to brush your hair differently. It is much too respectable as you have it brushed now. Whoever heard of anybody with a devilish streak in him parting his hair in the middle? You must brush it straight back. Here, use some of this pomade."

"But I haven't a devilish streak in me," the young man protested.

"You are going to have," Mr. Hazeltine promised him.

He lost patience with Elmer presently, and took the brushes in his own hands. He brushed and brushed; he applied pomade, and finally he stepped back and admired his handiwork.

"That," he announced, "is much better. And now, Elmer, I want you to sit over there in that chair."

"What for?" bleated Elmer.

"I want to study you."

Elmer seated himself as directed, and Mr. Hazeltine sat on the edge of the bed. He looked at Elmer for almost fifteen minutes without saying a word. Most of the time Mr. Hazeltine frowned. Several times he sighed, as does one who is confronted by a hopeless, baffling problem. He even swore softly under his breath.

"Smile, Elmer," he presently commanded.

"What for?"

"Smile, damn it, smile!" the lawyer snapped.

Elmer essayed a smile.

"That is a sappy smile," Mr. Hazeltine criticized. "What I want you to wear is a sophisticated, worldly smile. Like this." He illustrated the smile. "Try it again, Elmer."

Elmer tried it again. And again Mr. Hazeltine cursed softly, under his breath.

"Listen, Elmer. Imagine that you are confronting fifty pretty girls. Those girls have been told that you are a gay Lothario, a sheik, and a modern Don Juan. You have to smile in a way to impress them that it is the truth. Try that smile."

Elmer tried.

"That's it!" exclaimed the lawyer. "That's great! Now, practice that smile. No matter what happens to you, smile. There will be times when I will want you to use that smile for a purpose. Whenever I want you to use that smile I will say: 'Ah, Elmer!' Now try it. 'Ah, Elmer!'"

Elmer smiled. Mr. Hazeltine rubbed his hands with satisfaction.

"Now I want to teach you how to sit in that chair, to get across to any one who chances to be looking at you the same idea that the smile conveys. Worldliness. Sophistication.

"Be more nonchalant. Don't be so stiff. That's better. Oh, we're making fine progress, Elmer. Ah, Elmer! Smile, damn it, smile! Ah, Elmer! That's better. Now you may rest for awhile, and we will have another lesson."

Most of that afternoon Mr. Hazeltine tutored Elmer in the arts of smiling and sitting on a chair in a worldly, sophisticated manner. During dinner the lesson continued.

And after dinner, they entered the roadster again and drove through back streets to the Herendon Arms. On the floor beside Elmer's feet was photographic apparatus; a camera, a tripod, and a flash light pistol.

Mr. Hazeltine carried these into the ornate lobby of the Herendon Arms. There Mr. Yover, nervously smoking a cigarette, met them. He glanced dubiously at Elmer.

"This," said Mr. Hazeltine, "is Mr. Wirple, Addison. You, Elmer, are Mr. Yover's tenant."

Elmer only nodded dumbly. It was no use asking questions.

The three men ascended to the twelfth floor in an elevator, walked down a long hall, and stopped before a door numbered 1212.

Mr. Yover unlocked it, and they went in. It was really a dream of an apartment, with arched doorways and beautiful fixtures. Furniture was piled all about, chairs, and tables, and davenports, and parts of beds, and rugs.

"Lock that door," said Mr. Hazeltine, "and let's get busy. Take off your coats. We've got some hard work ahead of us."

The three men removed their coats and, under Mr. Hazeltine's direction, they began sorting out the piles and heaps.

They worked diligently for three hours, and at the end of that time the apartment was ready to be lived in—if you cared to live in that kind of an apartment.

It resembled, at first glance, the apartment of an imaginative sultan. The furniture was ornately carved, and of an Oriental appearance; the rugs were brilliant Oriental pieces. Sarongs and bright tapestries ornamented the walls.

"This," said Mr. Hazeltine, after he had washed his hands, "is your apartment, Elmer. How do you like it?"

Elmer said nothing. He looked tired and unhappy.

"Ah, Elmer!"

A sophisticated smile broke out obediently on Elmer's lips.

"Now," said Mr. Hazeltine, "let's take these pictures. There is so much to be done."

He looked at Elmer critically, and told him to sit down over there on that divan. It was really a sort of box couch, heaped with pillows of bright colors. Elmer threw himself down willingly enough, and the lawyer set up his camera, and loaded the flashlight pistol.

"Ah, Elmer!"

Elmer smiled. The flash light flashed.

Mr. Hazeltine posed him again. He posed him in all the rooms, and in a variety of positions. But in each pose, Elmer was smiling.

"That smile," said Mr. Hazeltine, as he packed up his photographic apparatus, "can be improved on, Elmer. You must practice it, and practice it. I think that will be all for to-night. You're going to stay here to-night, Elmer."

"But I haven't my pyjamas," Elmer protested.

"Perhaps Mr. Yover can help you out."

"I'll bring up pyjamas, bed linen and bathroom supplies," said Mr. Yover.

Mr. Hazeltine started briskly for the door. With his hand on the knob, he turned.

"Elmer, if you should be broken in on during the night, remember I am behind you to the last ditch."

Elmer gulped.

"Who—who would break in on me?"

"Well—the police might."

"What for?" Elmer wailed.

"Elmer, I do wish you would get over the habit of saying 'What for.' It's irritating. Aren't there any synonyms for 'What for' in your bright lexicon?"

"What would the police break in on me for?" Elmer bleated.

"It's like this, Elmer. Last night you unfortunately strayed off the straight and narrow path of rectitude, didn't you? Yes, you did.

"And once you have strayed off the straight and narrow path of rectitude, all sorts of things may happen. But even if you are arrested again, don't worry. No matter what the charge is, remember you are under my protecting wings."

"But what would they arrest me for?"

"Elmer, once you let the police suspect that you are a dangerous character, a menace, they are apt to arrest you for almost anything. Even, murder."

"Murder!" Elmer yelped.

"Yes, even murder. But even if they should, don't worry. And if they lock you up, have me notified first thing. I will be at home. Say nothing. Tell them, no matter what they do or say, that you will say nothing without consulting your attorney. And practice that smile, Elmer. You must perfect that smile."

"I don't like this," muttered Mr. Yover.

"And I don't, either!" Elmer snapped.

"The destiny that shapes men's ends," said Mr. Hazeltine, "often works in queer and devious ways its marvels to achieve. Goodnight, Elmer."

Left alone, in this bizarre, Oriental apartment, Elmer sank down on a chair with a moan, and buried his face in his hands. What was going to happen to him? What strange, terrible destination lay at the end of this queer, twisting road he was following?

9

IN AGAIN

GILLIAN HAZELTINE DROVE home regardless of the traffic laws. The elaborate trap he had been working so hard on all day long was now ready to be sprung. Every detail of his scheme had been polished to perfection.

Checking back over his activities, he could not see where any loopholes existed. He could not have improved upon what he had done.

He did not put up his car for the night, because he was reasonably certain that it would be required more than once before the sun shone down again upon this world of vexation and disillusion. He parked it beside the side door, and proceeded at once to his dark room in the cellar.

He placed the dozen plates he had exposed in a holder, and lowered them in a developing solution. When they were developed, he fixed them in a hypo bath, and then placed them in swirling, rinsing bath.

He did not wait for them to dry, but made prints from the wet plates. The prints he developed in one batch, and when they were fixed and washed, squeegeed them on a ferrotype plate. This he placed upon an electric heater.

The photographing plant in a newspaper office could have rushed those finished prints through no more rapidly than did Mr. Hazeltine. When the prints were dry, he took them upstairs to his study, inserted them in a plain envelope, and addressed the envelope to Mr. Adelbert Yistle, Prosecuting Attorney.

He weighed the envelope on a postal scale, pasted on the required postage, and slipped the envelope into his coat pocket. Then he put on his coat and hat, went out, and entered his car.

He drove into the city, and rolled slowly down Spruce Street. He stopped at a mailbox to post the photographs to Mr. Yistle, then proceeded on down Spruce to the Witz-Raldorf. The time was now about one o'clock. The lobby of the hotel was, as it had been last night, practically deserted.

Mr. Hazeltine walked casually to the row of telephone booths, and entered one of them. Once again he called the home of the prosecuting attorney. Presently, a sleepy voice answered him.

"Listen," said the Silver Fox in the deep, rough bass voice he could employ on occasions, "the guy you want in connection with the Dorothy Murphy case is in room 1212 at the Herendon Arms. I'm tellin' you you better act quick."

Mr. Hazeltine replaced the receiver on its hook, and strolled back to his roadster. It had not been absolutely necessary for him to telephone to Mr. Yistle; but Mr. Hazeltine hated delays and, in the present instance, a bird in the jail was worth a dozen on the broad highroad.

Elmer, he feared, might fall to brooding. Elmer might decide to leave this place miles behind him.

The Silver Fox drove home and waited. He waited a little less than an hour before the phone rang.

"Yes," he said. "Yes. Yes. Oh, yes. What—again? What's that?—murder! I'll be right down, Steve."

Once again Mr. Hazeltine climbed aboard his faithful roadster. What a boon, he reflected as he started down the driveway, the automobile was. Without it, he could never have encompassed the tremendous amount of work he had tackled today.

He parked under the green light outside the Third Precinct police station, nodded to the sergeant as he went through the outer room, and proceeded into the jail. He found Elmer clinging to the bars.

"Well, Elmer," he said in a tone of surprise, "what does this mean?"

"That's what I want to know," cried Elmer in a voice pitched midway between a snarl and a whimper. "What does it mean?"

"Well," temporized the lawyer, "what have you done?"

"I haven't done anything! I was in bed, sound asleep, when five policemen broke the door down and made me get dressed at the point of their pistols!"

"But what made them do that? What are they accusing you of doing this time?"

"Murder!" Elmer wailed. "They arrested me for the murder of Dorothy Murphy!"

He pressed his white, strained face against the bars. The Silver Fox gazed at him.

"Well, did you murder her, Elmer?"

"Of course I didn't! You know I didn't! I never saw her!"

"Then what are you worried about, Elmer? If you're innocent, you haven't a thing to worry about. Brace up, Elmer. I told you something dreadful might happen, and it has. But you are innocent, and we are going into court and prove it!"

"I wish I was dead," moaned the young man.

"Cheer up, my boy. Remember, I am going to stand by you; and I've only lost three murder cases in my entire career."

"I don't want to be hung!"

"You won't be hung. Don't take it so tragically. You and I are going to have a lot of fun out of this."

"Fun!" Elmer gasped.

"Yes, sir; fun! You wait and see. You're going to be the leading figure in a great court room show. And—you're going to be acquitted. So don't worry."

"Are you sure?"

"I am positive. Practice that smile, Elmer. Have you spoken to any one, answered any questions?"

"No, sir; I said I wouldn't say anything without consulting my lawyer."

"That's fine. Keep on saying that—and stick by it. Reporters are going to begin buzzing around pretty soon. Say nothing. Tell them your attorney will answer all questions."

"All right, Mr. Hazeltine. But here's another thing. I know how expensive it is to have you as a lawyer. How—how much are you going to charge for handling my case?"

"Elmer," said the famous criminal lawyer emotionally, "I am not going to charge you a damn cent!"

"But—but you've got to be paid for your work," Elmer protested.

"Work?" cried Mr. Hazeltine. "This isn't work, Elmer;

it's pleasure. But if you insist, I'll take ten per cent of your income for the twelve months that follow the trial."

"But I probably won't have any income. Nobody in the world will give me a job after all the nasty publicity I'll get."

"We won't worry about that now," said the lawyer. "I'll bring you down the agreement to sign in the morning—when I come to bail you out. Go to sleep now, Elmer. You have an innocent conscience, and you ought to sleep like a baby. Good night, Elmer."

"Good night, Mr. Hazeltine. You certainly have been kind to me."

10

FOR THE PROSECUTION

THE OFFICE OF the prosecuting attorney, on the following morning, was a scene of almost frantic activity. The outer office became a citadel, stormed by reporters from all the newspapers in town. And in the inner, or private office, development after exciting development charged the atmosphere.

At eleven thirty we find Adelbert Yistle seated at his desk smoking a mellow cigar, his face wreathed in smiles of complacent self-satisfaction, telling his assistant that things seemed to be coming their way pretty nicely.

A square-built man, with a strong, judicial forehead surmounted by a mop of iron-gray hair, and a massive pair of jaws surmounted by an iron-gray mustache, Mr. Yistle was a commanding figure. He was extremely ambitious, and hoped some day to become Governor of the State.

"We have one of the finest, cleanest-cut cases that has ever come into this office," said Mr. Yistle to his assistant, Mr. Bullock. "The way high-class witnesses have been coming forward is enough to make anybody believe that God's in His heaven, and that all is right with the world.

"Have you read Browning, Mr. Bullock? You ought to read Browning for inspiration and reflection, Mr. Bullock.

He phrases himself so well. We are going to win this, Mr. Bullock."

"Absodamlutely!" cried Mr. Bullock.

Mr. Bullock was a pale, thin young man with kind blue eyes, a disappearing chin, and a prominent Adam's apple. Mr. Bullock looked like a yes-man, and he was a yes-man— to the tips of his thin, bluish-white fingers.

His yessing qualities provided Mr. Yistle with quantities of mild amusement. Once, in an idle hour, he had compiled a list of Mr. Bullock's synonyms for the word yes. It was by no means a complete list, but it included, among other, the following:

> Yes, indeed.
>
> Yes, sir.
>
> Absolutely.
>
> Positively.
>
> Absotively.
>
> Posolutely.
>
> Absodamlutely.
>
> You bet!
>
> Darned right.
>
> I should say.
>
> I don't mean maybe.
>
> Right-O.
>
> Yep!
>
> Sure thing.
>
> Of course.
>
> I'll say so.
>
> You said it.
>
> And how!

Mr. Bullock tried very hard to keep abreast of modern slang, and he was frequently ringing in new variations of his favorite word.

"We are going to send that skunk to the gallows!" declared Mr. Yistle.

"You tell 'em!" chirped Mr. Bullock, his Adam's apple diving down and bringing up that one without the slightest difficulty.

"The way I am beginning to size up the situation," Mr. Yistle went on, "our offense should be based on the fact that these sheiks are becoming more and more of a menace. They must be wiped out! Our fair city must be purged of these vermin."

The eyes of the State's attorney were glistening. He spoke with an eloquence. He was already framing his message to the jury.

"The time has come when a decent, respectable girl dares not venture out upon the streets after dark without an armed escort," Mr. Yistle proceeded. "She may be pounced upon by one of these limousine lizards. Of course, it wasn't a limousine he used; it was a roadster, wasn't it, Bullock?"

"Yes, Mr. Yistle: a lavender roadster."

"A love chariot!" cried the prosecuting attorney. "Mr. Bullock, I simply can't get over my delight at the intelligent way these witnesses have come forward, and the willingness they show in wanting to be of assistance to us. Take that Mrs. Perkins. There is a woman who will make a perfect witness, Mr. Bullock."

"You said a mouthful, Mr. Yistle!"

"And take Harry Benedict, the Dulcier Big Eight sales manager. A clean-cut young fellow, Mr. Bullock. But I think Mrs. Perkins will be our star witness. What a story! What a woman! I think you'd better stir your stumps, Mr. Bullock, and round up a few more character witnesses.

"Those two girls he accosted on Spruce Street the other night will help. And you'd better drop in on that Mrs. Gibney, who runs the boarding house where he spent part of his time. We've got a Dr. Jekyl and Mr. Hyde type of scoundrel to deal with here, Mr. Bullock.

"Evidently he led a sane, respectable life at Mrs. Gibney's, but sound out the servants. Get witnesses who will blacken him, Mr. Bullock."

"I will, sir."

"There's no use in sounding out the office force at the Purity Pulverized Egg Corporation where he was employed. I talked with Mr. Wainright on the phone yesterday, and he said that Wirple was one of the most modest and self-effacing men in his employ, and that he had no opportunity to filch funds. We've got to look elsewhere for our evidence."

Mr. Yistle rubbed his hands with the gesture of a man who finds life filled to overflowing with good things. He picked up the photographs that had come to him, anonymously, in the mail this morning—the photographs of Elmer Wirple's love nest in the Herendon Arms. He shuffled through them, threw back his head, and laughed.

"Mr. Bullock, when I think of Gillian Hazeltine I simply have to give way to boyish laughter. Here is where his uninterrupted record of acquittals is badly bruised. He hasn't got a leg to stand on.

"I'll bet he's charging this Wirple sheik fifty thousand dollars to handle the case. He can't win. The cards are certainly stacked against him this time—dog-gone his hide!"

"Yes, sir," affirmed Mr. Bullock with nervous eagerness, "they certainly are. I understand he has Wirple out on ten thousand dollars' bail."

Mr. Yistle nodded. He became thoughtful. His smile slowly faded away. Then he continued:

"It doesn't pay to be too cocksure, Mr. Bullock. Hazeltine has got away with murder before. We must watch our step in this case with care, with infinite care, Mr. Bullock. We must plug up every crack. We must study every detail under a microscope.

"We must select a jury of unsympathetic men—not soft hearted saps, like the last one he slipped over on us. Yes, Mr. Bullock; we must have the right kind of jury. Do you know the kind of jury we want, Mr. Bullock? We want fathers! We want fathers of growing daughters!"

"There's a thought," Mr. Bullock complimented him.

"Yes, sir! We want a jury of fathers—fathers who are already worrying about this age that their girls are growing up in. Watch Hazeltine try to slip over a jury of bachelors on us! He'll try!

"He'll try to hand-pick a jury of old dissolute *roués,* Mr. Bullock, and then he'll pull some Clarence Darrow stuff on them. He'll try to prove that behind this murder was some good, justifying cause. Or maybe he'll plead insanity."

"There's another thought," said Mr. Bullock.

"We won't let him!" Mr. Yistle snapped. "I'll put three brain specialists on the stand to testify for every one of his. That Wirple is as sane as you or I are."

"Of course he's sane," cried Mr. Bullock.

"Mr. Bullock, that fellow Wirple, just between you and me, hasn't a chance. Not a Chinaman's chance. We are going to send him to the gallows if it's our last act on earth! Do you see a picture of that slinking sheik dangling from the end of a rope?"

"I do," cried Mr. Bullock.

"We'll hang that skunk!" shouted the prosecuting attorney.

"And how!" quavered his tremendously excited assistant.

11

AND THE SMILE STAYED ON

"AH, ELMER!"

"Aw, gee, Mr. Hazeltine, I don't feel like smiling. That crowd of reporters and photographers over at the court scared the life out of me. I wish I was dead. I—"

"Ah, Elmer!"

The man-of-the-world, man-about-town smile came reluctantly to Elmer Wirple's pale lips.

"That's better," said the Silver Fox.

They were lunching again in the Lawyers' Club, sitting at a small table for two against the wall. All about them lawyers and their guests were chattering.

Many glances were darted in their direction, and whenever a glance became lengthened into a gaze or a stare, Mr. Hazeltine would have Elmer smile. It was essential to Hazeltine's plans that Elmer employ that sophisticated smile in the very face of death.

They had reached dessert when Mr. Hazeltine stiffened slightly. Swiftly he leaned forward.

"Brace yourself, Elmer!" he snapped.

There was no time for more. The square, judicial forehead of Mr. Yistle was already bending over them. The face of Mr. Yistle wore a knowing smile. From Mr. Hazeltine he glanced at Elmer.

"Howdy, Adelbert," said Mr. Hazeltine cheerily.

"Good morning, Gillian," the prosecuting attorney acknowledged. "So this is my victim, is it?"

"Elmer," said Mr. Hazeltine, "shake hands with Mr. Yistle, the State's attorney. He is the man who is going to try you."

Mr. Yistle shook hands with Elmer.

"So this is the sheik!" he murmured.

"Sheik—ah, Elmer?"

Elmer smiled.

"So this is the fellow," Mr. Yistle went on, "who I'm going to send to the gallows! This is the next unfortunate who I am going to see hang by the neck until he is dead!"

"W-wuh-what?" blurted Elmer.

"That," exclaimed Mr. Hazeltine angrily, "comes under the head of unethical practice, Adelbert. Haul your carcass away from this table before I sock you a pretty one!"

"Now, don't get sore, Gillian," sputtered Mr. Yistle. "It was only a little pleasantry."

"And just for that," growled the Silver Fox, "I'm going to bend every effort to making a sucker out of you in the court room, Adelbert. I was going to go easy on you this time, but you've asked for war—and it's going to be war!

"I'm going to make you the laughing stock of this town. You're nothing but a stuffed shirt, and I'm going to go out of my way to prove it."

"Listen, Gillian—"

"Run away from here before I lose my temper entirely. You're nothing but a fourflusher, Adelbert Yistle, and I'm going to go out of my way when this case comes up to prove it. I'm giving you fair warning."

"I'll say just this before I go, Gillian Hazeltine," growled the State's attorney, drawing himself up to his full height with great dignity, "when I get through with you in the court this trip, you're going to go back to law school and learn law.

"Fourflusher, am I? Stuffed shirt, am I? Fair warning, eh? Well, I'm going to give *you* fair warning. I've got an air-tight, water-tight case. This sap here is going to swing; and when I'm through with you, you'll be glad to sell yourself for thirty cents on the hoof."

Mr. Hazeltine started to rise, and for a moment Elmer was sure blows were going to be exchanged. But evidently Mr. Yistle thought better of it, and he beat a hasty retreat.

Elmer looked back at Mr. Hazeltine, and was astonished to see a twinkle in his eyes, and a crafty little smile at his lips. So great was his astonishment that Elmer gasped.

"You mustn't let little things like that disturb you, Elmer," the lawyer said confidentially. "Court room battles are not always won in the court room. I've been trying to think of some way to get him worried. And I've done it.

"If he starts worrying, he's apt to overlook little details, and there are a great many little details I want him to overlook. Now, Elmer, stop looking so sad. Smile. Keep on smiling.

"Every moment you're in the court room you must wear that smile. You must convince the jury, the public and the reporters—particularly the reporters—that the whole proceeding is vastly amusing to a man of your worldly experience. Ah, Elmer!"

Elmer obediently smiled. Under Mr. Hazeltine's direction, he practiced the smile. And he practiced sitting with nonchalant ease and grace in a chair. He did not know what it was all about, and Mr. Hazeltine would answer no questions.

That day and the ones that followed were exciting and bewildering ones for Elmer Wirple. Never before had he basked in the limelight; now he was all but blinded by it.

Mr. Yistle gave out to the newspapers the photographs of his exotic apartment. Elmer could not venture out upon the street without hearing the click of Graflex shutters, and the merry whir of movie cameras. He bought newspapers with fear in his heart, and icy chills on his spine. At first, every photograph he saw of himself was like a whiplash on his face. He winced at the photographs, and he shuddered at the captions under them.

He saw himself referred to as a modern Jekyl and Hyde, as a love pirate, as a sheik, a Don Juan, a Lothario. All of the photographs were retouched. His eyes were made sinister. His smile was exaggerated. The newspapers made a satyr of Elmer.

It was all strange, and baffling, and bewildering. Then his new clothing was delivered. Mr. Hazeltine patiently valeted him the first time. And when Elmer saw himself in a pier glass, he shrank as if a blow had been delivered to his solar plexus.

But Mr. Hazeltine was firm. He insisted. And the time came when Elmer did not mind the ultra-smartness of his new clothing. The time came when he became accustomed to gray bowler hats, to flashing neckties, to spats. The time even came when he liked them.

In clothing that, let us say, a movie lover might have graced, Elmer sat for hours at a time on a stiff-backed chair, nonchalant, graceful, and easy, under Mr. Hazeltine's untiring direction. The smile was beginning to become a part of him.

"You're a murderer!" Mr. Hazeltine would roar at him. And Elmer would glance cynically at him, and smile his worldly smile.

"No matter what is said," Mr. Hazeltine repeated over and over, "you must never forget that smile.

"Supposing you should look among the spectators in the court room, and should see the face of Carrol Jameson. What would you do?"

Elmer's answer was his Adolph Menjou smile.

But his smile, at that reference, was more of a mask than it would be under other circumstances. As he became more and more accustomed to his smart clothing, as he became more and more inured to the horrible photographs and captions in the tabloids, the ache in his heart became more and more difficult to endure.

He had, he knew, lost Carrol Jameson forever. The night they had parted—that terrible night of disillusion with its fatal consequences—he had been within reaching distance of her. She had been merely startled by the unexpectedness of his proposal. With a little time, Carrol would, he was sure, have fallen in love with him.

Now, with all the world against him, it would have been so nice to be able to turn to her for sympathy and comfort. He pictured her taking him into her arms, and soothing him, and saying: "Don't worry, Elmer, dear, everything will come out all right."

But she was not there for him to turn to. There was, in fact, no one for him to turn to.

He began watching his mail in hope that some word might come from her. His mail grew larger, day by day. All of these letters were mash notes from silly girls and sillier women; but in the daily growing heaps of scented pink, and lavender, and mauve envelopes, there was no word from Carrol.

His adoration of her became an obsession. Mr. Hazeltine wanted him to keep himself shut up in his apartment at the Herendon Arms, and Elmer obediently kept himself locked in. He was given ample opportunity to brood.

And day after day, Elmer stayed in his apartment, brooding over his loss of Carrol. He knew now that the vision of their life together in a little white cottage had been a foolish vision; his suffering had enlarged his horizon sufficiently so that he could realize how little that picture appealed to her.

He had, accordingly, refashioned his dream. He did not care where they lived or went, so long as they were together.

And one day, in the pile of mash notes, he came upon a plain white envelope containing a very brief, very curt, note from her:

> Dear Sir:
>
>   You have broken my heart. I will never forgive you for your double-faced actions. I knew you were a sheik all the time. You didn't fool me for a minute. You took, me to the movies the very night before you murdered that poor girl. You beast!
>
>   Yours sincerely,
>
>   Carrol Jameson.

Elmer almost wept when he read it. She had loved him. Of course, she could never love him again, but it was some consolation to know that she had cared a little—back in those sweet, uneventful days before he had sown his wild oats on Spruce Street.

He tried to compose an answer to that heartbreaking little note. He used up an entire box of stationery, but he could not say what he wanted to say. He dared not say it was all a mistake, because if she knew the truth she would call him a refrigeratin' papa again.

And if he wrote acknowledging that the things the papers were saying about him were true, she would continue hating him. He was between the horns of a dilemma, between Scylla and Charybdis.

In the end he wrote nothing. His heart was breaking. His little world had fallen about him in ruins.

He was seated at his secretary, and the wastebasket beside him was filled with crumpled sheets of paper on which were the beginnings of answers to her note. Never had bitterness filled him so completely.

On the wall beside him hung a large French mirror. By chance he glanced into it. He was smiling! Even at the lowest ebb of his unhappiness, he was wearing that fixed, cynical smile.

Elmer dropped his face into his hands and wept. His shoulders shook with sobs.

He looked into the mirror again. His nose was red. His eyes were blurred with tears. Tears coursed down his cheeks.

But the smile remained. Not even tears would wash that smile away—that smile which said how terribly, terribly amused he was by it all!

12

COMING "OUT IN THE WASH"

THE PREPARATIONS FOR the trial of Elmer Wirple went forward without a hitch. The State's attorney was a little baffled during the impaneling of the jury by Gillian Hazeltine's indifferent attitude.

His interrogations of the talesmen were most casual. He did not seem to care whether they were fathers, bachelors, or widowers. He offered no objection when Number Eleven admitted with a redmouthed leer that he strongly favored capital punishment, or when Number Twelve admitted that he was the father of two daughters, still in high school.

Elmer sat at the counsel's table beside Mr. Hazeltine. He looked composed. At least, he smiled continuously. And he looked, to the crowded court room, very much like a composite photograph of all their favorite movie lovers.

There was a little of John Barrymore in him, a little of Ramon Novarro, a little of Ben Lyon, and a little of Adolphe Menjou. And he was much handsomer than we have ever seen him before.

He had, under Mr. Hazeltine's barber's aid, permitted his sideburns to grow. He had diligently brushed his hair straight back from his forehead. And for the past ten days

he had been taken by Mr. Hazeltine to a violet-ray special-
ist every day, until now his face was healthily brown, as if
from sunburn.

In his excellently cut brown tweed suit, with a golden
necktie, a golden handkerchief to match, and spats, he was
a striking figure. He was a nonchalant, graceful, debonair
figure. He looked like the kind of man who would have a
love nest in the Herendon Arms; he looked like the love
bandit that the papers said he was.

The court room, of course, was packed. And in the very
first row, as Elmer glanced smilingly at the closely-crowded
faces, he saw the white, strained face of Carrol Jameson.

Her eyes, in that white, drawn face, were startlingly large,
and they were fixed upon him as if he were some strange
creature from another world, as if he were, for example, a
man from Mars.

There was not the slightest trace of recognition in them.
She simply stared; and Elmer's heart fell leadenly. If she
had only smiled a little; if her face had only softened a little!

The impaneling of the jury occupied but the one day.
And that night Elmer, under Mr. Hazeltine's shrewd direction, gave out his first newspaper interview. The lawyer
brought Beatrice Fairview up to his apartment. Miss Fairview was an effusive woman with the appearance of forty,
and the coy, gushing manner of sixteen.

"You have loved a great many women?" she asked him.

"Uh—" Elmer began.

"He has loved an untold number of women," Mr. Hazeltine helped him.

"And an untold number of women have loved him!" said
Miss Fairview brightly.

"Look at that pile of letters from them," said Mr. Hazeltine.

It seemed to Elmer that all the questions were pretty silly. As if he'd been a regular sheik! But he fell into the spirit of it presently, and before the interview was half over, he was going strong. Was it true that the Duchess of Blenhurst had once followed him across the continent?

"And she threatened to commit suicide because I spurned her," Elmer added.

It was really sort of fun, kidding this gushing woman along. At the interview's conclusion, she grasped his hand convulsively.

"I don't blame the women for adoring you, Mr. Wirple," she gushed. "I—I could easily adore you myself!"

Elmer laughed when she had gone, but he did not laugh the next day when he read the interview she had written for the *Evening Gazette:*

LOVE BANDIT'S CONQUESTS LEGION!

The facing page was full of photographs of Elmer, with close-ups of his already famous smile, and with pungent captions under them all.

The interview itself made him a little sick. There were frequent references to his seductive smile, his alluring smile, his knowing smile, his lover's smile, his sinister smile.

"I don't know why they adore me," said Mr. Wirple with his champagne smile.

"Gosh," said Elmer to himself, after he had finished reading the interview, "the first thing I know I will be believing all this stuff myself. It just doesn't seem possible that it can be me!"

It made him still sicker to realize that Carrol would read the interview, and would hate him more than ever.

The last few lines of the interview were a shock to him:

> "Did you kill Dorothy Murphy?" I asked the love bandit.
>
> "Positively not!" he declared. "I did not know Dorothy Murphy. I never saw her in my life."
>
> The love bandit is confident of an acquittal. He is serenely, smilingly undisturbed by the grave charge against him.

On his second day in court, the trial got quickly under way. Everybody in the court stood up as the judge took his place on the bench. He had white hair and a coppery complexion, which he had probably acquired at golf, and a very pleasant smile. He looked exceedingly well fed.

A bailiff was droning:

"Oyez! Oyez! Oyez!" His voice became a blur of meaningless words.

The judge said: "You may call the jury," and a sheriff went out of the room. Presently twelve good men and true filed in and took their seats in the jury box. Then came the roll call, and when each juryman had answered to his name, the clerk read the charge.

Elmer, smiling cynically, heard himself accused of murder in the first degree. As soon as the ringing voice stopped Mr. Hazeltine was on his feet, dramatically pleading not guilty to the charge.

Mr. Yistle earnestly stated that he would prove that the

accused, Elmer Wirple, had deliberately brought about the death of Dorothy Murphy.

His first witness was the coroner. A gray-haired man with tired-looking eyes behind gold-rimmed spectacles, the coroner answered the questions put to him laconically, as if he were not greatly interested in these proceedings which had so excited the press not only of the city, but of the nation.

Elmer might have been impressed had he known that a network of telegraph wires, extending into the uttermost parts of the United States, were thrilling to little electric impulses carrying the account of this trial; that from Los Angeles to New York, extras were being published at half-hour intervals; that the world knew what he had eaten for breakfast, and that he was wearing to-day a smart herringbone tweed with a bright blue tie, a bright blue handkerchief, gray spats, and black oxfords.

And that, at this moment, at tremendous cost, photographs of his famous wicked smile were being transmitted over the telephone wires by ingenious machines, that the waiting world might see how Elmer Wirple looked when the charge was read.

"Did you find marks of violence on the body?" Mr. Yistle asked the coroner.

"I did."

"Will you kindly describe them to the jury?"

"There was a bruise on her chin which showed that the girl had been struck there."

"Would you say that she had been struck by a fist?"

"She might have been."

"Would you say, from your experience as a practic-

ing physician, that such a blow would have rendered her unconscious?"

"I would," said the coroner.

Mr. Yistle now picked up from the table in front of him the gold bracelet, with its encrustation of semiprecious stones. He held it before the coroner's eyes.

"Have you seen this bracelet before?"

"I have."

"Will you tell the jury where and when and under what conditions you first saw this bracelet?"

"This bracelet," the coroner obliged, "was on the left wrist of the body when I examined it. I removed it, and found on the inside the name of Dorothy Murphy engraved."

"I wish," said Mr. Yistle, "to have this bracelet introduced into the testimony as Exhibit A for the State."

Mr. Yistle now bowed to Mr. Hazeltine.

"You may take the witness," he murmured.

Mr. Hazeltine arose slowly and smiled. Three forbidden cameras clicked. He looked thoughtfully at the coroner.

"How soon after the body was found did you find this bracelet on the wrist of the dead woman?"

"The next morning, at about five," the coroner answered.

"When was the body found?"

"The previous evening, shortly prior to sundown."

"That will be all," said Mr. Hazeltine.

Mr. Yistle looked slightly astonished. He had come to court prepared to have every witness torn asunder, to be put together again with loving care by himself on redirect examination.

The next witness was Jake Horton, the watchman at the city morgue. He testified that he had been called to the Iron Ore docks by policemen, that he and his associate had taken it to the morgue.

"Was the bracelet on the girl's left wrist when you removed the body from the water?" asked Mr. Yistle.

"It was," said Jake Horton.

"That will be all," said the State's attorney.

"Cross-examination waived," said Mr. Hazeltine.

Again Mr. Yistle looked surprised. But he called his next witness. The court room stirred with interest as she took the stand. She was a tall, handsome, blond girl with the air of a princess.

She gave her name as Marguerite Murphy. Mr. Yistle smiled at her engagingly. She was his most important witness in the establishment of the identity of the corpus delicti.

"Are you Dorothy Murphy's sister?"

"I am," answered the girl in her full, rich voice.

"You are the proprietor, or proprietress, are you not, Miss Murphy, of an exclusive dressmaking establishment on Spruce Street known as Madeline Sœurs?"

"I am," the handsome girl answered.

"Until the night of March 3, you were in partnership, were you not, with your sister, Dorothy?"

"I was," said the girl.

"On the evening of March 3, she disappeared, did she not?"

"She did," Miss Murphy replied.

"Will you kindly tell the jury such details of that evening as you remember—I mean, those details pertaining to Dorothy's disappearance?"

Marguerite Murphy turned to look at the jury.

"We had finished supper, and we had washed up the dishes," she told them. "My sister complained that she had a slight headache, and was going to take a little walk. She said she felt stuffy. The time was about seven thirty. She put on her hat and left the apartment. That was the last time I saw her."

"Alive?" prompted Mr. Yistle.

"I have not seen her since, dead or alive."

The State's attorney nodded. "You visited the morgue, did you not, on the morning after her body was recovered?"

"I did."

"Will you describe that visit?"

"I went to the morgue, and the coroner met me in the outer room. I told him I was Dorothy Murphy's sister, and that I had read in the paper that her body had been found.

"He told me it would not be necessary for me to identify the body, because the bracelet on her wrist identified her sufficiently. I think he wanted to spare me the shock of seeing her. He showed me the bracelet he had taken off her wrist, and I recognized it immediately."

Mr. Yistle handed her the bracelet.

"Do you identify this as the bracelet?" Miss Murphy examined it.

"Yes, this is the bracelet. My sister was wearing it on her left wrist the night she disappeared."

"You saw it on her wrist?"

"I did. She always wore it."

"That will be all." Mr. Yistle bowed to Mr. Hazeltine.

Mr. Hazeltine looked the witness square in the eyes. He seemed to glare at her, and the girl gazed back at him coolly.

"You say your name is Marguerite Murphy?" he snapped.

"I do," answered the girl, instantly on the defensive. So promptly did this apparent antagonism spring up between them that it would have been difficult, indeed, to believe that they had dined most merrily together in her apartment the night before.

"You say your shop is called Madeline Sœurs?"

"I do!" she snapped.

"Why is it not called Murphy Sœurs?"

"Because my sister and I bought the shop from three sisters. Their name was Madeline."

Mr. Yistle had come quickly to his feet, prepared to object. He looked a little puzzled. He looked still more mystified when Mr. Hazeltine waved his hand, to indicate that he had nothing more to ask the witness.

Mr. Yistle was not worried; he was simply perplexed. His opponent was offering absolutely no battle, and usually Gillian Hazeltine tormented every witness he placed on the stand. His perplexity was destined to increase as the trial progressed.

The next three witnesses were of the character-blacken-ing order. With the stories of two of them we are already familiar.

In their turn, Minnie Schwartz, switchboard operator of the Witz-Raldorf, and Charmaine Dulcimer, the vaudeville singer, took the stand and told of the night on Spruce Street when the love bandit had accosted them; and they laid great stress on his efforts to lure them into the lavender roadster parked at the curb near-by. In both cases, Mr. Hazeltine waived cross-examination.

The third character witness was Tilly Gorner, a chambermaid in Mrs. Gibney's boarding house. She was a weird-looking girl, with wispy, oily hair, buck teeth, and bulging, very pale blue eyes. She had scarcely any chin, and her forehead sloped back strangely from her eyes. Her eyebrows were so pale as to be almost invisible.

She told haltingly of Elmer Wirple's wolfish attempts at putting his arms about her in darkened hallways. Elmer stared at her with amazement when she made these revelations—until to-day Tilly had been, to him, a minor shadow in the boarding house—yet he managed to maintain his cynical, amused smile.

The girl had a silly titter; her mind wandered. She contradicted her own statements.

Mr. Hazeltine, in cross-examination, questioned her briefly and cruelly.

"Tilly, I want you to answer me honestly," he said. "Have you ever had your picture in the tabloids?"

"No, sir," she chirped.

"You expect to, don't you?"

"Yes, sir; I hope so."

"Tilly, don't people sometimes call you Silly Tilly?"

Tilly turned pink. "Yes, sir, everybody calls me Silly Tilly."

"That will be all," said Mr. Hazeltine.

Elmer, seated at his counsel's table, appeared to be continuously amused by the testimony; he was amused when the bailiff banged on his high desk and demanded order in the court; he was amused when a movie camera-man was ejected from the court room after trying to take a photograph of Elmer with a telephoto lens.

In fact, every detail of the trial appeared to tickle that cynical, sophisticated humor of his. He smiled at the jurors. He smiled at the judge. He smiled at each witness—smiled persistently. Once he did not smile, and that was when he darted a scared glance at Carrol Jameson and saw tears in her large, beautiful eyes.

Then the corners of his lips went down irresistibly. He wanted to rush over there and tell her it was all a mistake, that he wasn't really guilty, that he loved her and had never loved another woman.

Court was adjourned for lunch. On his way out, Elmer was all but mobbed. He was caught in a terrific jam in front of the courthouse, and everywhere he looked were enemies. Camera men, movie men and newspaper men, were perched in trees, on rooftops, on the roofs of auto-mobiles, shooting away at him.

Reporters were pressing about him. Curious people were trying to get close enough to touch him. Near-by in the crowd he saw Carrol. She was staring at him, as she had in the court room. And her chin was trembling. He tried to call to her, but the babble of voices about him drowned out his own voice.

"Mr. Wirple—" It was a perspiring reporter. "I want to know—"

A whistle sounded sharply. The crowd gave way reluctantly. Eight policemen fought their way through the crowd, with a sergeant at their head. They composed the riot squad.

"Stand back! Stand back, you folks!"

The sergeant reached Elmer's side. He saluted Elmer.

"Where do you want to be escorted to, Mr. Wirple?" he asked respectfully.

"I want my lawyer," Elmer answered.

"Here I am," shouted Gillian Hazeltine.

The riot squad proceeded to form a squared circle about Elmer and Mr. Hazeltine, and a way was fought through the crowd to the Lincoln roadster.

But a girl broke through the cordon just as Elmer was about to step into the car. She was a beautiful girl, but she was a stranger. Without warning, she flung her arms about Elmer's neck, and kissed him heartily on the mouth.

"I love you, too!" she cried.

Cameras clicked. The crowd cheered.

Mr. Hazeltine held down his hand on the horn button, and drove ruthlessly toward the crowd. They scattered. The roadster fled up the street.

Elmer settled back against the upholstery with a sigh.

"These women," he said in bored accents.

"Most annoying," agreed Mr. Hazeltine dryly.

"Damnably bothersome," said Elmer. "It's getting so I can't turn without some woman throwing her arms around my neck."

"Oh, you'll get used to it," the lawyer reassured him.

"Let's stop at the next newsstand and get the noon papers," Elmer suggested.

Mr. Hazeltine stopped the car at the next corner and shouted to a news dealer, who came trotting over with copies of the latest editions.

As they drove on, Elmer Wirple considered them frowningly. A black headline arrested him:

GUINEA PIG WOMAN TO TAKE STAND!

"Who," Elmer demanded, "is the guinea pig woman?"

"Mrs. Perkins," answered Hazeltine.

"Why is she going to take the stand?"

"It will all come out in the wash," was Mr. Hazeltine's enigmatic reply.

13

FORGING THE FATAL LINK

THE FIRST WITNESS to be called after the noon recess was Harry Benedict. He approached the stand nervously. His eyes darted here and there, and, when he seated himself, he nervously fumbled with his fingers. Mr. Yistle addressed him in the soothing voice he reserved particularly for fidgety witnesses.

"What is your occupation?"

"Suh—sales manager of the Dulcier Motor Car Company in this district."

"Do you recognize the man who is sitting over there—the one in the gray tweed suit with the blue necktie?"

"Yes, sir."

"Do you know his name?"

"I do. It is Elmer Wirple."

"Have you ever had a business transaction with him?"

"I have."

"Kindly explain this transaction to the jury, Mr. Benedict."

Harry Benedict looked warily at the jury.

"I sold Mr. Wirple a Dulcier roadster for three thousand two hundred and seventy-eight dollars on March 1. He had wanted a special paint job done, and I didn't charge him for it. I had the paint job rushed, and the car was delivered to him the next day."

"With the permission of the court," said Mr. Yistle, bowing, "I wish to have this roadster rolled into this court room."

"Permission is granted," ruled Judge Manning, "if it is possible physically to bring the car in here."

Mr. Bullock, as if at a cue, opened the doors at the end of the middle aisle. The radiator and front mudguards of the lavender roadster were visible. A man was at the wheel. Two other men were at the rear, pushing.

The long, dazzling vehicle came rolling into the court room.

Mr. Yistle faced the witness.

"Do you identify this car as the one you sold the accused?"

"Yes, sir; that's the one."

"You're sure there can be no mistake about it?"

"I'm positive. It's the only lavender roadster in this whole territory."

"That will be all."

Gillian Hazeltine arose with a thoughtful frown, and slowly approached the glittering roadster. With every eye in the court upon him, he opened the door, stepped in, and sat down behind the wheel. He bounced up and down on the seat, switched the lights on and off, and got out again.

The bailiff hammered with his gavel for order. The merriment subsided.

Mr. Hazeltine faced the witness.

"How fast will this car go?"

"It will go eighty-five miles an hour," answered Mr. Benedict.

"Has it four-wheel brakes?"

"Yes, sir; it has."

"Has it the proper accessories on the engine so that the oil, air and gasoline are filtered properly?"

"Yes, sir; the Dulcier Big Eight has every modern improvement in keeping with the simplicity of upkeep and ease of operation."

"Is the chassis easy to oil?"

"Yes, sir; we have one of the simplest and most thorough chassis lubricating systems on the market."

"Is the upholstery real leather?"

"Yes, sir; it is guaranteed Spanish, thoroughly tanned leather—not imitation."

Mr. Yistle was listening suspiciously. He opened his mouth to object, and he slowly closed it again. The ways of Gillian Hazeltine were growing more mysterious.

"And you are positive, are you, that this is the roadster you sold to Mr. Wirple?"

"Yes, sir; absolutely positive."

"That will be all," said Mr. Hazeltine.

The witness stepped down. And an excited murmur ran through the court room as the next witness made her way to the stand. This was a tall, nice-looking old woman with white hair.

The spectators were already familiar with Mrs. Perkins from her photographs in the papers. She was the so-called "Guinea Pig Woman," from whose lips the most startling disclosures were expected. She was the star witness of the prosecution.

Elmer watched her mount the stand with his worldly smile. The interest in her was similar to that which is centered on the participants in the main bout of an evening of prize fighting.

She settled herself placidly in the witness chair, and was duly sworn to tell the truth, the whole truth, and nothing but the truth.

"Your full name is Henrietta Perkins?" Mr. Yistle began in a crooning voice, and he looked at her lovingly. On her testimony he was going to send Elmer Wirple to the gallows.

He was so sure of sending Elmer Wirple to the State capitol to be hanged by the neck until he was dead that the smile of victory was already upon the State's attorney's lips.

"It is," Mrs. Perkins answered.

"Where do you live?"

"On my farm," she said amiably, "about fifteen miles from here on the Sangamo River."

"What is your occupation?"

"I raise guinea pigs."

A ripple of excitement passed through the court room. The famous guinea pig woman—famed from coast to coast—was on the witness stand at last!

"Do you spend most of your time at your house?"

"I seldom leave my house, except to ride over to Cloverdale to buy the little things I need."

Mr. Yistle now unfolded a large sheet of paper on the table before him. It proved to be an elaborate, colored map on a large scale of the Perkins farm.

The road leading from the River Boulevard was indicated. The river was shown, a broad ribbon of silvery blue. The cottage was indicated. Emphasis, in artistic coloration, was laid upon the cliff behind the old oak tree, the oak tree which, by nightfall, would be known from one end of America to the other.

"I wish to introduce this map of the Perkins farm," said Mr. Yistle, "as Exhibit C for the State." He draped the map upon a frame near the lavender roadster, so that the witness and the jurors could see it plainly. As he talked he wielded a long ruler. He pointed to the brown square on the map.

"This is where you live, Mrs. Perkins?"

The old lady squinted and nodded.

"Yes, I live right there."

"And this road which goes past your house—that road terminates at a cliff, does it not?"

"It does. Yes, sir."

"And perhaps ten feet in from the edge of the cliff there is an old oak tree, is there not?"

"Yes, there is an old oak tree."

Mr. Yistle was now pointing to the old oak tree, which would, before nightfall, be known throughout the nation as "the old necking tree."

"Now, this cliff, Mrs. Perkins; it drops sheerly to the river a distance of about fifty feet, does it not?"

"It does, yes, sir; it's a very steep cliff."

Mr. Yistle drew a deep breath.

"You do not care to take your exercise in the form of pedestrianism, do you, Mrs. Perkins?"

"In the form of what?" replied the old lady.

"I mean, you are not overly fond of walking, are you?"

"No, sir; I'm not fond of walking."

"Well, when you go to Cloverdale, how do you get there?"

"I ride my bicycle."

"This bicycle?" asked Mr. Yistle.

Mr. Bullock was walking up the center aisle of the court room with a serious mien. He was pushing along a bicycle, but not the kind of bicycle seen now and then on our highways and city streets to-day. This was the kind of bicycle our grandfathers rode. It was a high-wheeled bicycle. Yes, it was an old and rusted high-wheeled bicycle.

"I wish to introduce this into the evidence," said Mr. Yistle when the excited murmur had subsided, "as Exhibit D for the State."

Mr. Hazeltine was on his feet.

"I should like to ask the eminent counsel if he intends to convert this court room into a museum?"

The court room burst into laughter. Judge Manning grinned. But the bailiff banged resolutely for order, and finally it was restored.

"Perhaps," Mr. Yistle retorted, "a museum for antiquated criminal lawyers!"

When order was again restored, he went on:

"This is your bicycle, is it not, Mrs. Perkins?"

"Yes, that's my bike."

"You are so used to riding it that you employ it on even short errands about your farm, do you not?"

"I do. I save myself as many steps as possible."

"Now, Mrs. Perkins, I want you to tell the jury if this road, this lane, that runs back from your house to the edge of the cliff is used by any one but yourself."

Mrs. Perkins faced the jury, and smiled pleasantly.

"It is; yes, sir."

By whom is it used, Mrs. Perkins?"

"It is used by people who come in automobiles."

"At night, or by day?"

"At night, sir."

"What do you presume that these automobiles come to the lane for?"

"Objection!" snapped Mr. Hazeltine.

"On what grounds?" asked the judge.

"The witness is not testifying on presumption, but on what she actually has heard or has seen, your honor."

"The objection is sustained. You may phrase that question differently, Mr. Yistle."

"Very well," said Mr. Yistle, smiling affably. "Have you been in a position to hear or to see what the drivers of those automobiles were up to when they went to the end of the lane under the old oak tree on the cliff?"

"I have been," Mrs. Perkins stated.

"Kindly tell the jury what you have seen or heard."

"Well, I've seen these autos go down to the end of my lane, and there's always only one couple in them. They usually go down there on moonlight nights, when the view across the river is simply beautiful. They are mostly young people.

"Once or twice I've been curious, and I've ridden down there on my bike, and I've heard them making love, and I've seen than making love."

"They were necking under the old oak tree, eh?"

"Yes, sir; we used to call it spooning when I was a girl."

The court room tittered.

"Now, Mrs. Perkins, I want you to look at this lavender roadster here. I want you to look at it very closely."

"Yes, sir; I am."

"Have you ever seen this car before?"

"Yes, sir; I have."

"When did you see this car before?"

"On the night of March 3."

"On the night, to be exact, that Dorothy Murphy disappeared from the flat she and her sister were occupying, and was never seen alive again?"

"Yes, sir; I remember the date very well."

The court room was so silent now that you could have heard a pin drop. The chains with which the prosecuting attorney would drag Elmer Wirple to the gallows were being forged to the final link. It was the guinea pig woman who would forge the final link.

"At what hour, Mrs. Perkins, did you see this roadster enter your lane?"

"It was just about eight forty-five, sir."

"How do you fix the hour?"

"I always go to bed at eight thirty, and I was in my bedroom starting to undress, when I heard the purr of an automobile coming up the road and I looked out. It was a bright moonlight night, and I saw this car turning into my lane."

"Tell the jury what you did then, Mrs. Perkins."

"I just sat there at my window, looking out—the night was so beautiful. You could see for miles. Then I heard voices—low voices. It sounded like quarreling.

"I'd forgotten about the lavender roadster, and I thought of my guinea pigs. Some had been stolen the week before. I hurried and got into my clothes, and went downstairs and got my flash light.

"I went outside and looked, but I didn't see anybody near my guinea pig houses. But the voices were still loud. It was a girl's voice and a man's voice. So I got on my bicycle, and I rode down the lane to the old oak tree. There was a man and a girl in the car."

"Could you see their faces?"

"I could!"

"How could you see them?"

"By the light on the dashboard of the car."

"Who was the man?"

"The man was the young man sitting over there."

"This young man?" And Mr. Yistle strode across the court room, and laid a hand on Elmer's shoulder. Elmer was smiling his cynical smile.

"Yes!" cried Mrs. Perkins.

"And who was the girl?"

"The girl was Dorothy Murphy!"

The court room burst into an uproar. It was *so* dramatic. Link by link, the clever prosecuting attorney had forged that chain which would drag Elmer Wirple to the gallows. And still Elmer Wirple wore that amused, rather bored, rather tolerant smile.

The bailiff banged his desk with his gavel. It was at least five minutes before order was restored.

Then Mr. Yistle went on:

"What were they quarreling about?"

"I didn't wait to hear. I supposed it was a lovers' quarrel. I got back on my bike without them seeing me, then halfway back to the house, I stopped, because I'd heard a scream. Then I waited, and I heard a heavy splash in the river— right at the bottom of the cliff! Then—silence!"

In the tense, electrified silence, Mr. Yistle shot his next question:

"What—happened—then?"

"The roadster started to back up," said Mrs. Perkins. "I got off the road so he could drive by. I guess I was hidden by a clump of bushes. Anyway, he turned around as fast as he could, and he drove out of the lane toward the city."

"Was Dorothy Murphy with him?"

"No, sir; he was all alone."

Mr. Yistle bowed to the jury; he bowed again to Judge Manning; he bowed a third time to Mr. Hazeltine.

"The State rests," he said.

It was, literally, a coup d'etat. With only a handful of witnesses Mr. Yistle had forged the chain that would drag Elmer Wirple to the gallows. Newspapers throughout the country said so in feverish resumes of the trial; they declared that Gillian Hazeltine hadn't a loophole to crawl through. Elmer Wirple was doomed!

But, even now, he smiled his amused, cynical, worldly smile. Newspaper photographers, risking jail sentence for contempt of court, snapped their cameras at him.

Mr. Hazeltine was on his feet, frowning. His cross-examination of Mr. Yistle's star witness was brief, and, it seemed, utterly without point.

"You say you raise guinea pigs?"

"I do," said Mrs. Perkins.

"And that this spot where you claim you saw the lavender roadster on the night Dorothy Murphy disappeared is accessible by a good road leading out from this city?"

"Yes, sir; the road is good all of the way. For fifteen miles it is new, wide concrete. Then you take a left turn on a good dirt road, and that brings you to my house."

"That will be all," said Mr. Hazeltine. He now addressed the bench.

"Your Honor, the hour is now four o'clock. It is Friday afternoon. I beg that this hearing be postponed until Monday morning, to give me sufficient time to marshal my witnesses. I did not expect the State to finish so soon."

Judge Manning bent toward the prosecuting attorney.

"Have you any objection, Mr. Yistle, to a postponement until Monday morning?"

"None at all," said Mr. Yistle jovially. "He can have as many postponements as he wants. Take your time, Gillian. Take your time!"

14

STRAIGHT TALK

ELMER WAS RUSHED out of court by the back door, and spirited to his apartment in a closed car that was waiting for him. Mr. Hazeltine joined him. Elmer was not smiling as they were whisked through the streets to the Herendon Arms.

"How," he wanted to know, "are you going to get me out of this mess, Gillian? You keep saying that everything will come out all right, but how in the world can everything come out all right, when you sat there like a log and let that Yistle convict me in the eyes of the world for killing Dorothy Murphy—who I never saw before in my life?"

"You will be a free man by Monday noon," Mr. Hazeltine promised him, and he would say no more.

"I don't understand you at all," Elmer complained.

"Everything will be as clear as a crystal by Monday noon," said the Silver Fox.

And he ignored Elmer's further questioning. Elmer was beginning to assert himself. He was beginning to enjoy the role he was playing.

At the entrance to the Herendon Arms, a reporter from the *Evening Gazette* was waiting for him. He wanted to publish the story of Elmer's conquests. The *Evening*

Gazette was prepared to pay Elmer five thousand dollars for the rights to his life story.

A competent literary artist would write the story for him by data furnished by him, and the *Evening Gazette* would guarantee simultaneous publication of the story in newspapers throughout the United States and Canada.

"Nothing doing," said Elmer.

"But it will be great publicity," the reporter persisted. "And practically every man, woman and child in the country will read it. They want to know about you. I don't believe you realize what a great public figure you've become, Mr. Wirple."

Elmer flicked an ash from his fifty-cent cigar.

"I am annoyed by it all," he said in bored tones. And pushed on past the other reporters to the elevator, with Mr. Hazeltine following modestly behind.

Mr. Hazeltine locked the apartment door. The telephone was ringing. Mr. Hazeltine answered it.

"No," he said, "you cannot talk with Mr. Wirple. This is his attorney. What's that? A conviction? Listen, Jimmy; you can turn your best rewrite man loose on this: When court opens Monday morning, a sensation is going to be sprung.

"I'm going to spring it. It will shake the nation to the core. Get that? To the core! Nope. No details. You'll find out all about it Monday morning. So long, Jimmy."

He knew that that statement would presently spring forth over telegraph wires to every city, town, and hamlet in the country; and he knew that Adelbert Yistle would sneer, and say: "Old stuff! We've got him hog-tied!" It would all make good reading.

Yes; Mr. Hazeltine was a great lawyer, and he was a great showman.

For fully an hour Mr. Hazeltine paced up and down in the exotic drawing-room of the love bandit's apartment, chewing vehemently at a dead cigar. He had sprung one trap; now he must spring another. He arrived presently at a decision. And he walked briskly to the telephone, and called a number. He was saying presently:

"I want to talk to Mr. Hamilton."

Mr. Hazeltine was quite pale, but those bright blue eyes of his were keener than ever. They seemed to have dancing flames in them.

A sharp voice came into the receiver.

"Is this you, Hamilton?"

"Yes"—a snap.

"This is Gillian Hazeltine."

"Well?"

"I'm giving you until to-morrow noon to clear out of town." Mr. Hazeltine's voice had become a harsh grating, and his face was livid with what looked, to the startled Elmer, as hatred.

"You've pulled that bluff before," snarled the voice at the other end.

"I'm telling you you're going to be out of town to-morrow noon, or you're going to be dead by twelve-thirty."

There was a short, hard laugh. "So you're getting around to rough stuff, are you, Hazeltine? Well, let me tell you—"

"You can't tell me a damned thing," barked the Silver Fox. "I'm giving you fair and honest warning. This town is too small for you and me. One of us has to clear out. Get me?"

"You'd better pack up," the man at the other end said, with another hard laugh.

"You will observe," growled Mr. Hazeltine, "when you leave the bank to-night, that four men will be watching you climb into your sedan. Those four men are Chicago gunmen. They've got orders from me to blow the roof of your head off—after twelve-thirty to-morrow noon.

"The open season on Jason Hamilton starts then. Get that? Have them pinched and I'll bring in twelve. Have those twelve pinched, and I'll import fifty—with machine guns! Do you get that, Hamilton?

"I'm through treating you like a man. From now on you're a wild animal that's going to be exterminated—unless you get out of this town and stay out. Fair warning! Good-by!"

He hung up the receiver. He was as pale as a ghost. His eyes were staring. Great beads of perspiration clung to his forehead.

Elmer gazed at him with something akin to terror.

"Gee whiz, Gillian; who was that?"

"That," said Mr. Hazeltine, "is the dirtiest, lousiest skunk alive. He is the crookedest scoundrel in the world. He is the vice president of the Fourth National.

"For ten years he has had this town under his thumb. He's responsible for all the dirty politics. He's been behind every rotten administration. He's a menace, a sneak. I've been trying to screw up my nerve to make that speech to him for two years."

"You don't mean that about the gunmen!" Elmer bleated.

"I don't?" Mr. Hazeltine snapped. "Why in hell don't I?"

For some time Elmer sat staring at him worshipfully in silence.

"I think it's just wonderful," he said, "the way you've got the interests of the community at heart."

"Oh, hell," said Mr. Hazeltine.

15

WHO WAS WITH ELMER?

THAT WEEK-END WAS replete with excitement. Even the more conservative newspapers were compelled to devote columns and columns to the sensational developments in the Love Bandit trial.

And in the less conservative newspapers, pages were given over to the testimony of the Guinea Pig Woman; to the confusion of Silly Tilly; to the unshakable calm, the cynical smile of the accused. There were photographs by the square yard not only in town, but in nation-wide profusion.

The love bandit had become a by-word. Editorial writers generally agreed that men like Elmer Wirple ought to be shot on sight. They were a menace to the nation.

Another stirring piece of news broke on Saturday. But this was local. One of the most prominent citizens of the community had committed suicide.

In the ordinary course of events, the news would have occupied the commanding front page position; but, in most cases, Elmer Wirple's sensational trial crowded it back to an inside page. Jason Hamilton had committed suicide.

He had taken a large dose of veronal on Friday night, and had been found dead in his bed on Saturday morning.

One newspaper spoke feelingly of his untimely demise, but the others were frank. Their obituary editorials were thinly veiled statements to the effect that Jason Hamilton's removal from this world was nothing to weep about. He had been a malignant power; he had corrupted not only the city but the State politics.

On Monday morning, thousands fought for admission to the court room, where the famous criminal lawyer defending Elmer Wirple would spring his promised sensation—if any.

The jury filed in. Judge Manning, pink and composed, took his place. Adelbert Yistle looked pale and thoughtful. Since he had been told that his crafty opponent had promised a sensation, he had been going over and over his witnesses' testimony.

To him, the case was iron-bound, watertight, and mothproof. Mrs. Perkins, whose credibility was beyond question, had seen Elmer Wirple and Dorothy Murphy in the death car or, as it was sometimes referred to, The Lavender Love Chariot, on the night of her disappearance.

Mrs. Perkins had heard them quarrel, had heard the splash of her falling body as it struck the river, and later the body of Dorothy Murphy had been found in the river.

It was a clean-cut case. And the jury, he knew with his sixth, or courtroom sense, was with him to a man.

He doubted that Gillian Hazeltine had anything up his sleeve. He believed that Gillian Hazeltine realized he was licked from the start, had taken the losing end for the free publicity he would get. Yet Mr. Yistle was more than a little concerned over Gillian's show of confidence. Damn him; he fairly oozed confidence and assurance!

The first witness for the defense was a real sensation, however. For the first witness was the accused himself.

Elmer took the stand with his cynical smile, and the air of the courtroom seemed fairly to crackle with high-voltage electricity.

"You have heard the testimony given against you in this trial?" Mr. Hazeltine asked.

"Yes, sir; I have."

"You heard Mrs. Perkins state that she saw you drive into her lane in your roadster on the night of March 3 with a young woman; you heard her state that you drove to the end of the lane, and that you quarreled with the young woman.

"You heard her further state that the quarrel stopped, and that shortly thereafter there was a splash in the river below, as of some heavy object having been thrown from the cliff; and you heard her state that when you drove away from the oak tree you were alone. You heard her say all that?"

"Yes, sir; I did."

"Will you tell the jury whether or not you knew Dorothy Murphy?"

"I did not. I never saw Dorothy Murphy."

"Who was with you in the car on the evening of March 3?"

"Another young lady."

"What was her name?"

"I prefer not to tell."

"Why do you prefer not to tell?"

"Because a gentleman does not kiss and tell."

A roar of excitement burst out in the courtroom. Ten

minutes passed before the examination—so carefully rehearsed over the week-end—could proceed.

"Did you have a quarrel with this unnamed young lady?"

"I did."

"What did it concern?"

"A bundle of old clothes."

"Why were you quarreling over a bundle of old clothes?"

"I was preparing to cast off a dual role that I had been playing. I had been a lowly clerk by day and, by night— well, I suppose I was what the newspapers call me something of a sheik.

"I had taken my old clothes, the clothes I wore in my clerk role, and intended throwing them away. The young lady quarreled with me over what she termed my ridiculous extravagance. But, in the end, I threw the clothes away."

"Where did you throw them?"

"Over the cliff."

There was a smile on every face in the courtroom now. Mr. Yistle was beaming. Mr. Bullock was trying hard not to laugh. The jurors were grinning. Even Judge Manning was smiling. It was simply too preposterous, too ridiculous.

"What happened then?" asked Mr. Hazeltine.

"The young lady became angry. In fact, she wept. I turned the car about, and started for town. Mrs. Perkins was on my side of the road—that is, on my side as we drove past her. The young lady was huddled beside me on the seat. That, I presume, is why Mrs. Perkins thought there was no one in the car but myself."

"I see," said Mr. Hazeltine. "Let me ask you this, Mr. Wirple. You can answer it or not as you see fit. Did the young lady in the car resemble Dorothy Murphy—I mean, did she resemble the photographs of Dorothy Murphy you have doubtless seen in the newspapers?"

"She did," said Elmer. "Very much, indeed. She had dark hair and brown eyes, and her face was of very similar proportions."

"That will be all," said Mr. Hazeltine.

Mr. Yistle arose with a jovial, benevolent smile. He chuckled a little.

"I waive examination," he chuckled, and the courtroom chuckled with him. "It is a shame that the young lady who accompanied Mr. Wirple on the night of March 3 on that historic ride down the Rustic Lane to the old Necking Tree in the Lavender Love Chariot is not brave enough to come to his defense. No, I do not wish to cross-examine this witness. He is excused."

Elmer got down, and returned to his seat at the counsel table. He still wore that debonair smile.

The next witness was a shabby, thin man of middle age with lackluster eyes, and a yellowish skin. Defeat, tragedy stood out in every line of his prematurely old face, in every wrinkle of his shoddy clothing.

He gave his name, under oath, as Ezra Johnston. He spoke in a dead voice. It was almost as if his voice emerged from a dead body.

"Where do you live, Mr. Johnston?" Mr. Hazeltine gently asked him.

"I live on a farm about ten miles north of Cloverdale."

"On the Sangamo River?"

"Yes, sir; on the Sangamo; right on the banks of the Sangamo."

"You are, or were, the father of a twenty-year-old daughter named Annette?"

"Yes, sir, I—I was. She was my daughter."

"Will you kindly tell the court what happened to your daughter Annette on the night of February 28?"

"Yes, sir; I will. My daughter Annette—she had a sort of quarrel with me. She wanted to leave the farm and go to the city, and I said the city was no place for a young, innocent girl. And we had quite a set-to about it.

"Right after supper she went out of the house, and I saw her go wandering off down t'ward the river. It was the last I ever saw of her—until to-day."

"You say, you saw her again to-day?"

"Yes, sir—I—I saw her to-day."

"Where did you see her?"

"I saw her in Donaldson's Undertaking parlors, on Spruce Street."

The courtroom was as silent as a tomb now. Ezra Johnston's words were barely audible.

"You identified her, did you not, as your daughter?"

"I—I did, sir."

"By what identification?"

"There was a birthmark, a mole, on her right upper arm; there was another birthmark, a red mark shaped like a moon in the second quarter on her left shoulder blade. It—it's her all right. She—she jumped into the river!"

His eyes were staring, unseeingly, straight ahead. His voice had risen almost to a shout. He was clutching the arms of the witness chair.

"You were accompanied by the coroner, were you not, Mr. Johnston?"

"Yes, he went along; and he told me the body was Dorothy Murphy! It wasn't! It was my—little—Annette!"

Tumult broke out in the courtroom again. Gillian Hazeltine had punctured the prosecution's iron-bound, water-tight case! The excitement reached a fever pitch when Ezra Johnston gently slumped forward, and slid to the courtroom floor in a dead faint.

Mr. Yistle was on his feet, clamoring.

When order was restored, Mr. Hazeltine said, soothingly:

"You can cross-examine him later, if you wish, Adelbert. Let me get through with my next witness—and you can cross-examine him to your heart's content."

The next witness was a slender woman in dark blue. She wore a heavy black veil. Another dead hush fell upon the courtroom as she slowly, gracefully walked to the witness stand. An excited whisper buzzed in the rear. The bailiff's gavel came down with a sharp thud.

Heads were lifting; eyes were staring; mouths were open. Was this mysterious, veiled woman the sensation that Gillian Hazeltine had promised to disclose?

The woman seated herself. Slowly, oh, so slowly, she lifted the veil from her face.

From a hundred lungs burst the shocking words:

"Dorothy Murphy!"

She was a bright-faced girl, with fine, brown eyes, and curly, brown hair. She was smiling sweetly.

Mr. Yistle looked at her in stunned astonishment. Never, in his experience, had the corpus delicti walked unaided to the witness stand. His lower jaw seemed to become unhinged. It hung down, and it stayed there.

Elmer Wirple looked at her with his wise, debonair, cynical smile. The path to freedom was being paved with great rapidity!

"You are the sister of Marguerite Murphy, and an associate in the business of Madeline Sœurs?" Mr. Hazeltine asked.

"I am," said the sweetly smiling girl.

"Will you kindly explain to this courtroom, and to these patiently waiting reporters why you left this city on March 3?"

"I left this city on March 3 because my life was threatened, and I dared not stay," the witness answered.

"Who threatened your life?"

"Jason Hamilton!"

"Why did he threaten your life?"

"He wanted me to marry him. I was in constant terror of him. He was a thoroughly bad man. He said he would have me trailed if I tried to run away. He said he would get me in the end. I knew he would.

"On the night of March 3, I disguised myself as I am now, and slipped out on the nine o'clock train for Chicago. I have been in hiding there since. I would not return until Jason Hamilton was dead. I did that on the advice of my attorney."

"That is all," said Mr. Hazeltine. "Adelbert, I wish to know if you care to cross-examine my beautiful witness?"

"I wish to know," snarled the defeated prosecutor, "who her attorney is."

"I," said Mr. Hazeltine, "am her attorney."

"I am going to have you debarred for this!" shouted Mr.

Yistle. "You rigged it all up. From the very outset, you knew Dorothy Murphy was alive!"

"But I could not prove it until the proper time, and by due legal procedure," the Silver Fox said, grinning at him. "Adelbert, I told you I was going to make a sucker out of you, and I—"

"There was a murder on that cliff at the guinea pig farm," shouted Mr. Yistle, "on the night of March 3. This scoundrel did throw a body into the water. I'll get to the bottom of it yet! I'll—"

A clear, ringing voice interrupted him.

"You are mistaken. There was no murder that night on the guinea pig farm. I was the girl in the car with Mr. Wirple!"

The clear, ringing voice came from the front row of spectators. Every one stood up for a glimpse of this melodramatic heroine. And Elmer Wirple looked at her with misty, baffled eyes as he smiled his debonair, worldly smile.

The girl was Carrol Jameson!

16

WESTWARD HO!

SIDE BY SIDE in a drawing-room of the Overland Limited speeding toward Hollywood, California, sat Mr. and Mrs. Elmer Wirple. His arm was about her slender waist, and her shining head was upon his exquisitely-tailored shoulder.

With dreamy eyes they were gazing at the contract which called for his services as a leading man in the Super Features Film, Inc., at a salary of two hundred and fifty thousand dollars a year.

Elmer withdrew his eyes from it presently, and gazed at his bride.

"Carrol," he said in muffled accents, "you will never realize how I adore you!"

"More than all those other women?" she shyly questioned.

"Carrol," he said, this time clearly and very sternly, "I must ask you never, never again to refer to my affairs. They are of the past. You are the one woman whom I can truly and everlastingly love. The past is dead. Do you promise?"

"I promise," she whispered as, with a little contented sigh, she settled into his arms.

"But who *was* the girl in the Lavender Love Chariot

with you that night under the Old Necking Tree when the Guinea Pig Woman came down on her High-Wheeled Bike?"

"A gentleman," he reminded her, "never kisses and tells."

And while the happy couple speeded over the miles to the land of glittering opportunity, Mr. Hazeltine was just returning to his office from a well-earned vacation.

He sat down immediately at his telephone, and put in a call for Mrs. Henrietta Perkins.

"This," he said, "is Gillian. I've wondered what's been happening in my absence. What has happened?"

"Gillian, I put up the fence as you directed. Ever since the day I took the stand, there has been a constant procession of motoring parties who want to look at the cliff from which the body was thrown, and the old Necking Tree, and the High-Wheeled Bike.

"The total paid admissions up to last night were eight thousand, seven hundred and sixty-three dollars, and fifty cents. I sold the last guinea pig this morning. I have been charging five dollars a pig.

"And I have just sent off telegrams to all the guinea pig farms in America to rush me all the stock they have on hand. By the way, I have bought the Lavender Love Chariot!"

Mr. Hazeltine's next call was the salesroom of the Dulcier Big Eight, queen of the road. A brisk and businesslike voice answered him.

"Well, well, well, Mr. Hazeltine, how are you?"

"I'm fine, Harry," said Mr. Hazeltine. "How's business?"

"Mr. Hazeltine, it's just booming! I've sold thirty-five cars since the trial," said Harry Benedict enthusiastically.

"And ten of them were Lavender Love Chariots. Yes, sir, old man Barnum could certainly steal some tricks from you!"

Mr. Hazeltine now put in a call for Addison Yover, the owner of the Herendon Arms. Mr. Yover was fairly boiling over with enthusiasm.

"Business?" he cried. "Gillian, if business gets any better, I am going to have a nervous breakdown. Every apartment is taken. I have rented the Love Nest for enough money to pay my taxes on the entire building!"

Mr. Hazeltine's final call was the exclusive dressmaking shop of Madeline Sœurs.

Dorothy answered the telephone.

"Gillian!" she exclaimed. "You old darling! When did you get back?"

"Just this afternoon," said Gillian. "How is business?"

"Gillian," she bubbled, "we have had to take on a dozen new seamstresses. We have all the worthwhile trade in town. You are wonderful. You've got to come up and have dinner with us to-night."

"I'll bring a quart of that nineteen twelve champagne," Gillian agreed.

He sat, looking at his cigar for some minutes after he had hung up the receiver. His expression was puzzled. Dorothy, or Marguerite? Golden hair and eyes of blue, or chestnut curls and eyes of brown?

Which of the two would become the next Mrs. Hazeltine? There was so much to be said for each!

WHO DID KILL EZRA KLAGG?

1

GILLIAN HAZELTINE, IN the course of his career as a criminal lawyer, was accused of a great many things. He was accused of corrupting juries. He was accused of buying judges. He was accused of unfair court room methods, of various and sundry kinds of malpractice. But no one was ever known to accuse him of taking a case for which he was not adequately compensated.

Yet that statement in itself is subject to various and sundry interpretations. What is "adequate compensation?"

Perhaps with tongue in cheek Gillian Hazeltine would have said that he was not paid a thin dime in actual cash for his services in this case and that, but that he had been amply repaid in spiritual satisfaction. On the face of a gray-haired old mother, he would say, he had replaced tears with a glorious smile, for having secured for her rascal of a son, charged with murder, an acquittal.

That, he would say, was ample compensation. Spiritual satisfaction! But, after all, just what is spiritual satisfaction?

However we approach Gillian Hazeltine, we are more than apt to find ourselves soon bogged down in a morass of contradictions. By his enemies he was declared to be a consummate rascal. By his friends he was declared to be one of nature's noblemen. "You pays your money and you takes your choice."

Viewing him by his results—he seldom lost a case and he was tremendously in demand by those seeking freedom.

They called him the Silver Fox because of his cunning and because his black hair was peppered with silver. Before we proceed to the baffling mystery of Ezra Klagg and try to determine by an honest examination of the testimony who *did* kill that wretched man, it may be well to mention two examples of Hazeltine's cunning. By his works shall ye know him.

You must take them with a grain or two of salt. They are a part of the legendary heritage which every great man of sharp practice leaves for the youngsters to laugh at, to marvel about, and to puzzle over.

They must not be scrutinized too sharply. As legends they are charming; as characterizing episodes they are perfect.

One had to do with murder, the other with mayhem, the latter being a crime seldom met with in these enlightened days. One dealt with a cookie, the other with teeth. There may be a grain of truth in either.

He was defending, in the first instance, a man named Balter against a charge of murder in the first degree. The motive was revenge.

Balter was accused of having poisoned a man named Wharton. According to the testimony of State's witnesses, Balter and Wharton were enemies as the result of a land deal in which Wharton bested Balter.

Balter, the prosecution claimed, had brooded over a fancied wrong until it became an obsession. He planned the death of his enemy with diabolical cunning.

He bought a cook book (Exhibit C for the State), and perfected the technique of baking ginger cookies, of which Wharton was inordinately fond. When his plans were ripe, he baked a batch of these cookies and sent them anonymously to Wharton.

Wharton ate the half of one cookie and died that night.

The prosecution offered the remaining half of the cookie in evidence. It became Exhibit A for the People.

A chemist took the stand and swore that he had analyzed crumbs from the cookie and found them to contain enough poison to assassinate an elephant, if given time to digest. With this testimony the State rested.

Gillian Hazeltine put his client on the stand. Balter freely admitted that he had baked a batch of cookies and sent them to Wharton. He firmly denied that he had put poison in them.

"Why did you send the cookies to the deceased?"

"Because he liked ginger cookies, sir. I was anxious to become friends with him again."

Amid the titters Gillian Hazeltine seized the half cookie.

"This is my answer to the elaborate *persecution* prepared by the *prosecution* against this poor, innocent man!" he cried.

Whereupon he stuffed what remained of the cookie into his mouth, hastily masticated, and swallowed it.

"The defense rests," he said in a contemptuous voice, and walked slowly, imperturbably from the horrified court room.

Gillian promptly repaired to an office where a stomach pump was in readiness. He was ill for a week, but no one knew it. And Balter, of course, was freed.

The other case, the mayhem case, concerned a notorious underworld character charged with having bitten off another man's thumb in a brawl. The name of the defendant was Simons.

He was known, in his intimate circle, as "the Shuffler," because of his curiously bearlike walk. The Shuffler was commonly supposed to be the member of the riverfront gang—the "wharf rats"—a powerful underworld organization made up of bootleggers, river pirates, and stick-up gentry, mysteriously under the protection of the political ring.

Shuffler Simons was taken before the grand jury,

indicted for trial before General Sessions, and his case put on the calendar. For reasons known best to himself, Gillian secured, on one technical ground after another, postponement and postponement and postponement.

Eventually, after much time had elapsed, the case came to trial. The prosecuting attorney had sworn to make an example of the Shuffler; the press of the city was clamoring for a clean-up of the waterfront gang.

The Shuffler was an occasional offender, and the press wanted him put away where he belonged for a long, long time.

The prosecution had eyewitnesses, some of them reputable people, who had, they declared on oath, seen the Shuffler chew his victim's thumb off. The stump was exhibited in evidence.

Gillian Hazeltine waited until the witnesses for the State had had their say. He then commanded his client to take the stand.

The Shuffler did so. He told the Shuffler to face the jury, which the Shuffler did.

Gillian's fine rich voice now rose in oratorical periods.

The cruel injustice of bringing this poor, innocent man before the bar! Would the jury and his honor pardon his wrathful indignation? He dwelt for some time upon the general theme of persecution, while the judge, the jury, the prosecution and the full court room wondered what it was all about.

Gillian's voice rose and rose until it attained the qualities of a bull's roar. Finally he bellowed:

"Open your mouth!"

The Shuffler opened his mouth. He was toothless!

Not without good reason had the Silver Fox obtained those various postponements.

These incidents—regardless of what their legal worth may be—are cited here to illuminate the character of the man with whom we have to deal in the baffling mystery of Ezra Klagg's murder. Such facts in that absorbing case as are presented herein were secured from obvious sources—court records, reliable witnesses, and so on.

Deductions are left entirely to the reader. The author has conscientiously endeavored to bridle all tendencies toward the expression of his personal viewpoint, and such theories bearing on this or that phase of the case as are presented are plainly labeled as such and may be accepted or rejected at the reader's discretion.

Here are the bald facts in the case:

Some time between the hours of seven thirty and nine o'clock on the night of June 6, 1927, Ezra Klagg, a farmer of miserly habits, was shot through the heart and instantly killed.

Investigation brought to light the fact that Ezra Klagg lived alone in a little farmhouse on an infrequently traveled thoroughfare known as High Rocks Road. His nearest neighbor, in either direction, was about a quarter of a mile away.

He was his own cook and handy man. He worked his farm unhelped. Ezra Klagg was, at the time of his death, forty-eight years of age.

Other facts follow:

The bullet which pierced his heart and passed on through his body was found lodged in the mattress of a bed in the next room. It was carefully removed and given over to experts, who upon examination pronounced it to be of thirty-eight caliber, having been fired, in their expert opinion, from a Colt revolver.

A young man named Theodore Jopling, who owned and lived on the farm adjoining Klagg's, was promptly arrested, charged with the murder. The evidence against him, while circumstantial, was very strong.

Theodore Jopling—or Teddy, as he was familiarly called—had quarreled with Ezra Klagg for months over a boundary line which affected their abutting land. Klagg had arbitrarily moved the fence over fifty feet along two hundred yards of pasture land which Jopling claimed as his own.

On the afternoon of the murder the two men had almost come to blows. Teddy Jopling was heard to threaten, in the presence of several men in the Bolivar post office, that he would "get even with that old scoundrel."

At a little after seven that evening, Teddy Jopling and his wife, Marie, were seated on their front porch discussing the matter with banker Torrence of Bolivar, when Teddy leaped up and declared that he was "going down and have it out with that old crook."

Neither his wife nor Torrence had objected or attempted to dissuade him, because Teddy Jopling was somewhat celebrated for his peacefulness and his self-control. Many proofs of this were recited later.

According to his own testimony, Teddy walked down High Rocks Road toward Ezra Klagg's house; but when he neared the house, he thought better of the project and walked on past with the intention of calling on Tom Howard, a farmer who lived a quarter of a mile farther along. His object, he insisted, was to get Tom Howard's advice.

When he reached Tom Howard's house, he found it locked. It then occurred to him that there was a meeting going on that evening in the town hall at Bolivar.

Still, according to his own statements, for no one saw him at any time, he started for home again. He was perhaps a hundred yards past Ezra Klagg's house when he heard a shot.

He presumed that Klagg was out in back somewhere shooting at a stray quail. At all events, he attached no importance to the shot until, later that evening, a constable arrested him, charging him with the murder of Ezra Klagg.

How it came about that the killing was discovered so soon after it had been committed was explained then and later by Tom Howard himself.

At about ten o'clock, on his way home from the town meeting, he stopped in to ascertain what Klagg's opinion would be on a new road tax which had been proposed at the meeting. He was the one man in the section who was on friendly terms with Klagg, and the town fathers had hoped that Howard could persuade him around to vote for the tax when it came up at the next meeting.

He found Ezra Klagg sitting upright in a chair in his meager sitting room with a bullet hole in his left breast.

Tom Howard promptly returned to Bolivar and notified the constable. The constable secured the services of old Dr. Fleming, and the Klagg farmhouse was visited again.

Dr. Fleming, after a brief examination, announced that Ezra Klagg had been shot approximately two or three hours ago, and later gave irrefutable proof to uphold his assertion. He was a shrewd old man. He had examined murder victims before; he knew just what the law would want him to look for.

Within an hour Teddy Jopling was in the Bolivar jail, charged with the crime. He was held over for the grand jury. The grand jury, after the briefest of examinations, indicted him for murder in the first degree, and the State's attorney, Mr. Adelbert Yistle, went ahead with the case.

All of the pertinent facts have so far been presented. Teddy Jopling had stuck to his story. Each involved witness had stuck to his story.

Teddy Jopling occupied a cell in the city jail, waiting for justice to take its course.

2

SOON AFTER HE had been committed, a beautiful, modestly dressed young woman presented herself at the outer gate of Gillian Hazeltine's busy law offices and requested an interview with Mr. Hazeltine. When she stated that she was the wife of Teddy Jopling, she was admitted to the famous criminal lawyer's private office without delay.

She told him, of course, that she wanted him to take her husband's case. Her accent was strongly foreign; she admitted, under Mr. Hazeltine's delicate and sympathetic questioning, that she had been born in France, and that there, in the town of Courvot, she had met and become engaged to Teddy Jopling while he was serving as a lieutenant of artillery in the American Expeditionary Force.

For purposes of simplicity, no attempt will be made here to reproduce her accent. Her English was quite good.

They were married, she said, immediately after the signing of the armistice and had gone to America as soon as he had received his discharge.

"Teddy had grown up on a farm," said Mrs. Jopling, "and I agreed that it would be very nice for us to have a farm of our own. He had inherited this farm from an uncle; I myself had lived on a farm the greater part of my life, and the idea of working our own farm appealed to us.

"We had had our farm and lived on it about six years before Mr. Klagg was killed. I will not give you any details, but I will only say that my Teddy was a hard working man, a very peaceful man, a man who has always been respected by every one. Of course I love him very much. And I don't have to tell you that I am absolutely confident of his innocence."

Gillian Hazeltine had taken her in very thoroughly. He saw that, although she created the impression of being well groomed, her clothing was inexpensive.

She was a girl of excellent taste, perfect poise, irreproachable manner. And she was beautiful, as the girls of southern France are beautiful.

She was neither thin nor plump. Her color was olive and rose. Her eyes were exceptionally dark, large and lustrous. Her lips were full and deep red. Her short hair was blue-black and softly curling.

Here, in brief, was a charming, dignified, beautiful young woman who would exert a tremendous appeal upon the sympathies of any jury. You could, Gillian knew instantly, pick your jury blindfold—as long as no juror was affected with astigmatism.

"You have not mentioned whether or not you have any children," he said.

The beautiful girl lowered her eyes. She had, he now saw, very long, curving black lashes.

That pose, he promptly decided, was to be her fixed court room pose. It made you want to take her in your strong, manly arms; to soothe her, to cuddle her.

He guessed the cause of her reticence as quickly as he guessed all other familiar human secrets.

"When will the child be born?"

"In about five months," she answered softly, and glanced up to find him smiling confidently. She, too, it now appeared, had a brain that worked with flashing speed.

"I want you to understand, Mr. Hazeltine, that if you take this case it must go into court on its pure merits."

"Of course I understand!" said Mr. Hazeltine, to whom clients sometimes said things like that.

"I don't want him got off by any maudlin appeals to the jury, nor does he. He has told the truth, and he is going to stick to the truth. Shall we go over and talk to him?"

They went over to the city jail and got permission to talk to the prisoner.

Mr. Hazeltine, looking at Teddy Jopling through the grilled-iron door, was a little surprised to find the young man, with evidence so weighty bearing down upon him, so clear-eyed and in such wholesome spirits. Most prisoners, the guilty and the innocent alike, were hardly more than hollow shells of themselves at this stage.

"My darling," said Marie Jopling in a tone that was truly touching, so deep was its tenderness, "Mr. Hazeltine is going to handle our case."

Mr. Hazeltine liked that, too. She didn't say "your case"; she said "our case."

"That's bully," was the prisoner's comment. "Needless to say, Mr. Hazeltine, we wanted to retain you because you're known as the greatest jury lawyer in the State."

"And naturally you want to get off," said the Silver Fox.

Teddy Jopling managed a small smile at that pleasantry.

"I will get off," he said in tones that rang with assurance.

Indeed, Mr. Hazeltine could not recall when any prisoner had revealed such complete faith in his cause. The young man's eyes were clear blue and honest. His whole make-up was that of the young man we are fond of calling a typical American.

He was of the blond type and he was one of the blondest blonds that Gillian had ever gazed upon. Never, in fact, had Gillian seen such sharp contrast as the young husband and the young wife presented.

His coloring was very high and fresh—like the freshness of peach blossoms, and his hair was of a silvery blondness. Her dark, rich beauty and his slim, blond handsomeness had a curious effect, one upon the other.

Each brought out the other's distinctive features, his blondness, her darkness. She became darker and more beautiful; he became blonder and handsomer.

It was obvious to Mr. Hazeltine that the deepest, most passionate, most abiding kind of love existed between these two. Their faith in each other attained to the dignity of a religion.

He was much impressed by it. He was sure that any jury would be equally impressed by it—if the case could be properly presented.

That, he presently discovered, was going to be the rub—presenting the case to the jury as it must be presented, if this beautiful young pair of lovebirds hoped for an acquittal.

"There is not very much time to waste," he told Teddy Jopling. "The prosecuting attorney is already at work on his witnesses, and, from what I have read of the case in the papers, you might, on the surface, have a hard time to escape the electric chair. At the best, they can prove no more than a circumstantial case against you and it is merely our job to create in the jury's mind a reasonable doubt of your guilt."

"I don't think there will be the slightest difficulty in creating that doubt in a jury's mind," said the confident young man. "I am absolutely confident that justice will be done."

"And I, too!" murmured Marie.

"Just what is your story to be?" Gillian then asked him.

"It will be simply and wholly the truth," stated Teddy Jopling. "I did not kill Ezra Klagg. You have only to look at me to know that I am not the killing kind. Anyhow, what had I to gain by killing Ezra Klagg? The argument between us related to the boundary line between his property and mine. That question is still in dispute, is it not? I'll still have it to fight out with the heirs, will I not? Any intelligent jury will realize that I had nothing to gain by killing Ezra Klagg."

"Juries are not always intelligent," Gillian demurred.

"I have absolute confidence that justice will be done."

Gillian nodded thoughtfully. Never in his experience had he encountered such an air of overwhelming, wholesome innocence.

You could not believe wrong of Teddy Jopling. You knew that he was not the murderer of Ezra Klagg; could not have been the murderer of Ezra Klagg. Men with his kindly, honest, fine eyes did not fly into homicidal furies; nor did they plan diabolical, cold-blooded killings.

If Gillian had been younger and much greener, he might not have argued. But he knew juries. He knew prosecuting attorneys. He knew the power of the yellow press.

"I have been reading some books on the legal side of the case," the young man went on. "She brought them to me." What ineffable glory and holiness he compressed into his pronunciation of that little word *she!*

He went on:

"It says that an accused man entering a court room does so with a presumption of innocence on his side. The State must cast out that presumption of innocence and prove beyond reasonable doubt that the prisoner did commit the crime with which he is charged."

"That is what it says in the law books," agreed Gillian. "Years ago I came across phrases like those in law books myself. For almost thirty years I have been waiting to see those phrases mean something—anything. And it has been thirty years of very vain waiting.

"If you wish me to handle this case, you must submit to its court room presentation as I dictate, Mr. Jopling. I don't want to seem arbitrary. Let me say, more simply, that I am an expert. You are in need of my expert assistance. I am very adept at getting acquittals for people who are charged with crimes.

"You come to me for my expert assistance, just as you go to a doctor for his expert assistance when you want your appendix taken out. You don't tell him how to go about removing your appendix, do you, Mr. Jopling, in spite of the fact that you may have read up on the technique of appendectomies in textbooks? No, you do not. You put yourself at the surgeon's mercy—just as you are going to put yourself at my mercy—if you want to save yourself a short, disagreeable stroll to a piece of furniture containing in the neighborhood of thirty thousand volts."

"I will not go into court with a lot of faked evidence, if that is what you're trying to say," affirmed Teddy Jopling firmly.

"Never!" cried the lovely Marie.

"You can call a spade anything from an excavator to a steam shovel, if you wish," said Gillian. "I am simply giving you an expert's point of view."

"And I insist, Mr. Hazeltine, that I am going into court with the true, simple story. I know that the truth will find its way through all the ugly things the prosecution says. I do not need to lie to save myself—and I will not lie!"

"Never!" upheld the charming girl.

"Just what story is the one that will shine through the insults and implications and sworn statements of the prosecution with the light of holy truth?" Gillian ironically wanted to know.

"The story that I told on the night of the murder," exclaimed the dauntless prisoner. "I will not vary it by a hair."

Gillian stroked his nose and nodded thoughtfully.

"Supposing," he suggested, "that you had visited his house—"

"But I did not go near Ezra Klagg's house that night!"

"Well, let us suppose that you did. Let us suppose that there was a quarrel. Let us further stretch our imaginations to suppose that, in the course of the argument, toward the end of it, threats of physical violence were made—by Ezra Klagg."

"Such suppositions are utterly false!" cried Teddy Jopling.

"Utterly!" added his lovely wife.

"But let us presume, for sake of argument, that they are

not false. We presume, then, an argument ended by threats of physical violence which were, in turn, succeeded by Ezra Klagg reaching out for the loaded shotgun which stood in a corner near where he sat when found dead.

"He was a man who went about with that shotgun tucked under his arm all day long. Forewarned being fore-armed, you provided yourself with a loaded revolver purely for purposes of self-defense when you made your call—"

Teddy Jopling was slowly, emphatically wagging his head; so was Marie Jopling; but Gillian went earnestly on:

"—and we will further presume that he pointed that loaded shotgun at your head, maniacal with wrath—a condition into which a score of witnesses will honestly testify that he fell on the slightest provocation—"

"I did not kill Ezra Klagg!"

"My dear boy, but if you killed him in self-defense—"

"I did not kill him!"

"No!" cried Marie.

"I must tell you again," said Gillian patiently, "that your idealistic conception of justice must go down before the hard, practical facts if you wish to escape the electric chair. No twelve men in the world will believe your story. You disclaim all guilt. My proposition is to build in their minds a picture of the miserable, hot-headed wretch that Ezra Klagg actually was—so that the jury will heartily forgive you for having shot him down in self-defense."

"I did not shoot Ezra Klagg, and I will not let any one convey the impression that I did," said the stubborn young man.

"My dear boy, I admire your pertinacity, but the time comes when an attorney must enjoy the absolute confidence of his client. That time, I believe, has arrived. You say you did not kill Ezra Klagg. Your fine young wife says you did not kill Ezra Klagg. In union there is strength and so on. All very well and good. But, just between us, the lawyer and the client—what did you do with the pistol after you shot him? I mean, are you sure it is well hidden? Those damned things are so easily traced!"

"How dare you!" cried Marie Jopling.

"Look here," growled the man behind the grilled door, "if I were out of here, I'd knock your block off for saying that! Why, you're accusing me of murdering Ezra Klagg!"

Gillian was growing irritable.

"I am not the first," he said. "Nor will I be the last. I wonder, Mrs. Jopling, if you will excuse us for a moment?"

She hesitated, then, with dignity, withdrew, walking away down the corridor.

"Now," said Mr. Hazeltine, "let us get down to brass tacks, Jopling. The flag waving is all over. America is a glorious, free country where the innocent are rewarded and the guilty are consummately punished. Let us freely admit all that and go on to the very important question of how we are going to handle your defense in this case.

"I know that you are going to make an excellent witness. All that remains for us to do, to bring you in a verdict, is to decide on the story we are going to stick to through hell and high water. Stop glaring at me. Remember that I am interested only in making you a free man once more."

Teddy Jopling did not stop glaring at him. Instead, he only glared the harder, while the color almost entirely left his face and his blue eyes seemed to become bluer and bluer.

"Will you kindly call my wife back?" he asked.

"Certainly," Gillian obliged and went after her.

"Marie," said the prisoner to her in a deadly low voice when they had returned, "I want you to find a lawyer who has faith in my innocence. I have no desire to retain this shyster. Good day, Mr. Hazeltine!"

3

IT HAD BEEN a good many years since any one had dared call Gillian Hazeltine a shyster. They had frequently called him a rascal and a scoundrel and a crook, but no one had recently called him, at least to his face, a shyster, and for a moment his head spun with the vertigo of aroused fury.

But he did not let his feelings be known to this rude and arrogant young man. He bowed curtly and said in a low voice:

"I wish you the best of luck—you'll need more than one carload of it!" And started down the corridor.

He heard a low, momentary exchange of words behind him, which his fury made unintelligible, then the sharp tapping of small high heels on the floor.

Marie Jopling was beside him, breathless and pale.

"Mr. Hazeltine, I want one more word with you—"

He snapped: "I absolutely wash my hands of this whole matter!"

"But you'll at least let me walk back to your office with you."

Mr. Hazeltine said nothing, which she construed as an encouraging sign.

"I want you to handle my husband's case, Mr. Hazeltine. You are the greatest criminal lawyer in this State. I won't trust the case to any less experienced hands."

"I won't touch the case."

"I think you will," said Marie Jopling, "when I have finished talking."

Her assurance was so startling, in view of what had just passed, that Gillian flashed an angrily surprised glance down at her. Her great dark eyes were aglow with purpose.

"In the first place," he said irascibly, "I will not take a case into court that is certain to be lost—certainly not, under the present circumstances."

"By the present circumstances," she picked him up, "you are referring to your fee, are you not?"

"Partly that," Gillian admitted. "I will not deal with a client who is not amenable to reason. Your husband is deliberately walking into the electric chair. I take great pride in the fact that the great majority of the cases I take into court are acquitted. I cannot afford the black mark of a conviction in a case so obviously open and shut as this one."

"You mean, from your point of view, he hasn't a chance to escape the electric chair?"

Gillian nodded.

"But we have the utmost faith that his innocence will spare him that awful fate."

"Your faith is in for a jolt," growled Gillian.

They emerged from the jail and started walking along Elm Street toward the office building where Gillian conducted his affairs.

"How much," Marie Jopling wanted to know, "would you have charged us if you had taken our case and handled it in your way?"

"I would have let you off easy," admitted Gillian, wondering what she was now driving at. "The case appealed to me. I would have let you off for five thousand dollars."

She walked beside him for a few seconds in silence.

"How much, Mr. Hazeltine, would you charge to handle the case as we want it to be handled?"

Gillian carelessly answered: "I wouldn't touch it for less than fifty thousand dollars. It would be worth that much to go into court and let Adelbert Yistle make a monkey out of me. Yes; my pride is worth fifty thousand dollars."

Marie Jopling said quietly: "I will give you fifty thousand dollars for handling the ease as we want it to be handled."

Gillian stopped in his tracks and glared at her.

"If it isn't impertinent, Mrs. Jopling, where are you going to lay your hands on that much money?"

"My father," the girl answered, "is a very rich man. Teddy has never permitted me to accept money from him; he would not even permit me to bring him a dot; it was his wish that we make our way without help—and we have. But in this crisis I will cable my father without even consulting Teddy. I will have fifty thousand dollars in your hands as soon as a cable can reach France and an answer will be received. I will come to you with the money, Mr. Hazeltine."

"I will take your money without a qualm," said Gillian, "but I wish you would tell me—truthfully, Mrs. Jopling, truthfully—just why, if you have such implicit confidence that your husband's story in court will acquit him—do you want to pay me the exorbitant fee of fifty thousand dollars, when a cheaper lawyer—yes, even a law student fresh from his books—could obtain the identical results that I can obtain."

"Because," was Marie Jopling's quick answer, "I have the utmost faith in your ability."

"That," demurred the lawyer, "is, *in petto,* a qualified answer. I am noted for so many different kinds of ability. If you are referring to my ability to sway a jury, let me disillusion you now, Mrs. Jopling. The story your husband is determined to tell on the witness stand would nullify the oratorical ability of an Alexander Hamilton. And I trust, sincerely, that you are not referring to the brutal and baseless accusations of my enemies."

The girl with the quick mind seemed confused.

"You know, no doubt," he elucidated, "that I have been accused of bribing judges and buying juries. I hope you have not put credence in those lying tales."

"I had not even heard them," said Marie Jopling.

"You infer then, that you are betting fifty thousand dollars on your childlike faith in my record as a criminal lawyer?"

Marie Jopling gave him a swimming, oblique glance. It said much. It said nothing. It was an admission of her agreement that they had reached some subtle, sophisticated understanding; it was her assent to his unvoiced suggestion that they had become partners in collusion.

Or it was merely a ray of her holy faith in the innocence of her husband. It was anything the recipient wished it, or construed it, to be.

And it may be that at about this juncture the *actual* mystery attached to the murder of Ezra Klagg entered. That is only a supposition, without much to go on.

We may assume that Marie Jopling was a young woman of great and simple faith; we may also assume that she was no fool. But we must assume that she loved her husband ardently and would go to what lengths to save his life.

"To what lengths" implies a recourse to any expedient. Well, it is hard to know just where to draw the line. A woman with a clever brain who is ardently in love can, in this situation, provide plenty of food for speculation.

And no end of speculation can be based on Gillian Hazeltine's acceptance of the fifty thousand dollars, which Marie Jopling brought to his office in the form of a packet of new thousand-dollar bills on a later day. We can wonder whether or not Gillian Hazeltine accepted that small fortune without a twinge of conscience, knowing full well that, as matters stood, his greatest oratory could not save Ted Jopling from the chair.

We can wonder whether or not he had a hand in the amazing development which occurred in the course of the trial. And we can only wonder.

It is not likely that we will ever know. Perhaps the mystery at no point touched either Marie Jopling or Gillian Hazeltine. Taking into consideration the position in which the girl was placed and the methods for which Gillian was famous—or infamous—we can only wonder and speculate and suspect. And the human mind when it leaves facts behind to soar in the airy realms of conjecture is so apt to be led astray!

4

THE OFFICES OF Mr. Yistle, the prosecuting attorney, were emanating a murmur of activity reminiscent of beehives in August. Witnesses were coming and going, detectives were coming and going, and as each came and went the pile of evidence that would crush Theodore Jopling grew higher and higher.

"We have made the mistake in the past," Mr. Yistle, the district attorney, was saying to his assistant, "of having too clean cut a case against the murderers Gillian Hazeltine has defended. A case that is too clean cut is, by its very completeness, often distasteful to a jury, who, being human, like to supply a few details from their own imaginations. That is simply sound court room psychology."

"I absolutely agree with you," asserted his assistant.

Mr. Yistle's assistant was an eager, nervous, thin young man who rejoiced in the name of Bullock. No matter how great the crisis, Mr. Bullock could always be depended on to say yes in a ringing voice.

He had perfected the technique of the yes-man to an extent where he could, with little effort, now say yes in upward of thirty different ways. As such, he was invaluable to Mr. Yistle, who liked to work along positive lines— possibly because his was a negative nature.

Any proposition he put to Mr. Bullock was always

greeted with a hearty affirmative. Given a little time, Mr. Bullock always proceeded to embroider his affirmatives.

But in the present instance there was no time.

"There seems to be some mystery," Mr. Yistle went on, "as to the whereabouts of the revolver Jopling used. I have had seven of the best detectives on the police force combing the countryside for that revolver, Mr. Bullock. Possibly we can get along without it, but it would strengthen our case immeasurably if we had it in our possession.

"Aside from the legal aspects, there is no evidence half so weighty as the weapon with which the crime was committed. I am firmly convinced that if the sash weight with which Gray and the Snyder woman killed Albert Snyder had been disposed of in such a way that the prosecution could not find it, that the case against them would have been tremendously weakened."

"Quite so," yessed Mr. Bullock. "I have thought of that, too. In fact, it had occurred to me—"

"The *corpus delicti* is, of course, indispensable in a murder case," went on the prosecuting attorney. "But next to the *corpus delicti,* the most important piece of evidence is the weapon with which the crime was committed. It exercises, in the court room, a powerful effect upon the jury. Well, in short, Mr. Bullock, we must find the revolver with which Ted Jopling shot Ezra Klagg."

"It will be found!" cried Mr. Bullock.

He was always saying dramatic things like that.

But as the day of the trial drew nearer and nearer, that important link in the evidence against Theodore Jopling was still unfound. Detectives, acting under the eager direction of Mr. Bullock, literally left no stone unturned.

They went through the fields and the barns, on the Klagg farm and on the Jopling farm. They went so far as to try to pry up boards in attics and to remove bricks in cellars. But to no avail. The revolver was still undiscovered on the day the trial opened.

The impaneling of the jury was done in a perfunctory manner. And it was evident that neither Mr. Hazeltine nor Mr. Yistle attached much importance to the character of the jurors.

It was a newspaper reporter who made the discovery, when twelve good men and true had finally been selected, that all twelve men enjoyed one trait in common; rather they looked as if they enjoyed one trait in common. They looked imaginative.

Perhaps for the first time since they had been engaging in court room tilts, the two enemies wanted the same kind of jury. Later, Mr. Yistle admitted that he wanted a jury with enough imagination to see Teddy Jopling committing that murder as it was sketched before their eyes by witnesses and himself; later, Mr. Hazeltine admitted that he had wanted a jury with enough imagination to see Teddy Jopling doing anything in the world but killing Ezra Klagg.

Gillian Hazeltine entered a plea of not guilty for the defendant, and the trial began.

Mr. Yistle, in his opening speech, stated that he would prove beyond a reasonable doubt that Teddy Jopling was the fiend who had "brought to the doors of death this upright, kindly gentleman.

"For," he went on as he faced the jury, "it is essential that you be convinced beyond a reasonable doubt that Theodore

Jopling did kill that defenseless old man. Killed him in a fit of fury insanely inspired by revenge. Killed him after cold-blooded deliberation by shooting him through the heart as he sat there in his chair. Killed him in such a manner, after such premeditation, that in only one way can you, gentlemen, expiate that wrong: by bringing in a verdict of guilty of murder in the first degree."

5

MR. YISTLE PLACED old Dr. Fletcher on the stand as his first witness.

Dr. Fletcher told the jury in simple, straightforward language of how he had been taken to Ezra Klagg's house by Tom Howard; how he had examined the body, and ascertained that Ezra Klagg had been killed some time between the hours of seven thirty and nine.

"How far away would you say that the murderer was standing when he fired the shot that killed Ezra Klagg?" Mr. Yistle wanted to know.

"He was standing at a greater distance than ten or twelve feet," Dr. Fletcher answered.

"How could you tell?"

"Because I examined the clothing adjacent to the bullet hole, and it was not singed or burned."

"Would it be your opinion, based upon the position of the body and upon the fact that the clothing adjacent to the bullet hole was not singed or burned, that there had been no hand-to-hand fighting which might have prompted the firing of a revolver at close quarters?"

"I object to that question as leading," interposed Gillian Hazeltine promptly.

"The objection is overruled," said Judge Manning.

"Exception!" snapped Gillian.

The judge nodded to Mr. Yistle and said: "The witness will answer the question."

"I should say," answered Dr. Fleming, "that there had been no hand-to-hand fighting."

"That will be all," said the prosecution.

"Cross-examination waived," said Gillian.

"Next witness!" cried a bailiff.

The next witness was Tom Howard. He took the stand and stated, in response to Mr. Yistle's questions, that he was forty-two years of age, a farmer by occupation, and that his nearest neighbor was—or had been—Ezra Klagg.

Then he recounted the incidents of the night of the murder; how he had dropped in to see Ezra Klagg and found him dead; how he had then gone to fetch a constable and Dr. Fletcher. He was an intelligent-looking man, with the red, seamed face which men who wrest their living from the soil often acquire.

Gillian Hazeltine asked him three questions in cross-examination.

"Mr. Howard," he said, "on the night of the murder, when you dropped in to see Ezra Klagg to ascertain whether or not he would vote for the road tax issue, why did you not drop in on the defendant? Is he not also a voter?"

"I had already talked to him about it," was Tom Howard's answer. "In fact, it was Ted Jopling who suggested that I speak to Ezra Klagg."

"When did the defendant make that suggestion?"

"A day or two previous."

"Not the day of the murder?"

"No, sir; not the day of the murder."

"That will be all."

Mr. Yistle now introduced the witnesses by whose testimony he confidently expected to send Ted Jopling to the electric chair. There were seven of them, all men prominent in business of one kind or another in Bolivar.

Each in turn testified that he had heard Ted Jopling making threats. Silas Winters said he had heard him say: "I'm going to get even with that old skunk if I hang for it." Jim Prentice had heard him say: "A man like that doesn't deserve to live." John Jacobs had heard him say: "The day I attend Ezra Klagg's funeral will be the happiest day in my life."

But the testimony of Ebenezer Hoag was the most damaging of all. He was the Bolivar postmaster, and he repeated with fidelity the threats Ted Jopling had made in the post office the afternoon of the murder.

Ted Jopling had come into the post office, fuming over Ezra Klagg's effrontery in moving over the fence.

"I'm going to teach that old snake not to trespass on my property," Ted had said. "I'm going to hit him on the head with a crowbar. Then I'm going to chop him up into little pieces. And after that I'm going to go down there and shoot him every morning for a month."

"Those threats were, obviously, exaggerations," said Mr. Yistle. "What other threats did he make?"

"He said he was going to get even with Ezra Klagg if it was the last act he did on earth," answered the Bolivar postmaster.

"That will be all," said Mr. Yistle. "My distinguished colleague may take the witness."

Gillian Hazeltine apparently had little more interest in

this witness than in the preceding ones. His cross-examination was very short.

"How long have you known the defendant, Mr. Hoag?"

"About seven years," answered the postmaster.

"Did you ever see him give any exhibitions of hot-head-
edness?"

"No, sir. I don't recollect any."

"Did you ever see him engage in a fist fight?"

"No, sir; I never did."

Mr. Hoag was apparently anxious to please Mr. Hazeltine. His manner was warmer; with Mr. Yistle he had
seemed uneasy and guilty. In fact, no witness had given
his testimony as if he had enjoyed doing so.

Involuntarily, they created the impression that it seemed
a shame that Ted Jopling was on trial for this crime; that
they liked him; that they were only here because it was
their duty or unavoidable.

And Mr. Hazeltine's purpose seemed to be merely to
keep them in that frame of mind. He did not try to upset
their statements; did not bully them; did not even try to
confuse them. His only object seemed to be to create in
the minds of the jury the impression that Ted Jopling was
a fine young fellow.

Teddy Jopling, his fair hair shining like an aura in the
dusty, dark court room, sat at the table with Gillian and
fixed his clear, blue eyes, unafraid, upon witness after
witness.

The newspapers seemed undecided whether to ascribe
his attitude to the shining qualities of his innocence or to
the most brazen audacity that had ever been witnessed in a

court room. His air was that of an innocent man absolutely confident of an acquittal.

Marie Jopling sat, day after day, in the first row of spectators, as close to him as the law allowed. Her face likewise shone. By now, the dark little beauty who sat in the same place day after day was known as Ted Jopling's wife. Never, in the face of the most damaging testimony, did her confidence falter.

It was interesting to watch the jury as the trial went along. Ted Jopling went into the court room presumptively innocent. Generally, that phrase is a hollow one, but in this case it seemed literally true.

Ted Jopling did look innocent. The jury, looking at him and at his wife, reflected in their faces that he was innocent; their expressions seemed to say that it would take a great deal of testimony to convince them that he wasn't.

And, day by day, you saw this reflection of the prisoner's innocence replaced by another look. The jury glanced less frequently at the prisoner and his beautiful young wife, and toward the end they glanced at Ted and Marie Jopling hardly at all, or with the most furtive sidewise glances. They hated to look at this young couple; they had sworn to do their duty, and their duty was beginning to look only too plain.

Yes; Mr. Yistle, with Mr. Bullock's help, had built up a case. Every scrap of it was, so far, circumstantial; no one had actually seen Ted Jopling kill Ezra Klagg; and the revolver—that most vital piece of material evidence—had not yet been found. Yet there could be no doubt in any one's mind but that Ted Jopling was the man who had brought Ezra Klagg's life to a sudden end.

Mr. Yistle kept witnesses going into and out of the witness chair steadily for four days. He then rested his case.

He was curious to know what Gillian's defense would be. He knew how tricky Gillian was; yet he could not conjure up in his own imagination any trick of Gillian's that would free Ted Jopling.

Secret information will leak out now and then from the best of regulated law offices, and when Mr. Yistle heard the rumor, from a reliable source, that Gillian had been paid fifty thousand dollars to handle the case, he promptly concluded that Gillian had simply taken a losing case for the fat fee.

He was further convinced of this when Gillian calmly informed the jury that he would put but one witness on the stand—the defendant!

6

NOT ONE JUROR looked squarely at Ted Jopling as he took the stand. They averted their faces. They looked elsewhere.

Plainly by their actions did they indicate that, much as they disliked doing so, they could not believe the earnest lies that this very blond, blue-eyed young man was about to utter.

The eyes of the court room flittered from Gillian to the prisoner, to his wife. Gillian was known to be full of tricks. He had freed more than one man in a tighter corner than this by thrilling tricks. And to a layman it seemed easy.

The sympathy of every one was with this handsome, confident young man in the witness chair. All Gillian had to do was to establish in the minds of the jury a doubt—a *little* doubt. How would Gillian go about it?

Gillian's first question, fell with crisp clearness upon the silence of the room.

"Will you please tell the jury just what you did on the night of June 6?"

Ted Jopling, in his rich, deep voice, began telling the story with which the judge, the jury, the entire court room were now so familiar. He told of walking along High Rocks Road with the intention of calling on Ezra Klagg; of changing his mind, and of going on down to Tom Howard's.

From beginning to end it was the same story. Not by a single word did he vary it from the story he had told on the night of the murder.

The court room was filled with an uneasy hush. No one believed that story. Not one spectator in the room believed it. Certainly the jury could not be expected to believe it.

That deep, clear, untroubled voice was slowly drawing before all eyes a picture of a blond, appealing young man seated in an electric chair.

The court room was warm and stuffy. Through the north windows behind Judge Manning the spotless blue sky could be seen, and the green foliage of a maple tree.

It lacked a few minutes of noon when Ted Jopling concluded his recital, and Gillian put the final questions to him. There would be a recess, and after the recess Mr. Yistle would take the witness for cross-examination. By to-morrow noon, Ted Jopling would know that he was going to be electrocuted.

"No, sir; I did not go near Mr. Klagg's house that evening."

Marie Jopling was leaning forward eagerly. Her lips moved as he talked, as if she were reasserting every word he uttered. How sublime her faith! And how tragic!

Gillian Hazeltine frowned and slowly paced to and fro with his hands knotted behind him, pausing now and then to put a question to the man on the stand. The State's attorney and his assistant conferred in whispers.

On their faces was triumph. At last—at long last—they were winning a case over the famous, the foxy Gillian Hazeltine!

"When you heard that shot, what did you do?"

"I thought Mr. Klagg was probably shooting a quail in his side yard. I really didn't think much about it. I simply walked on along home."

The drone of a fly buzzing against a window pane filled the tense quiet of the court room. Some one coughed.

Then heads began to turn, and a ripple of excitement ran through the spectators.

Two strange-looking men were walking up the middle aisle. Both had the appearance of tramps. The clothing of both was dusty and torn. Both were sweating. Both were badly in need of shaves and baths and haircuts. Both were gaunt and weary, indeed, both limped.

The one who led the way was perhaps twenty-eight or thirty. He had flashing, red-stained blue eyes and thick curly molasses hair. The man behind was older, perhaps thirty-five or six or seven. His hair was black and straight and matted. His eyes were black.

Straight up to the oak railing the two men limped. A bailiff stepped over to stop them, but something in the grimness of their bearing, some intense drama in their expressions, caused him to stand aside.

The court room now began to buzz with excitement. It was seen that the hands of the man who led the way were tied behind his back with rope.

A bailiff banged with a gavel for silence, and silence promptly obtained.

Ted Jopling had half arisen from the witness chair, his hands clutching the arms. Marie Jopling was likewise straining forward, one hand caught to her mouth.

"Warren Dimplo!" some one gasped.

And the name went from mouth to mouth.

Warren Dimplo! Through that sweat and caked dust, through the growth of stubble, they recognized the man with the roped hands as Warren Dimplo. His companion they did not know.

It was he who first broke the heavy silence of the court room. He pushed Warren Dimplo forward a step toward Judge Manning.

In a dry, harsh voice, a croak, he said: "I want this man to take the witness stand and tell you all he knows about the murder of Ezra Klagg!"

7

MR. YISTLE AND Mr. Bullock were already on their feet. Judge Manning was bending forward, frowning.

"This is very irregular," he said.

"I can't help it, your honor," panted the unknown man. "I've been trailin' this fellow through the woods ever since Klagg was shot. I want him to get up on the stand and testify. It's a crime to let that young fellow you've got there go to the chair."

Mr. Yistle broke in: "What is the nature of the testimony he wishes to give?"

"He killed Ezra Klagg, and he wants to confess it!" rasped the mysterious stranger.

Marie Jopling had leaped to her feet. Now she raced across the little space to the witness chair, where Ted Jopling had slumped. She caught his pale face in her hands and kissed him again and again.

The court room roared. A bailiff shouted for order. Judge Manning seemed bewildered. So did Mr, Yistle. So did Mr. Bullock.

And so, for that matter, did Gillian Hazeltine. But it was Gillian who immediately pressed, once order was restored, to place each of the strange witnesses on the stand.

Mr. Yistle promptly objected. He suspected trickery. He said so. Mr. Bullock confirmed him.

"It is absolutely irregular!" cried Mr. Yistle. "These men are a couple of tramps."

"That's a lie!" shouted Ebenezer Hoag, the Bolivar postmaster. "Warren Dimplo is one of the best farmers around Bolivar. Let him have his say."

Bailiffs attempted to straighten out the tangle. Ted Jopling was escorted back to his chair at the defense table. Marie Jopling was shooed back to her place in the first row of spectators.

Mr. Yistle continued strenuously to object when the pale, haggard, dusty Warren Dimplo limped to the witness stand and defiantly faced the court room.

Judge Manning made no ruling until Gillian spoke.

"It is certainly true, your honor," said Gillian, "that the advent of these two witnesses at such a critical moment is unprecedented—"

"It's one of your dirty, low-handed tricks!" shouted Mr. Yistle.

"That's what it is!" confirmed his faithful yes-man.

Gillian seemed amazed and hurt.

"One of my tricks?" he repeated. "Mr. Yistle, I am even more astonished at this unlooked-for turn of events than you are. Both of these men are total strangers to me. Before we make any decision in the matter, it seems only fair to me that we listen to their stories. As far as I know, both may be madmen."

"Your honor," cried Mr. Yistle, "I make a motion for mistrial!"

Judge Manning looked at him thoughtfully.

"Decision must be reserved until these two men have said what they wish to say. You may object later to their testimony, Mr. Yistle, after it has been rendered or as it proceeds, on such grounds as you may put forward. I myself will examine the witness, although presumptively he would be, in the nature of things, Mr. Hazeltine's witness."

He addressed the disheveled, defiant young man in the witness chair.

"What is your name?"

"Warren Dimplo."

"What is your age?"

"Twenty-nine."

"Do you swear to tell the truth, the whole truth, and nothing but the truth? Please raise your right hand. Do you so swear?"

"Yes—I do!"

"You are aware, of course, that you are about to give testimony in the case of the People vs. Theodore Jopling, who is on trial in this court, charged with the murder of Ezra Klagg?"

"Yes, I know all that. I'm here to tell the truth, and I'm going to tell the truth. I killed—"

"One moment, Mr. Dimplo," Judge Manning interrupted. "Before you make any statement of confession, as you are evidently desirous of doing, let me give you a warning. The circumstances attached to your appearance here are, to say the best for them, exceedingly curious. Let me warn you that I deal severely with perjurers."

"I am not a perjurer. I want to tell the truth!" cried Warren Dimplo. "I killed Ezra Klagg! That fellow—his name is Jason Greer—has the pistol with which I shot him. You've got experts who can tell whether a bullet came from a certain pistol or not, haven't you?"

Mr. Yistle answered his question. Mr. Yistle was pale and uncertain. Perhaps he was being swept away by the unconscious dramatic power of the unkempt young man on the stand.

"The bullet and the pistol can be examined by Dr. Whitely this afternoon," he said. "Dr. Whitely is at his laboratory."

The court room gasped as the strange man—Jason Greer—flashed from his pocket a blue revolver. He handed it butt foremost to Mr. Yistle, who accepted it.

"That is the gun," went on the grim young man on the stand, "with which I shot Ezra Klagg."

Teddy Jopling was staring at him. Marie Jopling was gnawing her fingernails.

Warren Dimplo brushed a lock of molasses hair from his eyes. It fell back across them. Again, impatiently, he brushed it away. The court room gasped. His every gesture seemed pregnant with some awful significance. Rapidly he began:

"I went down to Ezra Klagg's house that night—the night of June 6—to have a talk with him. I own land adjoining his on the north. A year ago I bought a ten-acre meadow from him, and he gave me a title to it that wasn't clear. That's why he sold it. I never bothered to have the title searched until a few days before—before I killed him, and then I found the title was no good, and I went up there to have it out with him.

"We had a pretty hot argument. I don't remember all we said. But we both kept getting hotter and hotter. Finally he reached for his shotgun and I reached for my gun—in my hip pocket. I shot him. That's all."

Mr. Yistle promptly objected.

"I object to Mr. Dimplo's entire testimony and ask that it be stricken from the record."

"On what grounds?" asked Judge Manning.

"There is a statute in this State, which I know exists and the exact reference to which I shall secure later, which provides that evidence must be produced to support a confession of crime. This man Dimplo—"

"That's just what I'm going to produce," barked the man named Jason Greer. "I saw him shoot Ezra Klagg. I was just comin' up the path from the road and saw it through the door. I saw him run as soon as he saw me. Ever since then I've been trailin' him through the hills. Last night I caught up with him!"

Judge Manning turned to the jury.

"Gentlemen," he said, "I must warn you that, in this amazing development, we must act without precedent. We are venturing, legally, upon unknown ground. I ask you to bear in mind that, while this testimony is being taken, it may be stricken from the record. You must weigh such facts as are proved with the most careful judgment."

"I move that the jury retire until the status of these two witnesses is established!" shouted Mr. Yistle.

"Objection!" snapped Gillian. "No evidence has yet been introduced tending to prove that these men are not properly qualified to testify. If they come in the nature of a surprise that is, of course, unfortunate. In fairness to the defendant, I move that the jury remain to hear what these witnesses have to say."

"I am constrained to uphold Mr. Hazeltine's objection," ruled the court.

"Exception!" muttered Mr. Yistle.

"Exception is noted," growled Judge Manning, who was beginning to lose his temper. He turned sharply to Warren Dimplo, who still occupied the witness chair.

"Have you said all you wish to say?"

"I haven't given any details," answered the confessed murderer of Ezra Klagg. "I'll answer any questions."

Judge Manning looked at Mr. Yistle.

"Have you any questions, Mr. Yistle?"

"Your honor, I object to this entire line of testimony."

"On what grounds, Mr. Yistle?"

"On the grounds that testimony taken under these conditions is entirely without precedent. I am convinced that Gillian Hazeltine is trying to railroad this case through—"

"Objection is overruled," said Judge Manning. "There is no evidence to uphold your contention. Mr. Hazeltine, have you any questions—"

"Then I move for a mistrial!" snapped Mr. Yistle. "On the grounds that the defense which will now be put forward diverges radically from that which was announced."

"I beg to point out to my distinguished colleague," snorted Gillian, "that the defense has announced no divergence in policy! This utterly unexpected development leaves me as much at sea as it does yourself, Mr. Yistle."

"You're a liar!" shouted Mr. Yistle.

"I must beg you, Mr. Yistle," roared Judge Manning, "to moderate your speech. You are obstructing this trial, Mr. Yistle. Your motion for mistrial is denied. Now, Mr. Hazeltine, if you wish to question this witness, will you do so?"

Mr. Yistle sank into his chair, puffing. He mopped his

white, glistening forehead with a large handkerchief and fell into whispered expostulations which Mr. Bullock eagerly affirmed.

"I have only one question to ask Mr. Dimplo," said Gillian. "Did you, while you were quarreling with the deceased, observe the defendant, Jopling, pass by the house as he has alleged?"

"The road cannot be seen from the porch," was Warren Dimplo's answer. "There is a sort of screen formed by poplars which run along inside the picket fence which parallels the road. No, sir; I saw nothing of Ted Jopling that evening."

"When was the last time you saw him?"

"It was about noon, that same day. I was in the post office at Bolivar getting my mail when he came in and told several of us about the trouble he was having with old man Klagg over their boundaries. I got mad about that. Klagg was nothing but a weasel. I am not sorry that I killed him. The only thing I am sorry about is that I put Ted Jopling to all this trouble. He is a good friend of mine."

Mr. Hazeltine: "Did you know that he had been charged with the murder?"

Dimplo: "No, sir; I did not."

Mr. Hazeltine: "You have been in hiding since?"

Dimplo: "Yes, sir."

Mr. Hazeltine: "That will be all."

Mr. Yistle: "I object to every line of that man's testimony."

The Court: "Overruled."

8

——

JUDGE MANNING INSTRUCTED a bailiff to remove the cords from Warren Dimplo's wrists. The bailiff did so. It was now Judge Manning's difficult task to decide upon Warren Dimplo's status. Was he a material witness?

Mr. Yistle solved the question.

"I move that the court issue a bench warrant for the arrest of Warren Dimplo on a—a charge of suspicion."

Judge Manning approved of this motion. The warrant was issued and Warren Dimplo, with a sheriff on either side, was taken through the corridor into the Greenville jail.

Jason Greer was now instructed to take the stand. He acceded with an air of eagerness and mechanically raised his hand to be sworn.

Mr. Yistle arose and began to pace up and down beside his table. He looked profoundly worried. From time to time he shot suspicious glances at Gillian Hazeltine, who remained seated beside Ted Jopling.

Gillian's air was one of childlike innocence; he appeared to be still bewildered and a little shocked by the turn events had taken.

"What is your full name?" Judge Manning asked.

"Jason Ezra Greer," answered the harsh voice.

The court room gasped. Ezra!

"What is your age?"

"Thirty-seven, your honor."

"What is your residence?"

"Detroit, Michigan."

"Will you tell the jury what you know of the murder of Ezra Klagg?"

"Yes, your honor. Ezra Klagg was my uncle. He was my mother's brother. I had not seen my uncle since my mother's death, about a year ago, and I had obtained a leave of absence from the Ford factory, where I was employed, to pay him a visit and tell him of my mother's last days. I walked across the fields from the Bolivar railroad station to my uncle's farm, and as I was going up the walk from the road I heard angry voices.

"I just saw this man Dimplo raise his arm and discharge a revolver in his hand as I was halfway up the walk. I ran in and found my uncle dead. Dimplo ran out through the kitchen and into the wheat field in back. I would have caught him then, but I tripped on a loose board on the back steps and fell and shook myself up pretty badly. When I got to my feet he was gone.

"I followed the path he had broken through the wheat. He was heading for the range of hills up toward the north—I don't know their name. I have been following him ever since. Last night I found him. Some farmer gave us a ride back to town."

The witness stopped. Judge Manning looked questioningly at Mr. Yistle. The State's attorney had paused in his nervous pacing. He now walked slowly toward Jason Greer and glared at him.

"You say you are Ezra Klagg's nephew?"

"Yes, sir; I am."

"Can you prove it?" Mr. Yistle snapped.

"Why, yes, sir; I have some letters here from him to my mother and from him to me."

"Let me see them," rasped Mr. Yistle.

Greer produced a small bundle of letters, dark from his pocket.

"I want to read these," said Mr. Yistle darkly.

"You may take your time," Judge Manning obliged him.

Mr. Yistle read each letter. Gillian, in turn, read them as Mr. Yistle finished. Gillian handed them, in this fashion to Judge Manning, who gave them to a bailiff who, in turn, passed them along to the jury.

A half hour was consumed in reading the letters. The noon recess was long since forgotten.

When the letter reading was concluded, Mr. Yistle growled:

"It is a question in my mind whether those letters are genuine or not."

"It seems to me," put in Gillian, "that the jury are intelligent enough to decide that point with the others."

"This jury," snarled Mr. Yistle, "are going to decide nothing. You can't get away with this, Hazeltine. Your honor, I renew my previous motion for a mistrial, on the grounds that the defense has departed radically from its announced plan and left the people high and dry without sufficient time—"

"Your honor," promptly interjected Gillian, "I must insist that you instruct my honorable adversary to refrain from his constant reflections upon my integrity. I am quite as dumfounded by the appearance of these two witnesses as is your honor and Mr. Yistle. Simply because what the jury may, at their discretion, decide has been a fortunate accident in favor of the accused is no reason why a mistrial should be ruled. Both witnesses are credible. Both have proved their credibility."

"I refuse to permit this case to go to the jury in its unfinished state!" shouted Mr. Yistle.

Judge Manning leaned forward. "Mr. Yistle, I must again instruct you not to arrogate to yourself the discretionary powers which are resident solely in this court. If you wish to produce fresh witnesses, produce them. Otherwise, this trial will go forward. You will begin your summation after recess, Mr. Yistle."

"I respectfully except," groaned Mr. Yistle.

"Exception and objection noted, Mr. Yistle. Gentlemen of the jury, we are about to take a recess until two thirty o'clock this afternoon. The court admonishes you not to speak about this case among yourselves or permit any one to speak to you about it. You will keep your minds open until the case is finally submitted to you. The defendant will retire."

Gillian strolled over to the wrathful Mr. Yistle.

"What are you going to do about Professor Whitely?" he wanted to know.

"You can do what you damned please about it!" snarled Mr. Yistle. "This case is not going to that jury—you dirty crook!"

"Sometimes, Adelbert," said Gillian pleasantly, "I think your mind works very, very slowly its wonders to perform."

Gillian consulted the judge, and from him obtained permission for Professor Whitely, the firearms expert, to compare the bullet which killed Ezra Klagg with the revolver which Warren Dimplo claimed had fired it. Mr. Yistle now strenuously objected to this proceeding.

But Judge Manning firmly denied him. He himself, he said, would take the bullet and the revolver to Professor Whitely.

9

PROFESSOR HAWTHORNE J. WHITELY was the first
and only witness of that exciting afternoon. He was a wisp
of a man, white-bearded and almost completely bald. He
wore gold-rimmed spectacles and spoke with slow, metic-
ulous care.

Judge Manning interrogated him.

Yes, answered Professor Whitely, he had made a careful examination of the bullet and of the revolver and was
prepared on his oath to state what relation existed, if any,
between the two.

The interrogations and responses follow:

The Court: "Will you tell the jury, professor, what result
you arrived at after a careful examination of the bullet and
the revolver?"

Professor Whitely: "I will, gladly, your honor."

The Court: "You may proceed, professor."

Professor Whitely: "There is absolutely no question in
this case. Sometimes the condition of a bullet makes it
difficult to compare the rifling on it with the rifling of a
gun barrel from which it may or may not have issued. But
in this case, the bullet was intact. It had entered, I believe,
after passing through the body of Ezra Klagg, a mattress.
It was hardly scratched.

"I should perhaps say that, to students of ballistics,

such as I am, every pistol and every rifle is found to have as distinct a personality as every man. Every one of ten thousand rifles of the same caliber turned out by the same factory will be different, in some slight respect, from every other. This difference is found in its rifling. By means of photography or an enlarging reflectoscope, it is possible to establish beyond any doubt whether or not a certain bullet has been fired from a certain firearm. In this case, there is no shadow of a question. This bullet was fired from this revolver!"

The court room hummed. Professor Whitely, by proving that the bullet that had killed Ezra Klagg had been fired by the pistol possessed by Warren Dimplo, had clearly established Ted Jopling's innocence.

Mr. Yistle was on his feet, again demanding that a retrial be ruled, before Judge Manning could frame his next question.

"I insist that a retrial is mandatory, on the grounds that the defense departed from its announced plan."

"Your honor," Gillian at once took him up, "the time has come to consider the charge that Mr. Yistle has repeatedly made. I wish to recall to Mr. Yistle's attention the original statement of the defense. I claimed that Ted Jopling was an innocent man. I said, in so many words, that the jury would discover this for themselves. I did not say how they would discover it for themselves. I will admit that I did not anticipate the happy miracle that has taken place."

"Rhetoric!" snorted Mr. Yistle. "Your honor, I again insist that a mistrial be ruled."

"I cannot grant your request," ruled Judge Manning. "If neither you nor Mr. Hazeltine wishes to examine Professor

Whitely, you may proceed with your respective summations."

"Summation waived," growled Mr. Yistle.

"I am not prepared for summation," said Gillian. "I, likewise, have been rendered almost speechless by to-day's developments. All I can say to you, gentlemen of the jury, is that my client's case is clearly established. He, obviously, is not the man who killed Ezra Klagg. It is proved by confession corroborated by credible testimony, all of which has been clinched by Professor Whitely's identification of the revolver and the bullet."

"I will say only this," said Judge Manning in his charge to the jury. "Regardless of the connection which Professor Whitely has established between the bullet and the revolver, you must be thoroughly convinced that the testimony of Jason Greer is reliable. On his credibility as a witness depends the worth—or the worthlessness—of Warren Dimplo's confession. Is Jason Greer the deceased's actual nephew? And does this combined testimony remove from your mind all reasonable doubt as to the guilt of the accused?"

He then explained the legal definition of "reasonable doubt" and the jury retired. They returned within ten minutes with their verdict:

Theodore Jopling was not guilty of the crime as charged.

Every last edition of every evening paper carried photographs of the handsome blond young farmer and his beautiful brunette wife clasped in each other's arms.

The same papers carried the news that Warren Dimplo was being held without bail for the grand jury, charged with the murder of Ezra Klagg.

Mr. Yistle telephoned Gillian Hazeltine at the latter's home that evening.

"I hear Dimplo has retained you to defend him," said the irate prosecutor.

"Your hearing is pretty good," Gillian complimented him.

"I think you are a crook and a liar," snarled Mr. Yistle. "I think this whole thing is a put-up job. I'm giving you fair warning, Hazeltine. I'm putting every detective in the city on this case—and before I'm through, I'm going to prove that you framed it up. I'm going to disbar you. I'm going to make you a laughing stock!"

"Go to it," Gillian cordially urged him.

"And if you think you're going to pull any trick to get Dimplo off, you're mistaken!"

"From the way things look," Gillian agreed, "Dimplo is guilty as hell."

"I'll bet you one thousand dollars," raged Mr. Yistle, "that I send him to the electric chair!"

"You're on," said Gillian. "We'll each put a thousand in escrow at the First National. If Dimplo burns, you get it all. If I get him off, I get it all."

"Another thousand says I'll have you disbarred before that trial is over!" shouted the State's attorney.

"I'll meet you at the First National with the money to-morrow at eleven," agreed Gillian.

Somehow the newspapers got wind of these wagers and printed a first page story concerning them and the new defendant.

Warren Dimplo, so zealous reporters had ascertained, was, in every respect, as fine a young man as was Teddy

Jopling. He was, they unearthed, a peaceable, industrious young farmer, with a reputation for minding his own business and letting other people's alone.

The son of a splendid old American family, he was a graduate of the Cornell Agricultural School and, by scientific methods, had made his farm one of the most successful in the county. It was little short of a showplace.

Reporters also uncovered the romantic information that Warren Dimplo was engaged to marry Jennie Anderson, the daughter of a Bolivar minister of the gospel.

He was, in short, as unlikely a murderer as was Ted Jopling.

Gillian often said: "It is not the accused I am defending—it is those who love him—his wife, his children, his mother or father or sweetheart. They are the ones for whom my heart bleeds!"

And Mr. Yistle had, on one occasion, snorted: "The lying hypocrite! There is no more blood in his heart than there is in a chunk of flint."

"Will he burn in the chair?" screamed the *Morning Gazette*, a tabloid newspaper. Below the headline was a "composite photograph," filling three-quarters of the page, showing Warren Dimplo, his face distorted with agony, seated in the electric chair.

The same eminent dispensary of news also printed a story dealing with an offer made to Theodore Jopling and his wife by a motion picture firm, which they promptly declined through their attorney, Gillian Hazeltine.

And in all the papers of that date appeared a record of the sale of Ezra Klagg's farm to the Joplings. Jason Greer was Ezra Klagg's sole heir. The price was ten thousand dollars cash, which Ted Jopling borrowed from Banker Torrence of Bolivar and paid into Jason Greer's hand.

To reporters, the nephew of Ezra Klagg was quoted as saying:

"It seems only fitting to me that this property, over which there has been so much bickering, should go to the man who has suffered so unjustly because of it. The property is worth more than twenty thousand dollars, but I am perfectly satisfied with the price Mr. Jopling paid.

"I will stay in Greenville. I will stay until after the trial of the man who so brutally murdered my dear uncle. Nothing could persuade me not to testify against this black-hearted scoundrel. I went through weeks of hardship in bringing him before the bar of justice, and I will do my duty as an American citizen. I will not leave Greenville until my evidence is given in court."

Three newspapers commented editorially, in substance: "The nephew of Ezra Klagg deserves the gratitude of the community for the zeal he showed, the hardship he suffered, the sacrifice he made in bringing to justice his uncle's murderer."

In short, public interest in the Ezra Klagg murder case was fanned to white heat.

Promptly, Gillian Hazeltine promised amazing revelations—the most amazing revelations in the history of American court procedure.

Just as promptly, Adelbert Yistle promised the people of his fair State an electrocution.

Once again the offices of the prosecuting attorney gave off a humming sound resembling that of many busy beehives in the honey season. Detectives came and went on all manner of mysterious errands.

And as time passed, the case of the People *vs.* Dimplo took on more and more the aspect of a sure thing—for the People. Mr. Yistle glowed with returning self-esteem, but he was suspicious of Gillian.

"There ought to be a particularly hot corner of hell where such reptiles as Gillian Hazeltine go when they die," he once confided to Mr. Bullock. "There is no trick mean enough, low enough, that he won't resort to, to get a client off. The man is positively a menace."

"There ought to be a law against such lawyers," affirmed Mr. Bullock.

"We've got some fine witnesses, Mr. Bullock. Aside from Greer, we've got Professor Whitely to establish, with enlarged photographs, that the revolver fired that bullet; and we've got credible witnesses who heard Dimplo making threats—worse threats than Jopling ever made. Then, of course, we've got Greer. He saw Dimplo do the killing!"

"And hunted in the hills till he found him!" chirped Mr. Bullock.

"And still I sometimes wonder," mused Mr. Yistle, "if there isn't a catch in this somewhere, still wonder if, with all the evidence we have, we have even laid our eyes on the actual murderer."

For once, Mr. Bullock did not say yes.

"What makes you say that, Mr. Yistle?"

"Hazeltine," was the prosecutor's simple answer. "He has tricked us before. He will trick us again. He may be tricking us at this very moment. What will his defense be this time?

What can it be? Self-defense? Another alibi? We will be prepared to smash either, Mr. Bullock!"

"And we will!" quavered Mr. Bullock, whose voice, in such exciting moments as this, became high and tremulous.

"I wonder," mused the State's attorney, "if we ought to go to the bother of tracing that revolver."

"It *would* be a bother."

"Oh, the devil with it!"

"That's what I say," his yes-man upheld him.

Which furnishes a reason why cases appearing to be sure-fire often fizzled out for poor Mr. Yistle.

Meanwhile, in the city jail, the young man accused of the killing of Ezra Klagg was saying to Gillian Hazeltine:

"I don't care so much for myself. It's Jennie Anderson I'm thinking about, Mr. Hazeltine. We—we were going to be married next month."

"You will be," said Gillian confidently. "Now—think—think—*think*—where did you get that revolver?"

"I—I just don't seem to remember."

10

IT HAD ALWAYS been one of Gillian Hazeltine's fixed beliefs, that bashful dogs do not grow fat. On the day before the trial, he announced through the newspapers that he was absolutely confident of Warren Dimplo's innocence and, accordingly, was confident that the young farmer would be acquitted.

On the same day he addressed a hearty personal letter to the dean of the State University urging him to send the entire senior class of the law college to the trial of Warren Dimplo.

"In all my years of law practice," said Gillian, "it has never been my good fortune to handle a case so replete with unique legal aspects. The defense of Warren Dimplo will be one of the most original, most surprising in the annals of the American criminal court. I cordially urge you, dean, to send this body of young students to the court room for the duration of the trial."

Somehow, this letter was seen by a reporter. It was reprinted in full in a box on the first page.

It may have been Gillian's intention to worry Mr. Yistle; it may merely have been his plan to annoy him. Perhaps he planned that a highly gullible public should swallow the letter as a proof that the forthcoming trial was to be an affair of great dignity.

Gillian seldom aimed a stone at only one bird. What was in his mind no one even knew.

The natural result of the letter's publication was, of course, that the court room was crowded to the doors from the moment the first panel of prospective jurymen was called. No one was surprised when a delegation of young men from the State University took their seats in a reserved section and, to a man, fixed their eyes reverently upon the commanding figure of Gillian Hazeltine. He was, in their eyes, a creature of mystery and power—a man any young law student could well pattern himself after.

Not knowing what Gillian's defense would be, Mr. Yistle selected a jury of unsympathetic looking men, men with hard eyes and firm chins, men who believed in capital punishment. Gillian used only three of his peremptory challenges.

The trial began. The defendant entered a plea of not guilty.

Mr. Yistle's first witness was, again, old Dr. Fletcher, who once more told of visiting the Klagg house with Tom Howard and the constable. Mr. Yistle proved, by his testimony, that the revolver had not been fired at close range. In that way he spiked any attempt of Gillian's to prove that the killing had been done in self-defense.

The next witness was Professor Whitely, the firearms expert, who, with enlarged photographs of the bullet and the revolver's rifling, established to a certainty that the bullet had been fired from that particular revolver. Bullet, revolver and enlargements were introduced as material evidence for the State.

Townsmen of Bolivar were next called to the stand to

testify that, in their hearing, the defendant had made various and sundry threats against the person of Ezra Klagg.

Mr. Yistle's star witness was Jason Greer. The nephew of the dead man gave his testimony in a clear, steady voice. He was not vindictive; he seemed merely firmly determined that the murderer of his uncle should be made to pay for his crime.

He gave in great detail his actions and those of the prisoner on the night of June 6. He told of leaving the train from Steel City at the Bolivar station at seven twelve; of striking across fields; of hearing the quarrel and seeing the shot fired.

His account of the man hunt through the Black Hills was gripping; he admitted that he was frightened. He was unarmed; he knew that the man he was hunting still possessed the revolver.

He described days and nights of following the trail, of losing it, of picking it up again, waiting, always waiting for the moment when Warren Dimplo, in a careless moment, slept and could be seized.

Gillian's cross-examination of him was brief. He wanted to know the exact time at which he had come up the path from the road; heard the bullet fired.

Jason Greer estimated the time at seven forty-five.

"Not seven thirty?"

"No, sir."

"Not eight?"

"No, sir."

"Did the defendant resist you when the capture was made?"

"Yes, sir, he did; he fought like a wild cat."

"And you subdued him?"

"I did. I tied his wrists."

"I think that will be all," said Gillian.

Mr. Yistle looked at him expectantly. The State had presented its case, and its case, looked at any way you pleased, was water-tight and iron-bound and copper-riveted.

It was a tighter case by far than Mr. Yistle had built up against Teddy Jopling. He had, he believed, overlooked no detail.

Gillian faced the jury in his habitual attitude; head thrust forward, hands clasped behind him, feet planted far apart.

"Gentlemen of the jury, by witnesses whom I will call to the stand, I will prove to you beyond the shadow of a doubt that the defendant was not the murderer of Ezra Klagg; could not possibly have been the murderer of Ezra Klagg, in spite of the testimony you have heard to the contrary; that the defendant was elsewhere when the killing occurred.

"You are supposed, gentlemen of the jury, to have come into this court room with clear minds, unaffected by prejudice, unswayed by what you may have heard or what you may have read in the newspapers. You declared, under oath, that that was so. Legally, it is so. Under the present circumstances it is difficult to believe that any one of you came into this court room in that state of mind. I am stating this so flatly because I wish you to realize too that I am fully aware of the difficult task confronting me—to prove to you honestly and fairly that the young man sitting there at that table is innocent of the crime of which he is charged.

"In the attempt I am about to make to convince you

that Warren Dimplo is innocent of the crime of murder, I wish to call to your attention that the defense about to be presented is unique in courtroom annals. My distinguished opponent will label it as trickery. I need only to mention that you, the peers of this defendant, are to decide that.

"I wish to add that, in my humble estimation, the defense about to be presented is so unique that I felt justified in inviting to this trial the members of the senior class of the State law school. This defense will be, I fully believe, a liberal education for these young men. On their behalf—"

Mr. Yistle crisply interrupted:

"I object to all this, your honor, as irrelevant."

"I expected you would," said Gillian pleasantly.

"Objection is sustained," ruled the court. "You will confine your statement to the issue, Mr. Hazeltine."

"I merely wished to point out," Gillian complied, "that the defense about to be presented is baffling even to the counsel for the defense—meaning myself. We are faced with the utterly fantastic situation of a defendant who does not know whether he is guilty or not; who must have it proved to his own satisfaction that he is not guilty. We have, in Warren Dimplo, a defendant who ran away from a crime which I will endeavor to prove to you he did not commit!"

11

AN EXCITED MURMUR went through the court room. Gillian Hazeltine's trials were always interesting; always full of surprises and thrills. He was apparently planning to outdo himself.

"From the very beginning—since Ezra Klagg was killed—we have been faced by mystery. We are faced by a ghostly problem. I have, frankly, burst into cold sweat more than once pondering it. It has always seemed to me there was something strange in the way Warren Dimplo walked into the court room during the trial of Ted Jopling and made his confession. This has been a case of precedents broken.

"In Warren Dimplo we have a man who believes in his own guilt. The plea I entered of not guilty is purely technical. Is he guilty? I believe that this mystery has reached beyond the point at which we lawyers—Mr. Yistle and myself—are to argue plain guilt or plain innocence. We are confronted by a fascinating problem. Who *did* kill Ezra Klagg?"

He swept the court room with his sparkling eyes.

"Is that man in this court room now?" he cried. "Or is that man following his normal pursuits on some farm, perhaps, in the vicinity of Bolivar? Ezra Klagg was known to have many enemies. You have heard witness after witness admit that he and Klagg were not friendly; that Klagg was guilty of this unkind deed, of that spiteful action. In the course of his lifetime how many enemies did Ezra Klagg make? Who is the man, where is the man, who killed him as he sat there in his chair on that evening in June?

"While all of this, in the opinion of my estimable opponent, is irrelevant, we cannot but permit our minds to run along these fascinating channels. You will smile, my distinguished adversary will sneer, when I advance the only theory which to me, in light of the evidence, is acceptable.

"My claim, which I will now endeavor to prove, is that no physical man killed Ezra Klagg. My claim, which I offer for what it is worth, gentlemen of the jury, is that the temporarily disembodied soul, the astral body, of Warren Dimplo, is guilty of the deed!

"What facts have we now to go on? Let us see. The first witness for the defense is Ebenezer Hoag. Will Mr. Hoag take the stand?"

Ebenezer Hoag walked stiffly to the witness chair with grimly set jaws and seated himself. He faced Gillian with cold blue eyes.

"You are the postmaster at Bolivar, are you not?" Gillian asked him, when Mr. Hoag had been duly sworn.

"I am," snapped the old gentleman.

"Now, Mr. Hoag, between the hours of twelve and twelve thirty noon, June 6, where were you?"

"In the Bolivar post office, distributing mail."

"To the best of your recollection, was the defendant in the post office at that time, between those hours?"

"Yes, sir, he was. I talked to him and heard him talk."

"To whom was he talking most of the time?"

"To Ted Jopling. The two of them were telling what they thought of old man Klagg, and everybody else was listening."

"At what time, if you recall, did the defendant leave the post office?"

"I closed up for lunch at twelve thirty. He left then," answered Mr. Hoag.

"Thank you, that will be all, Mr. Hoag. Do you wish to cross-examine, Mr. Yistle?"

"No," said the State's attorney, "but I want him to wait."

"I'll wait," said Mr. Hoag.

"The next witness," said Gillian, "is Mr. Robert N. Oliver. Will you take the stand, Mr. Oliver?"

A tall, gaunt man of about fifty, with fierce black eyebrows and a walrus mustache, stepped forward.

When he was sworn, Gillian asked:

"What is your occupation, Mr. Oliver?"

"I am the proprietor of the Bolivar hardware store," answered Mr. Oliver in a deep, rumbling voice.

"Are you acquainted with the defendant, Dimplo, Mr. Oliver?"

"I am. I know him well."

"Will you kindly tell the jury, Mr. Oliver, if Dimplo was in your store at any time on the afternoon of June 6?"

"He was. Yes, sir. He came to my store at about twelve thirty. I locked up and we went over to the Busy Bee for lunch. Then we went back to my store and talked until a little after three."

"What was the nature of your conversation?"

"Well, we talked about old man Klagg and what a dirty deal he had given Warren on that piece of land. And we talked about a new milking machine Warren was thinking of putting in for his dairy."

"What terminated your conversation with the defendant, Mr. Oliver?"

"A couple of young ladies did. One was Jennie Anderson, and the other was Mary Shaw."

"Kindly tell the jury, Mr. Oliver, what took place."

"Well, these two young ladies saw Warren, and they came over, and I think they asked him what he was doing in Bolivar. And as I recollect it, he said he'd come in to do some errands. Anyhow, one of them—Miss Anderson, I think it was—said they were showing a movie at the Strand that afternoon, and to come on along and they'd treat.

"There was a lot of laughing and joking about this treating business, and finally the three of them walked out of the store."

"What time was that?"

"That was about three."

"What you are saying, Mr. Oliver, is that you were in the defendant's company from twelve thirty to three on the afternoon of June 6?"

"Yes, sir—just about that length of time."

"That will be all. Do you wish to take the witness, Mr. Yistle?"

"I have no reason for taking the witness," answered Mr. Yistle testily. "His testimony, like that of your previous witness, is irrelevant. You are trying to prove a perfect alibi. I want all these witnesses to remain."

Gillian smiled. "My next witness," he said, "is Miss Jennie Anderson. Will Miss Anderson take the stand?"

A slender, pretty girl with large blue eyes came forward.

She was pale and nervous. She lifted her hand uncertainly, and in a low, husky, small voice swore to tell the truth, the whole truth, and nothing but the truth.

The court room rustled.

"Do you live in the town of Bolivar?" Gillian asked her.

"I do," she said huskily.

"Are you acquainted with the defendant, Dimplo?"

"I am."

"Will you kindly tell the jury if you saw the defendant Dimplo at any time on the afternoon of June 6, and if so, what transpired between you?"

"I met him," she answered, still in the same sweet, husky voice, "at about three o'clock that afternoon in the Bolivar hardware store. I was with Mary Shaw. Mary and I asked him to go to the Strand Theater. He argued a little and finally consented to go. The three of us went. We saw a picture called 'Chang.' The show was out at five thirty."

"Was Mary Shaw with you and the defendant during that time?"

"Yes, sir; I sat on one side of him, and Mary Shaw on the other."

"What did you do when you left the theater?"

"We went home—to my house—for dinner."

"You invited him to your house for dinner?"

"Yes, sir."

"And he accepted?"

"Yes, sir."

"And he ate dinner in your house?"

"Yes, sir."

"Who else was there, Miss Anderson?"

"My father and mother."

"Kindly tell the jury what happened after dinner?"

"After dinner he said he was going to the town meeting, and I said I would walk down to the town hall with him. My father joined us then and said he would walk along with us. He did. We left him—I mean Mr. Dimplo—at the front door of the town hall. That was the last I saw of him until to-day."

Her chin was quivering, and her eyes were bright.

"That will be all. Mr. Yistle, do you wish to take this witness?"

"I do not," snapped the State's attorney. "I want her to remain with the others."

Gillian walked slowly toward the jury.

"I am sure that it must be quite evident now, gentlemen, what I am trying to do," he told them. "I am trying to establish the fact that the defendant, Dimplo, was in the town of Bolivar continuously from noon on—that he did not leave Bolivar. We have followed him through the day from noon until seven o'clock. That is, we are now approaching, for the purposes of this trial, the most critical period of that day. My next witness is the accused. Mr. Dimplo, please take the stand."

The young man with the electric-blue eyes and the curly molasses hair walked slowly, carefully across the space to the witness chair and sat down. The newspapers later vied in descriptive comment of him.

They said there was something fantastic about him. One called him strange. Another asserted that he was faunlike. There was a curiously eerie atmosphere about him. Yet his gaze was level and his voice was full and firm.

Warren Dimplo was sworn.

"Mr. Dimplo," Gillian began in a low voice, "I want you to describe to the jury what took place, as you recall it, from the moment Jennie Anderson and her father left you at approximately seven o'clock on the evening of June 6."

The prisoner turned to the jury.

"I went upstairs in the balcony of the town hall," he answered. "I knew the meeting wouldn't start for half an hour, but I was sleepy, and I wanted to take a little nap before it began. So I sat down, and I guess I fell asleep right away. I could not have been asleep a minute or two, when I woke up, and I was thinking of old man Klagg. I had been sore at him all day, and I decided I'd pass up the town meeting and go out to his farm and have if out with him about that land he cheated me on. I guess you gentlemen read about that land deal in the papers.

"I walked down High Rocks Road to his house, and I went in, and he was sitting there in the chair. I—I'm sort of hazy on the rest of it; but I know we had a hot argument. It ended by his grabbing his shotgun. I knew he was going to shoot me. I saw it in his eyes. So I pulled out the revolver—"

"What revolver?" Gillian snapped.

"The one I had in my pocket."

"Which pocket?"

"I—I don't remember."

"Where did you get the revolver?"

"I—I don't remember."

"Did you have it when you left the town hall?"

"No, sir."

"Where did you get it?"

"I—I don't seem to remember."

"Very well. What did you do with the revolver?"

"I shot Ezra Klagg."

"Then what happened?"

"I—I think I ran out of the house. Everything is pretty confused. Next thing I knew I was somewhere back of Bolivar—just on the north side of the new paved road. I—I seemed to come to my senses. I knew I had to get away. Then I realized I was being followed. Everything gets pretty confused again after that. I had to get away. I mean, I'd killed a man. Well, I hid in the hills, and that man was after me all the time. He—finally got me."

"Did you have that revolver with you all the time?"

"I don't remember. I was just about crazy when I realized I'd killed Mr. Klagg."

"I only wished," said Gillian, "to have this witness relate this story which he has insisted on telling me over and over again, in spite of overwhelming evidence—"

"Objection!" snapped Mr. Yistle. "It has not been proved and it is summation."

"Your objection is sustained," ruled Judge Manning. "Do you wish to cross-examine the witness, Mr. Yistle?"

"I do!" said Mr. Yistle grimly.

He planted his fists on his hips and faced the young man in the witness chair.

"You say you didn't have that revolver when you left the town hall?"

"No, sir; I did not."

"Where did you get it?"

"I don't know."

Mr. Yistle grinned at the jury, and winked.

"It was handy when you got to Mr. Klagg's house, though, wasn't it?"

"Yes, sir; it must have been."

"You admit you shot him with it, don't you?"

"Oh, yes, I admit that."

Mr. Yistle breathed more freely.

"That will be all," he said affably.

"Will there be a redirect examination?"

"There will," said Gillian quite as affably; and he faced the witness.

12

"MR. DIMPLO, WILL you tell the jury whether or not you have, as a child or a grown man, been subject to somnambulism, or sleep-walking?"

"Yes, sir," the young man answered. "All my life I've walked in my sleep, always whenever I was particularly excited or worked up about anything."

"Do you at these or other times have vivid or what might be called violent dreams?"

The accused hung his head, as if he were ashamed, and a blush stole into his cheeks. But he looked up quickly.

"Yes, sir."

"You're ashamed of these dreams?"

"Yes, sir."

"Why?" Gillian snapped.

"I—I don't know, Mr. Hazeltine. You asked me that before. I don't know. I—I certainly don't go around telling people about them."

"In these dreams do you fight?"

"Yes, sir."

"Now, Mr. Dimplo, I want you to think carefully, and to answer very frankly, my next question. Are these 'fighting dreams,' as we might call them, sometimes so vivid that when you awaken you are sometimes confused as to whether you have actually fought or merely dreamed you fought?"

"Yes, sir; that is true. And it had bothered me a great deal."

"That's all," said Gillian. "Mr. Yistle, do you wish to take the witness for re-cross-examination?"

"I am not interested in dreams, day dreams, night dreams, pipe dreams—or any other kind of dreams!" Mr. Yistle laughed, and the spectators in the court room laughed with him.

A bailiff banged with a gavel for order.

My next witness," said Gillian, "is Mr. Joseph Finchley. Will you take the stand, Mr. Finchley?"

An erect, aristocratic looking old man walked briskly toward the witness chair. He had fine white hair and a crisp small mustache.

"Mr. Finchley," Gillian asked him, after the old man had been sworn, "what is your occupation?"

"I am the town treasurer of Bolivar," answered the old man in a high, birdlike voice.

"How long have you held that position?"

"Fifteen years, sir; fifteen years."

"Will you kindly tell us where you were on the evening of June 6 at about seven o'clock?"

"At that hour, sir," answered the obliging old man, "I was mounting the stairs to the balcony of the town hall."

"Did you see this defendant when you were mounting the stairs?"

"I did, sir. The young man was directly ahead of me."

"Kindly describe your subsequent actions and observations, particularly as they pertain to the defendant."

"Well, sir," Mr. Finchley chirped, "I followed him up into the balcony and took a seat just behind him. I saw him start to nod, as if he was sleepy, and pretty soon I heard him snore. About that time, Jake Burroughs came up and sat down beside me."

"Go on, Mr. Finchley."

"Well, Jake and I sat there, chewin' the rag, and pretty soon along comes Sam Benchley and Gil Stevens. The four of us sat in a row—"

"Behind the defendant?"

"Yes, sir."

"Listening to him snore?"

"Well, he stopped snorin' presently, and the town meeting started."

"The defendant was there in front of you all this time?"

"Yes, sir, right up to the end of the meetin'!"

A gasp of several hundred pairs of lungs burst upon the tense quiet of the court room. Then the air was filled with a clamorous buzzing.

Mr. Yistle had suddenly seated himself. He was pale and perspiring. Suddenly, now, he was upon his feet, shouting above the clamor of voices and the clatter of the bailiff's gavel.

"Your honor! Your honor!"

The court room quieted and Mr. Yistle grasped the edge of the judge's desk.

"Your honor, I move that Gillian Hazeltine be charged with contempt! He has defiled justice again and again and again with his cheap trickery. He has permitted this trial to go forward when, if he had wished, he could have communicated this unknown evidence to me. The very credibility of this witness proves the depths of Gillian Hazeltine's perfidity!"

"If the court please," Gillian broke in indignantly, "there are yet insufficient grounds for contempt. I am presenting this defense honestly. There is no trickery."

"You are a liar and a sneak!" shouted the State's attorney.

"Mr. Yistle—" roared the Court.

"Your honor, I beg—" Gillian began.

His fists were doubled. He expected the irate Mr. Yistle to charge him. Never, in the course of their endless feuds, had they been nearer blows than this. But Mr. Yistle recovered his lost poise; he faced the bench with hot, glittering eyes.

"Your honor, I respectfully submit that Mr. Hazeltine has deliberately frustrated the ends of justice by his trickery. I move for mistrial."

"My evidence is not yet in!" snapped Gillian. "If the court please, permit me to finish with the presentation of my case."

"Your motions, respectively, charging the attorney for the defense with contempt, and for a mistrial, must be denied, Mr. Yistle. Both will be considered later, if you wish."

"May I proceed, your honor?" Gillian breathed.

"You may proceed, Mr. Hazeltine."

"My next witness," said Gillian with a sigh of weariness and relief, "is Jason Greer."

To this there was no response.

"Jason Greer!" shouted a bailiff.

The witness did not respond.

"In place of Greer," said Gillian, "will be Abraham Lefkowitz. Will Mr. Lefkowitz take the stand?"

A broad shouldered man with a beefy neck strode heavily to the witness chair, where he was sworn.

"Mr. Lefkowitz," said Gillian, "what business are you in?"

"I am in the pawnbroking business," answered the witness.

"In what place?"

"In Steel City."

"I want you to identify this revolver," said Gillian, placing in his hand State Exhibit D.

The witness quickly glanced at the number stamped into the butt of the revolver. He now compared this with a sheet of paper he removed from his pocket.

He looked up, squinting.

"I sold this revolver on May 12 to a man who gave his name as Ezra Klagg."

Mr. Yistle was hardly paying attention. He was holding a whispered consultation with Mr. Bullock—and Mr. Bullock was not saying yes.

Gillian now extended to the witness a photograph—an enlarged photograph of Ezra Klagg's hard, mean features.

"Do you recognize this man?"

"Yes, sir; that is the man I sold the revolver to."

"That will be all," said Gillian. "Mr. Yistle, do you wish—"

"Cross-examination waived," said Mr. Bullock for the State.

"Are there any further witnesses?" the judge inquired.

"No more for the defense," said Gillian.

"No more for the State," said Mr. Bullock.

"The State may now proceed with summation."

Mr. Yistle arose stiffly.

"Your honor, I merely repeat my previous motion. I move for a mistrial. I move that the attorney for the defense is in contempt."

"I submit," put in Gillian, "that both motions pend until summations are concluded. I have still something to say."

"The State will proceed with summation," the Court decided.

"The State waives summation," snapped Mr. Yistle.

"The defense may proceed with summation," said Judge Manning.

Gillian looked tired and worn as he faced the jury.

"Gentlemen," he said, "my summation will be extremely brief. The facts of the case are before you. Did the defendant kill Ezra Klagg as he claims he did? Or was he asleep in the balcony of the town hall between the hours of seven and ten—as Mr. Finchley claimed he was? Did his disembodied spirit, the aura of his personality, visit and kill Ezra Klagg? And, if it did, is his physical body to be punished for that lapse?

"Was he the victim of a delusion? The problem fascinates me. If he did not kill Ezra Klagg, who did kill Ezra Klagg? Can you be sure that the murderer was the accused? I wish to assure you, gentlemen of the jury, that I have resorted to no trickery. That is all I have to say."

"To take up Mr. Yistle's two motions," said the judge, gravely, "this court holds that the attorney for the defense has not been proved to be in contempt. That motion must be dismissed. It seems to this court that Mr. Hazeltine, while presenting us with a knotty problem, has brought the light of his own intelligence to bear honestly upon it.

"I must also deny Mr. Yistle's motion for a mistrial. We are, to be sure, confronted by a fantastic array of evidence which you, gentlemen of the jury, must sift down. There is no precedent dealing with a man's astral self.

"To me, it is inconceivable that the astral self of this man left his body and somehow secured a revolver, owned, as proved, by the deceased, and with it shot him.

"You have heard testimony, on previous days, supporting the doubtful proposition that because the deceased was found with eyes open staring as if with horror, that he may have met his death by some supernatural means. I would say that any man faced by sudden death, whether natural or supernatural, would retain in his eyes an expression of horror.

"Now, the evidence produced to support the astral body theory is, to an imaginative mind, attractive. Yet the mind of a normal civilized man must reject theories based upon supernatural occurrences. You may retire now to deliberate these rather confusing points. And you may return with any one of five possible verdicts for the defendant.

"You may find that Warren Dimplo is guilty of murder in the first degree for the killing of Ezra Klagg in his home, near Bolivar, on the evening of June 6.

"Or you may find him guilty of second degree murder or manslaughter, first degree, or manslaughter, second degree. You can, finally, render a verdict of absolute acquittal."

Judge Manning then defined for the jury the meanings of first degree murder, second degree murder, first degree manslaughter, and second degree manslaughter.

The jury retired, and had to cast but one ballot to reach their decision. Their verdict was absolute acquittal.

"With the recommendation," added the jury foreman, smiling, "that Mr. Dimplo consult a good doctor to cure him of those bad dreams!"

13

A FORD TRUCK was parked at the curb in front of the courthouse, and behind the wheel sat Theodore Jopling. He scrambled out when he saw his old friend Warren Dimplo descending the courthouse steps, surrounded by reporters, fought his way to him and threw his arms about him.

The two young men posed for photographs, then climbed into the truck and drove away.

"Hazeltine," remarked Captain Jopling as they rattled along, "is a damned fine lawyer."

"They don't come any finer," agreed Lieutenant Dimplo.

The truck bounded and banged across a number of railroad tracks.

"What I want to know," said Lieutenant Dimplo, "is—who did kill Ezra Klagg?"

"If I knew," replied Captain Jopling, "do you suppose I would have let you rot there in jail all that time."

At a later hour that afternoon, Mr. Yistle unfortunately encountered Gillian Hazeltine in the smoking room of the Lawyers' Club. Unfortunately—for Mr. Yistle's already disturbed peace of mind. He had lost another case and two thousand dollars to Gillian, and it would be hard to say which grieved him the more.

"Look here," he snarled at Gillian, "just between us, and in the strictest confidence, who killed Klagg?"

"If I knew," answered Gillian gently, "I would consider it my duty, as a patriotic American citizen, to inform the prosecuting attorney of this fair county, namely—you! But I don't know, Adelbert; I have added a thousand gray hairs wondering. What is your theory?"

"In the first place," growled the disgruntled State's attorney, accepting one of Gillian's fine mellow Havanas, "I think you know or I wouldn't ask. As long as you won't tell, I'll guess: Jason Greer! Why did he skip town?"

"I'll tell you," said Gillian. "But that, too, is a theory. I should say that Greer skipped town because, as things looked to him, the hawk-eyed district attorney of this town was very apt to pounce on him next. You seemed to be having quite a run on industrious working men—and Greer is an industrious working man."

"You don't think there was a possibility of his killing his uncle? Look at his motive! He was the sole heir!"

"I thought of that, too," admitted Gillian. "But I don't believe he did the killing. I believe he saw the murder, as he claims; that he went dashing out into the wheat field and, over near the paved road, came upon the sleep-walking Dimplo, who promptly ran for the hills, while the real murderer escaped."

"But how," demanded the baffled Mr. Yistle, "do you account for that revolver? Did Greer pick it up? If he did, why did he insist that Dimplo—or whoever he saw do the shooting—ran away with it?"

"Adelbert," said Gillian, gently, "you are right back again at the hub of the mystery: who *did* kill Ezra Klagg?"

www.ingramcontent.com/pod-product-compliance
Lightning Source LLC
Chambersburg PA
CBHW031152020726
47499CB00002B/344